RAID

Once I'm done ransacking his camp, I grab the unconscious raider by the feet and drag him to my truck. I tie his hands and feet, gag him in case he wakes up, and throw him into the backseat.

With that done, I allow myself a moment to breathe, and re-tie my dark hair back into a neat ponytail. Then I climb into the driver's side, and smile at the roar of my truck coming to life. No matter how many times I hunt down a raider, it always gives me a special pleasure to make prey out of them.

By K. S. Merbeth

Bite
Raid

Praise for K. S. Merbeth and *Bite*

'A full-throttle, sand-in-your-eyes, no-holds-barred ride through a *Mad Max*-style wasteland where the bad guys become family. Finally, an underdog with teeth!'
Delilah S. Dawson

'Merbeth has created her own universe filled with destruction and not a small amount of grim, acerbic wit. Fans of Mira Grant's Newsflesh series will be pleased by the smart writing'
Library Journal

'Filled with dark humor, wit, and a realistic dystopian setting, *Bite* plays with the idea of who the good guys are in such a harsh world'
Booklist

'Merbeth's debut novel puts a unique spin on post-apocalyptic horror ... *Bite* flips the script'
B&N Sci-Fi and Fantasy Blog

'Pure undiluted high-octane anarchy ... If you enjoy movies like ... *Mad Max: Fury Road*, or games like *Fallout 4* and *Borderlands*, then *Bite* is the book for you. Gleefully unrestrained and unrelenting, strap yourself in and enjoy the ride. *Bite* is here, let the mayhem commence!'
Eloquent Page

RAID

K. S. MERBETH

www.orbitbooks.net

ORBIT

First published in Great Britain in 2017 by Orbit

1 3 5 7 9 10 8 6 4 2

A CIP catalogue record for this book
is available from the British Library.

ISBN 978-0-356-50773-6

Typeset in Baskerville by M Rules
Printed and bound in Great Britain by
Clays Ltd, St Ives plc

Papers used by Orbit are from well-managed forests
and other responsible sources.

MIX
Paper from
responsible sources
FSC® C104740

Orbit
An imprint of
Little, Brown Book Group
Carmelite House
50 Victoria Embankment
London EC4Y 0DZ

An Hachette UK Company
www.hachette.co.uk

www.orbitbooks.net

For nasty women

I
Hunters and Prey

Raiders always think they're the top of the food chain until I come along.

This one hasn't even noticed me following him for the past week. It probably never crossed his mind that he was being hunted until this very moment. I take out his legs first, a bullet in each kneecap before he can react. He falls forward, bleeding and snarling, rusty meat cleaver clutched tightly in hand. He still manages to crawl in my direction and brandish the knife, his ugly face contorted with pain and rage and hatred. I shoot him in the shoulder, twice for insurance, and he falls flat on his face and stays there.

I study the man, lying still in the dirt, and take a few steps closer with my gun trained on him.

His cleaver swings at my ankle. I step aside and slam

my boot down on his hand. I grind my heel into his fingers until he stops struggling, then lift it and kick the knife out of his reach. The fight bleeds out of him quickly after that. I wait a few seconds before flipping him onto his back, where he lies dusty and bloody and struggling for consciousness.

'Bitch,' he spits at me, his eyes half-shut. I ignore him and pull a crumpled wanted poster out of my pocket, smoothing it out before comparing the hand-drawn face on it to this ugly motherfucker. The picture was clearly drawn by some half-brain-dead townie, making it hard to compare, but that huge knife is easy to recognize.

'Beau the Butcher,' I say. Probably came up with the name himself; he looks like the type.

'You know who I am,' he wheezes out. 'Means you know who I work for. Means you know you're dead if you kill me.'

I crouch down beside him, grabbing a handful of his stringy hair and yanking his face up, closer to mine. His eyes find the burnt skin that twists up the left side of my face and widen in recognition.

'Clementine,' he says, his breath quickening, and I grin. 'You bi—'

Two hits are all it takes to knock him out.

I drop his limp body in the dust and grab his knife. It's a famous thing, this knife, both the namesake of this asshole and better known to people than his ugly face.

I admire it before tucking it into my pack with my own weapons.

Embers still smolder nearby, the remnants of the campfire that allowed me to find him last night. Idiot was too stupid and drunk on power to head somewhere safer to sleep, making him easy pickings for me this morning. I dump sand on the fire, smothering the last of it, and search through his small collection of belongings. I find a couple bottles of water and a can of food, which I stuff into my pack. There's also some dried meat, but I toss that aside; there's only one kind of meat to be had around here, and I refuse to partake.

Once I'm done ransacking his camp, I grab the unconscious raider by the feet and drag him to my truck. I tie his hands and feet, gag him in case he wakes up, and throw him into the backseat.

With that done, I allow myself a moment to breathe, and re-tie my dark hair back into a neat ponytail. Then I climb into the driver's side, and smile at the roar of my truck coming to life. No matter how many times I hunt down a raider, it always gives me a special pleasure to make prey out of them.

I throw the Butcher facedown in the dirt. The townies scatter as if expecting him to jump up and grab them, staring goggle-eyed first at him and then at me. Several of them back away, their eyes wide.

My mistake. I forgot I was dealing with *civilized* folks. At least, that's what they fancy themselves, hiding in their walls and ramshackle communities and clinging to scraps of what life was like before the bombs fell. They're not like raiders, who fully embrace the mayhem of the world and make their livings killing and looting. Townies would rather rely on scavenged canned food, rather stay half-starved than eat human flesh like the sharks do. I admire the way they stick to some semblance of morality, even in a world like this. I try to do the same, though I'm no townie – not anymore. Of course, I'm not a goddamn shark, either. I exist somewhere in between the two ways of life, apart from all of them.

The townies don't let me forget it, either. Right now, they're staring at me like I'm some kind of monster that wandered into their midst.

The two dozen standing in a half circle around me comprise the bulk of the population of Sunrise, a dingy little town on the edge of what we call the eastern wastes. The buildings of Sunrise are all stout and cramped together, not one above a single story high. It's like they're crouched in the dirt, afraid to lose their hold on the earth. Beau the Butcher lies still in the middle of the dusty ring the people of Sunrise call the 'town square.'

'Is he dead?' one man asks, after several moments of silence. He cautiously cranes his neck and then retracts it, like he simultaneously wants to get a better look and fears what he'll see if he does.

'Well, no,' I say, my eyebrows drawing together. 'Figured you'd want to do it yourselves.'

They ogle at me some more. One man clears his throat. Nobody meets my eyes.

'But he's one of . . . ' a townie starts, and stops. He licks his lips and drops his voice to a loud whisper. 'Jedediah Johnson's men.'

'Yes,' I say, not sure what that has to do with anything. 'And he killed your sheriff over a card game. So you wanted him dead. What am I missing here?'

There's another long stretch of silence, in which all the townies glance at each other and shuffle their feet and refuse to look at me. Finally, a woman steps forward. She's a solidly built, middle-aged woman, dusty and stout like the buildings of her town. The top of her head barely reaches my chin, but then again, my height rivals that of a decent amount of the men in town as well. I recognize her as the woman who made the initial deal with me – the wife of the recently murdered sheriff, who seems to be taking on the role of her dead husband.

'Well, there's a reason we hired you to do it,' she says. 'If word got out that we killed one of Jedediah's men, he'd burn this place to the ground.' She pauses, her eyes sliding across the scarred and burnt section of my face, the angry red skin that stretches across the entire left side. With my hair tied back, my burns are on full display. I'm not afraid to show them off, but if this woman thinks she can bring them into an argument, I'll blow her damn head off. 'We know what happened to Old Creek,' she says, and leaves it at that.

My lip curls in disgust. So they're willing to hire someone to kill a man, but not to get their hands dirty themselves. I knew that they hired me because they didn't have the means to take Beau out themselves, but it seems they also don't have the guts when the opportunity presents itself. I thought they'd relish the chance to deal out their own justice, especially this woman who lost her husband . . . but I guess I overestimated them.

In the dirt between me and the woman, Beau the Butcher starts to stir, lifting his head and looking around through the one eye that isn't swollen shut. When his eye lands on me, he chuckles, spitting out a glob of saliva and dust.

'Knew you wouldn't have the balls to kill me,' he says. 'Now, if you'll just untie me, we can talk about—'

I un-holster my pistol, shoot him three times in the head, and re-holster it.

'All right,' I say flatly. 'Pay up.'

The townies gasp and blink and step back. Some of them gag. But, to her credit, the new sheriff holds her ground and her stomach. When she gestures to a couple of the men, they manage to stop staring and disappear into one of the closest buildings. They return with arm-loads of canned food and bottled water. I make no move to take it from them, so they dump it all in a pile at my feet and retreat to the rest of the gathered townsfolk.

I separate the pile with my boot. All laid out, they've given me three bottles of water and four cans of food. I count again, ticking them off on my fingers, and fix the sheriff with my hardest stare.

'You said four and six.'

The woman doesn't flinch. She even raises her chin at me, though her lower lip wobbles as she does it.

'Ain't got six to spare,' she says. 'Still got to pay the tax this month.'

I sigh. Part of me admires the gutsiness, but I don't have time for this shit. Damn townies always use the tax as an excuse when it comes time to pay out. Sure, it sucks for them, giving up a share of hard-earned goods to the self-proclaimed ruler of the eastern wastes. But they know damn well that it comes every month, and they know damn well that they should take it into account when we make the deal, not when it comes time to pay me.

I know better than to try to talk sense into townies. Instead, I take my pistol out of its holster again and let it hang by my side.

'You'll find the rest,' I say. The sheriff hesitates. I press my lips into a firm line, tapping my gun against my leg.

Finally she nods and gestures to her men again. We wait in silence until they return with two more cans of food and one more bottle of water, and dump them on the dusty pile in front of me. I wait until they step back to join the others, count the payment once more, and slide my pistol back into its holster. I swear I hear a collective *whoosh* of the townies releasing breath, but maybe that's my imagination.

I keep an eye out in case they get any stupid ideas, but none of the townies move or even look at me as I stuff the goods into my pack. When I finish and straighten up, only the sheriff meets my eyes. The wobble in her lip is gone, and she stands with her posture stiff and her jaw set, looking up at me like she's waiting for me to demand more.

'I'm a fair woman,' I say. 'Just want what I'm owed.'

The townies stare at the ground with pinched faces, and I tighten my grip on my bag.

I wish I could say this kind of treatment is unexpected. It sure hurt the first time it happened, when I had just lost my home and I was so hopeful for a new one. I was sure the town would take me in after I helped them with their raider problem. After I got my reward, I stood there waiting for the inevitable *You know, we could use a woman like you around here* ... Instead, the sheriff said, *You've got what we owed you*, and the townies all stared at me like these ones are staring at me now.

As it turns out, towns aren't so eager to trust strangers. That's especially true when a stranger with a burnt face shows up after a local town is burned to the ground, and that stranger turns out to be particularly good at killing people. Towns do see me as an asset, but not the kind they want to invite in for dinner. Makes it hard to find a home when people view you as a necessary evil.

At this point I know better than to expect the townies to be welcoming, or even understanding, but they could at least stop acting like I've done something horrible by taking what they promised me.

I turn my back and walk away without another word. I keep my ears pricked and my eyes searching, just in case, but of course none of them have the spine to say or do anything. As I reach the edge of town I sigh, relax my shoulders, and reach into my pocket for my keys. Just as my fingers close around them, something on the horizon catches my eye and my blood runs cold.

Cars. Black cars, coming this way fast. And black cars mean only one thing out here.

'Oh, fuck me,' I breathe. For one moment, I consider running for my truck and booking it out of here. But instead I turn, run back into town, and skid to a dusty stop near the cluster of townies. They cluster more tightly together at the sight of me, wild-eyed with my hand on my gun.

'Incoming,' I say. 'Jedediah Johnson's men.'

II
The Reign of Jedediah Johnson

Once, Jedediah Johnson was just the leader of another crew of raiders carving their bloody way across the wastes. They were known as the toughest and the meanest raiders around, the scum among scum, but the scariest thing about them was their leader. People said he was some kind of mad genius, more wily than any raider before him; he was the reason why nobody saw them coming, and why no town stood a chance against them.

Of course, people also said that he could hear his name every time someone spoke it, that he could change his face every day, and that he gained the knowledge of every man he killed and ate. Rumors still run wild; nobody knows what the guy looks like, even now. But the genius part I believe. He and his men cut through the wastes in a way that had never been seen before.

One day, that infamous leader decided he'd rather be a dictator than a raider. He settled down in an old mansion in the town of Wormwood, told everyone he was in charge now, and started calling his raiding 'collecting taxes.'

At first, people laughed at him. When he actually showed up to collect, they fought him. Soon, those who laughed and those who fought were all dead. Everybody left didn't dare do anything but obey the self-declared king.

Even I know better than to fuck with Jedediah and his men. I'll pick off a stray if he's off on his own with a good price on his head, like the man I just killed, but that's risky enough, and it's as far as I dare to go. I've been killing raiders my whole life, but Jedediah's crew are a breed of their own. Better fed, better equipped, better organized. There's a reason they've been able to hold down this corner of the wastes for years, keeping townies under their thumb and fending off wandering raider crews as well. Jedediah holds all the power here.

So predictably, the townies lose their shit at my announcement. Most of them panic and flee to their houses. A few of the smarter ones remember the dead man lying in the middle of their town square – a dead man who worked for the very same dictator they're so afraid of. If Jedediah's men find that body here, they'll massacre these townies and burn their town to the ground.

'Just tax collectors,' the sheriff shouts, struggling to be heard above the general clamor. 'They don't know nothin', they're just here for the tax. Get what we owe, and hide the damn body.'

Two townies go to move the corpse, but I shoulder one of them out of the way and grab its feet myself. The sheriff hesitates, as if ready to tell me to leave, but thinks better of it.

'Get it inside and cover it up,' she says. We drag it to one of the nearby ramshackle homes, throw it onto the cot in the corner, pull a blanket over him – all the way over the head, since the multiple bullet holes in the face aren't exactly subtle.

A small collection of townies stays in the town square, including the sheriff and a handful of the bigger men. They surround her, which mostly just makes their leader look dwarfed and nervous. The rest of them cower inside their homes. They shut doors if they have them, cover windows with boards and blankets, and stay out of sight. When the townies move to cover the window of the house I'm in, I wave them off before they can finish, keeping a corner of it uncovered. None of them question me; they're too busy running to find their hiding spots. I crouch down next to the open spot, staying between the window and closed door, my gun in my hand.

I force myself to breathe deeply, trying to keep the wild beating of my heart under control. I've always heard about Jedediah's tax collectors, and seen the aftermath of their visits, but I've never been present for one.

Living out of my truck and never spending a night in any town means that I never get surprised. I engage with Jedediah's men on my terms only, like I do everyone else. But this ... this is unexpected, and I'm unprepared. I could take out one of Jedediah's men with the element of surprise, *maybe* two if I'm lucky, but any more than that and I'm fucked. And even if I can handle them, killing them here when they're out collecting taxes would make it far too easy to trace them to Sunrise, and then to me.

I need to lay low. Now is not the time to fight Jedediah's men, though it's hard to hold myself back. After all, killing raiders is what I'm best at. I've been doing it since I was eight years old.

The first was a huge brute of a man with a squashed face and a hissing voice. He was alone, but our town was young, many of us barely out of our bomb shelters, and we weren't prepared. One armed raider was enough to send everyone cowering. Ours was the third house he broke into, and nobody had dared raise a hand to stop him. Even at eight, I knew what would happen: He'd take everything we had, and probably kill us too. I was stupefied to see my parents cowering on the floor in front of this man. They looked at him and their brains told them *Cower, hide, let him take it, just let us live.* Behind his back, I looked at him, and I looked at the gun he had seemingly forgotten on the table, and my brain said: *Kill.*

I was proud that night, and so was everyone else. Afterward, the sheriff started giving me shooting lessons, and my pa gave me first pick of weapons whenever we found a new haul. I would strut around town with a pistol on my hip and people would smile at me when I passed by. 'The little hero,' they called me. But, as I eventually learned the hard way, there's a time and place to be a hero.

Right now, right here, is not it.

Outside, the town is dead silent. I lift myself up to steal a glance out of the peephole just in time to see Jedediah's men arrive. They're unmistakable, with their heavy black clothes and huge guns. One of them is a massive man, six foot four at least, and made of muscle. He's middle-aged, with a bushy beard and hard eyes that are constantly roaming the area around him. The top of his companion's head barely reaches his shoulder, but he's solidly built as well, with a mess of wavy blond hair and a shaggy beard. His face is nearly covered by hair, his eyes barely visible, and the skin that pokes out is ruddy and sunburnt. They approach the town square and stop a few feet in front of the sheriff. The men around her draw back as Jedediah's men get close. The sheriff stands alone, straight-backed, her chin raised.

'We've got your tax,' she says. 'Don't want no trouble.'

The two men study the sheriff and the pile of goods at her feet. It's easily three times what the townies paid me for the job, and I feel a stab of resentment at them for trying to hold back the extra goods they owed me.

'You're not the sheriff of Sunrise,' the shaggy raider says. He brushes his hair out of his eyes and squints at her. 'Where's what's-his-name? With the goatee?'

The big man mumbles something in a surprisingly soft voice, so quiet I can't make out the words.

'Yeah,' the shaggy one says. 'Sheriff Daniels.'

The new sheriff hesitates, considering how to answer. *Don't mention Beau*, I think. *Whatever you say to them—*

'He was killed last week by one of your men,' she says. 'Called himself the Butcher.'

Damn stupid townies.

'Oh,' the shaggy man says, letting his hair fall back into his face. 'Alrighty then.' Without further ado, he crouches down and starts counting the goods for Jedediah's tax.

The townie woman's face turns red, and then purple, while Jedediah's men pay no attention whatsoever to her. I grit my teeth, willing her to keep her mouth shut. She may have already fucked her people over by mentioning Beau. When he shows up missing, Jedediah's men are likely to remember this conversation.

'He killed him over a card game,' she bursts out

finally. 'Beau hacked his head off. It took him five hits.' The words pour out of her, like she can't help herself. 'There was no reason for it. Just cruelty.'

'Well, there's your reason,' the shaggy raider says, still counting. 'I don't need the details. Was just curious.'

'Aren't you going to do something about it?' the sheriff asks, her voice rising to a near shout. I wince, tightening my grip on my gun. Jedediah's men have killed people for less than raising their voice.

The shaggy raider pauses, then shrugs and keeps counting.

'Not my job,' he says. 'My job is collecting taxes … which you're short on. Need four more bottles of water and three food.'

The sheriff, still red in the face, looks ready to argue more, but the massive, quiet raider shifts his grip on his gun. She looks at him, and her shoulders slump.

'This is the amount it's always been,' she says, sounding more tired than argumentative.

'We need more this month.'

The townie woman says nothing, but doesn't move to collect the extra goods either. The rest of the townspeople shuffle their feet behind her, none of them looking at either her or the raiders. After a moment, the shaggy man sighs, straightens up, and raises his gun. He steps forward until the barrel rests against the side of the sheriff's nose, and taps it against her face.

'All right, I've had about enough of this shit,' he says. 'Get what you owe us. Now.'

The sheriff doesn't move or speak, just stares down the barrel of the gun at the raider. But the men behind her immediately scramble to do his bidding, disappearing into a nearby building for a minute before rushing back with the extra cans and bottles. They dump them hurriedly in front of the tax collectors and retreat, none of them daring to help their leader.

The shaggy raider is still staring at the sheriff's defiant face, his own expression impossible to read with his hair in front of his eyes. After a long few seconds, he lowers the gun.

'See? Not so hard,' he says, and gestures to his big companion. The huge man bends down and scoops up the goods. The pile looks small and paltry in his arms, but I can tell by the stricken look of the townies that it's a fortune to them. Still, they don't make so much as a whisper of protest as the men turn to go. I sink down, resting my back against the wall, and sigh out a long breath.

I wait until I hear the sounds of their vehicles starting up, and then wait a few minutes more, staying inside even after the townies have trickled out of their houses to gather in the square. Finally, when I'm sure that Jedediah's men are gone, I stand up, holster my gun, and head outside with the others.

The townies stand in a tight, worried knot in the middle of the square, speaking in lowered voices. They turn to stare at me as I emerge, and I pause. I can feel their eyes on the bag I carry, their minds no doubt on the food and water they handed over before the tax collectors came. I pull the bag tighter against my body and rest my hand on my gun.

'Thanks for the business,' I say. The townies say nothing, but continue to stare at me, hollow eyed, like I'm the one who did this to them. After a few moments, I turn my back on them and head for my truck.

Truth be told, if they asked nicely, I might hand over what they paid me. If they showed an ounce of compassion or understanding or trust in me, I might help them out. But they won't ask, and I won't give, because this place and these people aren't right. I need to save my supplies for when I do find my new home, or at least for the journey there.

Still, I pause for just a moment on the edge of town, as if I'm waiting for something. Gratitude is a long shot, but they could show some recognition for what I've done for them. At the very least, they could stop looking at me like I'm a goddamn monster just for taking what they owed me.

But it's been a long time since anyone looked at me like anything else, and I should know better by now.

III
The Collector

I drive until my truck is long out of sight of Sunrise or any other town. Once I'm secluded enough, I pull over and dig a can of food out of my bag, prying it open with my knife and slurping it down in a matter of seconds. I almost open up a second one, but stop myself.

Pickings have been slim lately. The more Jedediah solidifies his hold on the east, the more dangerous it gets to take out one of his men, and the stray raiders and thieves are few and far between out here. It's been harder and harder to find work bounty hunting. It took me a week to catch Beau somewhere secluded enough to take him down. I had to ration the last of my food, and even now that I've gotten paid, I doubt it'll last me until the next cash-out. Maybe I'll get lucky, but I know better than to count on that. For now, though, I'll allow myself a moment to relax.

Back when I started, when I was just a sixteen-year-old townie girl with a pistol, cashing in a bounty was always a grand affair. I'd claim my reward, head home and hand it over to the sheriff, and we'd all celebrate. There'd be claps on the back and smiles and thanks. *Our little hero.*

Now, I look forward to eating in my truck alone. It is what it is. Being alone isn't so bad, especially when I'm all wound up from talking with those townies. Dealing with people always proves to be more frustrating and more disappointing than I expect. They don't understand me, I don't understand them, and altogether it's never a good experience for anyone involved. After I lost my hometown, I quickly realized that all strangers see is a tall woman with a burnt face, a gun, and some rather unsavory skills. I soon learned it was better for me to keep my distance, spending nights in my truck and staying focused on my job.

I thought maybe my job was the key, and that building up a reputation for myself would help people see the real me. I've built up respect, to be sure – but it's respect out of fear, not out of liking. Still, the only thing to do is keep trying, and keep saving. Maybe one day I'll have a chance to prove myself; a town in need of supplies or protection, a person who asks me for help, an opportunity to show that I can be more than just a killer ... or maybe I'll just have to wait until I save up enough supplies to go somewhere new and get a fresh start.

But there's no time to dwell on that. There's still work to do. I left Beau's body with the townies, not wanting to lug it around after a near brush with Jedediah's men, but I still have his knife. So after a few minutes of soaking up the silence, I start my truck.

There are several bounty collectors in the area, all of whom have a price set for any member of Jedediah's crew, especially one as blatantly vicious as Beau the Butcher. But Alex the Collector is the closest, and one of my favorites, so I head to him.

His place is small but sturdy, a lone, stout building in the middle of nowhere, surrounded by a wire fence. It looks like another abandoned ruin to someone who doesn't know better, but I've been here many times before. The guard at the fence barely glances at me before waving me through. But Alex himself squints out from a barely cracked door, scrutinizing me thoroughly as if there's some trick involved. I bite my cheek and wait as he finishes his inspection and checks behind me twice before letting me inside.

With all the windows covered, the room is dim even with the sun still up. The place reeks of some kind of chemical – or maybe that's just Alex. The Collector is a squat, jiggly, nervous man with thinning hair. He's deathly afraid of the outside world, and I suspect it's been a long, long time since he's set foot out there. But once the door is shut and locked and it's just the two of us, his nerves give way to barely contained excitement. He trembles with it, barely able to restrain himself from immediately demanding to see what I've brought. I make him wait, taking my time looking around.

His center of operations is, if possible, weirder than the man himself. Alex is a collector not just of bounties, but of souvenirs. The walls are lined with dusty wooden shelves, the shelves lined with his mementos. I don't mind the weirdness; I appreciate the fact that Alex is a freak, because it means he doesn't look at me like I'm one. Dealing with him is much better than dealing with townies.

Still, staring at his souvenirs too long makes me uncomfortable. Some are fairly normal, like a boot sitting on a low shelf, or a sniper rifle hung high on the wall. But most venture far past the limit of the reasonable and into the land of the grotesque. A scorched femur, a skull split down the middle, an eyeball floating in a vat of murky liquid. Each one has a wanted poster framed next to it, announcing who the item once belonged to. Several of them came from my own collected marks.

'So,' Alex says, rubbing his hands together, his eyes bright. 'What've you got for me today?'

I dig the knife out of my bag, hold it up until I see recognition light his face, and deliver it hilt-first into his waiting hands. He turns the weapon slowly, admiring the rusty and bloodstained blade. His fingers find the small initials B. B. carved into the hilt and tap against them.

'Beau the Butcher,' he says, a smile splitting his face. I allow myself to smile back. He's one of the few people who appreciates my line of work, unlike the damn townies who treat me like I'm barely better than a raider. 'But no body?'

'You think I'm going to lug around one of Jedediah's men?' I ask, rolling my eyes. 'You recognize the knife. That's enough.'

'But how do I know that he's dead?' Alex asks, still admiring the knife. I stare at him until he glances up. As soon as he sees the look on my face, he blanches and lets out a nervous laugh. 'Right,' he says. 'Never mind. Will be a reduced payment, though, and I can't help that.'

'Fine,' I say. It's not worth the effort of arguing, especially when I'm already double-dipping for the reward – first the townies and now a collector. 'How much, then?'

'Hmm,' he says. 'Well, considering it's just the knife . . . ' His eyes flick upward as he no doubt considers how much of the bounty he can weasel out of paying. After a moment, his eyes flick back to me. 'Four and six.'

I frown, digging the crumpled wanted poster out of my pocket to double-check the listed reward. I hold it up for him to see.

'That's less than half.'

'Well, there's no body.'

I glare at him, and he takes a step back.

'Five and seven,' I say.

'Fine,' he says, so quickly I mentally kick myself for not asking for more. Before I can say anything he's already scrambling to the back room, the knife clutched in his greedy hands. He returns soon after with the goods wrapped in a plastic bag. I take them out to count.

'By the way,' Alex says, 'I've got an informant in Buzzard's Beak looking for you. I've worked with her a few times, she's never steered me wrong.'

I pause, and then resume counting, double-checking to ensure he gave me the right amount before returning my attention to him.

'She's looking for me specifically?' I ask, wary. That rarely means anything good.

'She's looking for the best of the best,' Alex says with a smile. I give him a dead stare, and he drops it. 'Well, looking for someone who isn't afraid of a hard job and won't let any personal feelings get in the way.'

'Fair enough. You send anyone else her way?'

'Only you,' he says, which I take to mean, *So far.* Alex is a cunning bastard, and he never places everything on one gamble. 'Huge payment, I hear.'

'For who?'

'She didn't specify. Just said it was a big job, a danger-ous job, and a huge payout. I'd get there quick.'

'I'll see what I can do,' I say. 'Got a lot on my plate right now.'

I count my reward for a third time, gather it up, and head out.

Buzzard's Beak isn't far, and I reach it by sundown. It's a dull little town full of dull little people, and tonight it seems even more dreary than usual. The townspeople are scuttling into their homes now that the sun's going down, and they all avoid eye contact and scoot out of my way as I walk down the street. Some of them must recognize me – I've done business here before – but nobody says a word of greeting. Judging by the mood, I'd guess Jedediah's men have been here. I wonder if they upped the tax here as well as in Sunrise, but don't care quite enough to ask one of the dead-eyed men or women trying to ignore my existence.

There's only one place in this town that stays alive after sundown: the saloon. In this case, 'alive' means there are two flickering lanterns keeping the room lit, and a whopping five people occupying the rickety chairs and stools. I sweep my eyes around the room, and it doesn't take long for me to find who I'm looking for. There's only one person out of place, one person who meets my eyes and isn't coated with three layers of dust and sorrow: a woman sitting in a corner with a half-empty bottle of water on the table in front of her.

I size up the dusty handful of townies in the room and scope out the dark corners, but it doesn't look like there are any surprises waiting for me. Once I'm confident that nothing looks suspicious, I walk over to the woman's table and take a seat on the slanted wooden stool across from her. She studies my face, idly toying with her bottle of water.

'I know you,' she says. 'Clementine, right?'

'Mhm.' I can't deny that it pleases me to be recognized, though *tall woman with a burnt face* isn't so difficult to remember. At least we can skip the part where I convince her I'm trustworthy.

'I've heard good things about your work.'

I almost smile, but suppress it. She's just trying to butter me up.

'Tell me about the job,' I say. 'Who's the mark?'

She hesitates, and my frown deepens.

'Are you a risk taker, Clementine?'

Though her face and voice show nothing, one of her hands taps out a nervous beat on the table. I stare at the hand, and she stops.

'I am if I'm paid enough,' I say, folding my arms across my chest. 'What, is it one of Jedediah's men?' I should be wary, but it's hard to keep the hunger out of my voice. I lean forward, and she leans with me, allowing me to drop my voice. 'I've taken out almost a dozen of them over the years.'

She studies my face, showing no hint of surprise at my words.

'So I've heard,' she says. 'But this isn't one of Jedediah's men.'

I lean back again, disappointed despite myself. There's a certain thrill to hunting down the scum who work for our not-so-benevolent overlord – the risk, the challenge, the sense of justice, and of course the more personal thirst for revenge. But I push those thoughts aside. A job is a job . . . and more importantly, I'm starting to wonder what mark would make the job such a challenge, if it's not one of Jedediah's underlings. There isn't anyone else who poses a threat around here; Jedediah's made damn sure of it.

The informant glances around the room, licks her lips, and gestures for me to lean forward again. I sigh, but oblige, and she leans in even farther so our faces are a mere half foot apart.

'The mark is Jedediah Johnson himself.'

My head snaps back. I'm shocked into silence for a moment – and burst out in a harsh bark of laughter that causes every head in the room to turn toward us. The informant sinks down in her chair, her cheeks growing red. By the time I finish laughing, all but one passed-out townie in the corner have fled the room.

In the silence following my laughter, the townie snores quietly.

'Well,' the informant says. 'Now that you've succeeded in drawing far too much attention to us, I think we're done here.' She stands up and moves to leave, but I grab her arm before she makes it far, yanking her back. She stares down at me, and I stare right back.

'What is this?' I ask. 'Some kind of convoluted scam? An ambush? What's the point of telling such a stupid lie?'

'I'm not a liar,' she says. 'I'm sure Alex told you as much, or you wouldn't even have showed up.'

I chew that over, relaxing my grip on her arm just a bit. While I wouldn't go so far as to say I trust Alex, he doesn't have any reason to waste my time. I bring in a lot of business, and a lot of his beloved souvenirs.

'Getting to Jedediah is impossible,' I say. 'He never leaves the Wormwood mansion, and he's surrounded by his goons.' I've looked into it, hunted for information that could lead me to him, even risked scoping out the place myself a couple times. I've wanted to kill him for years, but it's just not feasible. There are guards at every door of his mansion, armed patrols, impenetrable defenses. The place is a fortress.

The informant sighs. She pulls her arm back, and I let go after a moment, gesturing to the seat across from me. She slowly sits down.

'There's new information,' she says. 'From someone on the inside.'

My eyebrows shoot up.

'Why would one of his men betray him?' It doesn't make sense. Jedediah's men have it made, and they'd be dead if they went against him in any way.

'They say he's been acting strange,' she says. 'Upping the taxes, tightening his noose a little too snugly. The townies are pissed, and his men are taking the blame. There's been talk of dissent in the ranks, maybe even an uprising. Maybe they think they're jumping off a sinking ship.'

I've heard no such rumors of an uprising – but then again, why would townies tell me? They've made it pretty damn clear that they trust me just a hair more than they trust the raiders. And I know the part about raising taxes is true. I gesture at her to continue.

'Whatever the reason, this person came to me. And they told me there's something hardly anyone knows about the place. Something that, if you knew, would make it easy to get into the Wormwood mansion, right to Jedediah himself.'

She stops there. I know she wants me to ask more, but I'm still wary. I want to believe – want to believe so badly that I'm trying very hard to hold myself back. My mind keeps flashing to what a job like this would mean for me. Jedediah Johnson is the reason that my home is now a pile of ashes. He's the reason my family is dead and my face is burnt and my life is the way it is.

But taking him down would be about more than revenge, or honoring the memory of my people … It would be a chance to show, once and for all, that I'm on the good side. I could liberate the eastern towns, get rid of a tyrant, save people from this oppression. People would love me for it. No more unwelcoming stares, no more mistrust, no more looking at me like I'm some kind of monster. They would let me in with open arms.

I'd be a hero. I'd have a home.

But I'm getting carried away here. No matter how much this would mean for me, and how badly I want it to be true, I can't let that blind me. It's still highly unlikely that this is true, and far more likely that I'd be wandering into a trap.

'Fine. Give me the information and maybe I'll consider checking it out,' I say, even as I will myself to walk away.

The informant looks far too satisfied for my liking. She knows she's caught my interest. I plaster on a scowl, waiting for her to stop looking so smug and continue.

'Near the mansion is a scrapyard,' she says. 'Bunch of rusty, good-for-nothing old cars, all the good parts stripped. But beneath one of them – a red truck – is a hidden trapdoor.'

'Seriously?' I ask, rolling my eyes. This sounds more and more like another urban legend about Jedediah.

'Inside is a tunnel. A tunnel leading right under the Wormwood mansion, that opens up right in Jedediah's bedroom.'

I stare at her.

'There's no way it can be that simple.'

'Jedediah's a smart man. He knows he needs a way out in case shit ever goes down. But hardly anyone is allowed into his room, and nobody's going to bother to check under rusty old cars. Very, *very* few people know about this, as far as I understand.'

'And you're sure there are no guards waiting on the other side?'

'Like I said. Hardly anyone knows the tunnel exists, including his own men.'

I tap my fingers on the table. I still have so many questions, and so many doubts. And yet, I want so badly to believe it could be true, want so badly for there to be a chance to take out Jedediah. If there was even a half-believable shot, I would be willing to take it. And yet . . .

'What a load of bullshit.' I shove out my chair and stand up, shaking my head at her. 'Thanks for wasting my time,' I say dryly, and head for the door.

'Clementine!' she calls after me. I don't turn around, but she continues anyway. 'If you get him, get him alive. No one will believe you otherwise.'

I pause at the door, scowling over my shoulder at her.

'I'm not chasing some fairy tale,' I say, and leave without another glance back. I head to my truck, start her up, and hesitate for just a moment, my hands gripping the steering wheel tightly. The information has to be fake … it has to be. All signs point to this 'job' being absolute bullshit. And yet … what if it's not?

I jam my heel on the gas and head straight for Wormwood.

IV
The Tunnel

The tunnel is real.

I sit back on my heels, staring at it. It was waiting beneath a rusty old red truck in the middle of a scrapyard, exactly where the informant said it would be. The metal trapdoor was coated with dirt, making it virtually invisible unless you were looking for it, but it was here. The darkness of the tunnel stares back at me, an awful smell drifting out of its open mouth.

Goddamn do I wish the tunnel wasn't real. Would've made things a whole lot easier if I could've just dismissed the whole thing as bullshit. I could've laughed at myself for being stupid enough to believe it for even a second, for risking my life coming out to Jedediah's headquarters in Wormwood, hiding my truck, and sneaking past his patrols into this abandoned scrapyard. I could've walked away kicking myself about nearly falling for such a stupid trick.

But the tunnel is real. So now what?

I chew my bottom lip, keeping my gun aimed at the open tunnel just in case something comes crawling out of it, but inside it's still and silent. There's no hint of what's within, aside from the smell, and no hint about what's waiting on the other end. It could be an ambush. It could be a dead end. Or maybe, just maybe, it could be the self-declared king of the eastern wastes.

It seems far more likely that it's a trick ... but if I don't find out for sure, I'll wonder about this moment forever.

'Fuck it,' I mutter. I scoot under the car and lower myself into the darkness.

Inside, it's cramped and earthy, and I have to crouch to prevent my head from hitting the ceiling. The terrible smell is ten times worse than it was outside. I cough, and cover my mouth with one hand to stifle any further noise, the other keeping my gun aimed at the darkness in front of me. It's impossible to see anything ahead.

I remove my hand from my mouth and grope along the wall, pressing forward. After a couple minutes, the dim moonlight from the entrance is barely visible. Muffled sounds come from above – voices and footsteps. I must be directly underneath the Wormwood mansion. I pause, looking up and imagining Jedediah's men right above me. The ceiling of the tunnel trembles, raining dust whenever it gets too loud above. It's easy to picture the whole thing collapsing on me, burying me as punishment for my stupidity, but I brush the concern away. Clearly the tunnel has stood for this long, and it will continue standing tonight. I push forward, half-listening to the sounds above, just in case there's a clamor that means they may have found my truck, or the disturbed trapdoor, or some other sign of an intruder. None comes.

After a few minutes longer, I bump up against something. I step back, so startled I almost make the grave mistake of firing my gun, but it's just another wall. My stomach sinks at the thought that I've hit a dead end. Is this it? The end to my fantasy of killing Jedediah?

The ceiling groans, and I look up. There are footsteps above, and barely visible in the darkness, another metal trapdoor. I reach up to run my fingers over it, and my heart thuds wildly in my chest. I haven't hit a dead end after all. This is it: the exit, and the moment of truth.

Someone is right above me, in the room this trapdoor opens into. I listen carefully for a couple minutes, but I can only hear one set of footsteps. Perhaps not an ambush, then. But could it really be him? The raider king himself, Jedediah Johnson? Is this the moment where I prove myself an idiot for believing what the informant told me, or the moment where I prove myself a hero?

Time to find out.

Gun held ready, I push open the trapdoor, grab the edge with my free hand, and pull myself up to the other side.

V

The Capture of Jedediah Johnson

'Oh, hello,' Jedediah Johnson says, going slightly cross-eyed as he stares down the barrel of my gun.

I've imagined this moment a thousand times, in a thousand different ways, but it never played out quite like this. I thought the infamous Jedediah would be angry about being captured, or afraid, maybe even impressed. At the very least, I thought he'd be surprised. But instead, he just seems curious and progressively more cross-eyed.

He doesn't look the way I'd expected, either. Rumors abounded about his appearance, of course, mostly involving hideous scars and jewelry made of human teeth. I was more realistic; I knew he was the brains of his crew, with more than enough brawn eager to do his dirty work, and he wouldn't have to be huge and intimidating like his made-of-muscle tax collectors. But still, this guy looks like I could deck him with one good punch.

And he has a very punchable face, with a mouth that seems on the verge of smirking, even at this moment. He's surprisingly close to my own age, and has no scars, burns, tattoos, piercings, or any marks of the life of violence and depravity I know he leads. And he's *shorter* than I am. It's not unusual, but still, I would've assumed a man with such a towering reputation would top five foot ten. In a room full of strangers, I never would have picked this man as the infamous raider-turned-ruler. In fact, I wouldn't spare him a second glance for any reason.

But this is him. It must be. Against all odds, everything else the informant told me has been correct – and why else would there be a secret tunnel into Jedediah's headquarters, if not as an emergency escape route for the man himself?

'Get on your knees,' I say, gesturing impatiently when the gun in his face doesn't seem like enough of a clue for him. 'Put your hands behind your head.'

'Yes, ma'am,' he says, sinking to his knees on the carpet. I can't believe the bastard actually has carpet in his bedroom, plush and beige and offensively clean before my boots smeared a trail of dirt across it. He also has a real bed, with real sheets, and a closet full of clothes that look like they've barely been worn. It's exactly the life of luxury I would've expected an evil, conniving dictator to lead. At least that makes sense about this situation.

But his attitude is really throwing me off. He seems completely unconcerned, even with a gun to his head, even when I roughly jerk his hands down and tie them behind his back. He doesn't struggle, doesn't yell for help, just sits there patiently waiting for me to finish. Once his hands are secure, I circle around to the front of him, jabbing the gun in his face again. This time he doesn't go cross-eyed, but looks right past the gun and meets my eyes. One corner of his lips curls up.

'You don't have anything to say?' I ask. I know it's a bad idea to engage an extremely dangerous prisoner, but I can't resist.

'Oh, is this the part where I'm supposed to beg for my life?' he asks. 'Or ask how you got in here?' His eyes swivel to the trapdoor. 'I mean, that one is pretty obvious. I suppose a more appropriate question would be "Which traitorous asshole told you about the secret entrance?" but that's a mystery easily solved. There are a very limited number of people who know about it. It shouldn't take the crew long to figure out who spilled the beans, find them, and kill them.' He says it very matter-of-factly, and smiles as he turns back to me.

I stare at him. Maybe there's nothing fishy going on here after all; maybe he's just this damn arrogant.

'I thought about yelling for a guard,' he continues,

'but I figured you'd likely shoot me if I did that, and I'd prefer not to get shot.'

'So you think I'm not going to shoot you?' I ask, keeping my voice even and flat.

'Don't think so. I'm worth more alive, right, Clementine?'

I jerk at the sound of my name.

'How do you know who I am?' I ask, trying to hide how much it rattles me to hear my name from his mouth. I never thought the raider king himself would know about me. I thought he'd have his goons worry about things like bounty hunters, while he stayed holed up in this pretty little room.

'Oh, please,' Jedediah says. His eyes slide across the burnt half of my face, his gaze so penetrating I can practically feel its touch. His eyes reach the twisted corner of my mouth, pause, and shift up to meet my stare. 'You're prettier than I thought you'd be.'

I stuff my handkerchief into his mouth to make sure he's thoroughly silenced. He waggles his eyebrows at me, the corners of his eyes crinkling in amusement.

I have yet to decide if he's utterly insane or just ridiculously confident, but either way, I need to keep this job professional. Clean. The way I always do things. It doesn't matter that this is goddamn Jedediah Johnson I'm dealing with, and it doesn't matter that I've been dreaming of taking him down for years, and it doesn't matter that this could change my entire life. For now, all that matters is getting the job done, and getting it done right.

Collecting a mark usually means a lot of struggling and fighting and yelling, at least until I knock them out. I certainly wouldn't mind landing a couple of good punches on this bastard, but he's behaving himself remarkably well, and I'd rather avoid dragging him all the way to my truck if I can help it. Still, I'm not gentle as I shove him into the tunnel, my gun aimed at the back of his head. I jump down and pull the trapdoor shut behind us. When it closes, it's just him and me and the darkness of the tunnel. I can barely make out his shape ahead.

'Move,' I say. Jedediah balks, hesitant for the first time. I wonder if it's the sudden realization of his own helplessness, or that he's leaving the safety of his head-quarters, or maybe just the fact that his secret escape tunnel smells like something died in it a while ago and was never discovered. Regardless, a sharp jab with the barrel of my gun gets him moving again.

I move slowly, quietly, listening for any sound of a disturbance above or company joining us in the cramped tunnel. But I hear nothing; no one approaching, no sign that anyone has noticed my presence or Jedediah's absence. I'm listening so carefully that a sudden noise makes me jump. It takes me a few moments to realize what it is. Jedediah is . . . humming. Humming cheerfully under his breath like this is a pleasant stroll.

'Stop that,' I hiss once I've shaken off my surprise, poking him in the back of the neck with my gun. He shuts up, but I swear I hear muffled chuckling.

At the end of the tunnel, I make him wait behind. I pause, my hands on the trapdoor, listening for any voices or footsteps outside. When I hear nothing, I push it open – first just a few inches so I can peer around, and fully when the area appears deserted.

The trapdoor scrapes against the bottom of the car above as I open it. I climb out and reach back to help Jedediah up. Thankfully he's a scrawny bastard, and easy enough to pull upward. I move on my hands and knees to the other side of the vehicle, and glance around once more before dragging Jedediah out and pulling him to his feet. He coughs on dust, frowning, unable to wipe himself off after the drag through the dirt. I almost smile at the look on his face, but stifle it, reminding myself I'm still not in the clear.

Outside of Jedediah's mansion, which towers like a lone giant among the other buildings, Wormwood is much like every other town – dreary, dusty, on the verge of falling apart. It's quiet, perhaps a little too quiet, the doors all shut and the people sealed away. I guess Jedediah's crew keeps a tight watch over this place. I'm careful to keep quiet myself, creeping along with Jedediah ahead of me. He trips over a discarded car door, and a loud *clang* echoes through the scrapyard.

I pull him back and freeze, but the town remains silent around us.

My truck is parked a few minutes' walk away, hidden behind a decrepit building on the outskirts of town. I'm careful to stay behind crumbling walls and old buildings that seem unoccupied. The goal is to secure Jedediah and be out of Wormwood before his crew notices anything is wrong. But if I fail, I'll have dozens of angry, heavily armed raiders hot on my trail.

Thankfully Jedediah is quiet at the moment, and still cooperating. Probably a smart move, because right now I'm so jumpy that I very well might shoot him, intentionally or not, if he startled me. The night is still and calm, no sound other than our footsteps and my own heartbeat in my ears. I push Jedediah forward, gun never leaving his head. I know better than to underestimate him, despite how accommodating he's being about his own kidnapping.

Voices ahead.

I grab Jedediah's arm, yanking him back and dropping to a crouch. He lands on his ass beside me with a thump, a burst of dust, and a muffled groan of complaint. When he notices the voices, he turns sharply in that direction. There are at least two men, and they're moving this way.

Pulling Jedediah with me, I straighten up and move to a nearby building, pressing myself against it. I wait, holding my breath, wondering if the men heard us. But their conversation sounds casual, their pace leisurely. They don't seem to suspect that anything is wrong; they're just patrolling the area.

Ordinarily I wouldn't hesitate to take down two unsuspecting men, but I can't afford to raise a ruckus. And if I try to sneak by, I don't trust that Jedediah's compliant attitude will hold up with help just a shout away. Is this why he's been so smug and unconcerned? Did he know we would run into one of his patrols on the way out? I turn to him, my lips pressed into a firm line. He's staring in the direction of his men, his eyes narrowed as if carefully considering something, his muscles tense. He looks ready . . . for something. To run, to fight, to make a sound to attract their attention.

He looks over at me as he notices I'm staring, and his eyes widen, as if he can see my intention. He tries to say something, his words unintelligible through the gag.

I deck him with one good punch.

VI
The Sale of Jedediah Johnson

Halfway through the process of dragging an unconscious Jedediah to my truck, I almost regret my decision to knock him out. But, if I'm being honest, the satisfaction of my fist hitting his face was more than enough to make up for the annoyance. I really do try my best not to be overly sadistic while working, but this is Jedediah Johnson. Even setting the personal vendetta aside, I've heard more than enough stories about the things he's done. If I hadn't personally witnessed the results of his dictatorship, I would've thought he was an urban legend. But portions of hard-earned goods disappearing every month, people stolen in the middle of the night, rebellious towns burned to the ground – those are real, and they all have one name whispered in their wake: *Jedediah Johnson.*

I have about a thousand reasons to put a bullet in this man's head. Luckily for him, there's one very important reason not to. Like the informant said, no one will believe me if I lug in a body and claim it's Jedediah Johnson, considering no one knows his face. His men could easily cover up the death, since he spends his time holed up here anyway – and even if the information did eventually get out, by that time my name would be long forgotten. I'm staking everything on this. I need people to know it was me. I need to be the woman who freed the eastern wastes.

And with Jedediah unconscious, there's no one to stop me from getting away with it. The patrol is relaxed, noisy, and easy to avoid even when I'm weighed down by a body. I make it to my truck without trouble, tie Jedediah up, and throw him in the backseat.

'Damn easy job,' I mutter to myself with a smile, and start up my truck.

With that done, I ride toward freedom. First slow and steady, so I don't attract unwanted attention from the residents of Wormwood. But as soon as I pass the outskirts of town, I pick up speed, gradually and then suddenly, and grin at the roar of my truck's engine and the thought of what's to come. Soon, very soon, everything is going to change for me.

I'd be hard-pressed to find someone that *doesn't* want

Jedediah's head, but Alex the Collector is where I started this journey, so I show up at his door. It's the middle of the night, and his guard seems wary about seeing me again so soon, but they let me in when I show them I'm bringing in a mark.

Alex holds a lantern up to the crack in the door, providing a sliver of flickering light in the darkness. His thinning hair is in disarray, his eyes bloodshot.

'Well, well, Clementine. Back so soon?' He eyes me, and then the unconscious man I'm dragging behind me, raising his lantern to get a better look. 'Who's this?'

'Open up and I'll tell you,' I say. He licks his lips, peers around for any sign of someone following me, and lets me inside.

I drag Jedediah into the room, past the shelves of souvenirs. I note Beau the Butcher's knife already displayed in all its rusty glory. Next to it is another new souvenir, a freshly severed hand from a raider named Left-Hand. It makes me wonder what he'll take from Jedediah. I smile slightly at the thought.

I drop Jedediah and continue to the far wall. This one doesn't have collectibles, but is instead covered in current wanted posters. The lantern light flickers across names and sketched faces.

'So, who have you brought me?' Alex asks as he locks the door behind us. 'I don't recognize him.'

'Few people would,' I say. I can feel his questioning

eyes on the back of my head. I find the poster I'm looking for, the one that has nothing but a silhouette and a
question mark where a sketch would normally be. I'm
not the best reader, but this name is so imprinted in my
brain that I recognize it immediately. I rip the poster
off the wall and turn around, holding it up for Alex, a
broad grin on my face.

Alex raises the lantern to get a better look. He stares
at the poster for a long few moments, and then at me,
and then at the unconscious, dusty man sprawled out
on his floor.

'Jedediah Johnson?' he asks. He takes several hasty
steps away from the man, and shakes his head so violently I swear I hear his jowls flapping. 'No,' he says.
'No way.'

'It's him, all right,' I say. 'Your informant's tip sent
me right to him.'

Jedediah stirs. The timing is so convenient that it
occurs to me maybe he wasn't actually unconscious,
but just waiting for the proper moment to step into the
conversation. Alex jumps back like the man is a snake
uncoiling on his floor. Jedediah's eyes open slowly. They
land first on Alex, who stares back in utter terror. One
eyebrow rises. When his gaze sweeps over the shelves of
souvenirs, the other eyebrow rises to join it. Then he sees
me, and both eyebrows lower again.

'Mmmpfff,' he says, wiggling.

'What's he saying?' Alex asks in a loud whisper, refusing to take his eyes off him. His usual excitement over a bounty has shifted into the deep fear he normally reserves for the world outside. It seems I've brought a piece of the wastes a little too big for him to handle. 'Was that ... a threat?'

'I don't know or care,' I say. Jedediah shoots me an offended look, which I ignore. 'Look, do we have a deal or not?'

Alex chews his fingernails, finally tearing his eyes away from Jedediah and turning to me. He sizes me up and makes a noncommittal noise in the back of his throat.

'I want to hear what he has to say,' Alex says.

'I doubt that,' I say.

'Gag off, or no deal. I want to know what I'm getting myself into.'

I know this is a bad idea, but I can't do much when my customer is making a demand. I sigh, step closer to Jedediah, and yank my handkerchief out of his mouth, letting it fall to the ground. He sighs contentedly and leans his head back to look up at me.

'Wow,' he says, his voice earnestly impressed. 'You throw a hell of a punch.'

'More where that came from,' I say, eyeing him in case he decides to try something. But he seems as mellow as before, apparently unconcerned by where he is and what's happening. He grins at me, but as he turns toward Alex, the smile disappears. The Collector takes a step back. Jedediah stares silently.

'What's he doing?' Alex whispers, looking to me for answers. I shrug.

'I'm deciding how I'll kill you when I'm free,' Jedediah says brightly. 'Alex the Collector. I've heard of you. And now I'll know exactly how to find—' I step forward and give him a swift kick to the gut to stop him from saying anything else, but the damage is done. Alex lets out a sound like a wounded animal, his hand-wringing accelerating to light speed. I sigh and brush hair out of my face.

'Alex, he's—'

'No,' he says. 'No, no, no. I can't do it. He's too dangerous.'

'You're the one who sent me to the informant,' I remind him. 'Now you're saying you're not going to pay out?'

'I didn't know she would send you to Jedediah fucking Johnson! I was just the middleman!'

'You—'

'I can't, Clementine.' He throws up a hand to stop me from continuing, his voice growing firm. 'Think about what you're asking me. You're asking me to take *Jedediah Johnson* off your hands, in an area ruled by the *crew* of Jedediah Johnson. Do you see the problem?'

'Yes,' I say, grudgingly. 'I'm not an idiot.' I take a long look at Jedediah, who is still groaning after my kick, and back at Alex. 'What if I only take half the bounty, to make up for potential trouble?'

'Not happening.'

'A third.'

'I'm not getting anywhere near this, Clementine,' he says. 'I wouldn't do it if *you* paid *me*.'

I pinch the bridge of my nose. My dreams of adoration for this catch are quickly slipping out from between my fingers.

'Why offer a bounty if I can't cash it in?' I ask.

'No one thought it was possible to just waltz in and take him!' Alex says, throwing his hands up. 'I thought the only way this would happen was if his whole crew was taken out, or he lost his position, or ... I ... I don't know. But I didn't expect ... *this*.'

My heart sinks. Alex is right to be concerned about Jedediah's crew showing up on his doorstep, whether it be before or after we deal with Jedediah for good. Still, I never thought a collector would be so afraid that they'd turn him down. I think back to the way the townies stared at me when I asked if they wanted to kill Beau the Butcher, and shake my head. Every time I start to think I understand people, they surprise me with new depths of cowardice.

I look down at Jedediah, who has recovered from the

kick and is now humming under his breath while waiting for us to finish talking. I sigh, shift from foot to foot, put my hand on the gun at my hip. The feel of it beneath my hand is reassuring. But I see Alex eyeing me nervously as he notices me gripping it, and force myself to remove my hand and place it on my hip instead.

'So what am I supposed to do with him, then?' I ask, finally admitting to him as well as to myself that I have absolutely no idea where to go from here. I doubt I'll have luck with any other collectors. With anyone other than Alex, it'd be a real pain in the ass just to prove that this is the man I claim it is – and even if they believed me, they could turn me away. I can't just keep dragging Jedediah around. His crew will catch up to me eventually. Do I kill him, cut my losses, and be done with it? It would be satisfying, sure, but . . . I'd get nothing out of it. I'm not sure I could live with the knowledge I was so close to everything I'd ever wanted, and let it slip away.

Alex looks like he wants to throw me out in the dust here and now. But maybe he sees the desperation in my expression, because a few moments later his face softens.

'Look, Clementine,' he says. 'It's suicide for me to get involved in this, and you're not gonna have any more luck with anyone else in the area. But maybe you could reach a little further, past where people are so afraid of this guy.'

I drum my fingers on the butt of my gun.

'Turn in his bounty somewhere else?' I ask. 'All my contacts are here.'

Alex licks his lips, looking at Jedediah and back at me. I wait silently. After a few moments, he sighs and nods.

'Follow me,' he says, and walks into the back room. I make sure Jedediah's bonds are secure before following.

The back room is small, musty, and windowless. I've never been allowed back here before, but there's not much to look at. Just a ratty cot in the corner, where the Collector must sleep, and a wooden, half-broken desk and chair. The desk is piled with outdated wanted posters and other papers. I'm not a strong enough reader to get any information out of them at a glance, and a glance is all I get before Alex steps between me and the desk. He sets the lantern down on it, leans over, and rummages through one of the drawers. He plucks something out and places it atop the mess on the desk.

'A radio?' I ask, glancing over at him. 'Didn't know anyone used these anymore.'

'They usually don't,' he says. 'I'd just fiddle with it occasionally, for fun. But then I started picking up something.' He scrounges around on his desk until he finds a particular piece of paper, and holds it up. 'A broadcast. A real one, a nightly one, always the same guy, who calls himself "Saint." It was a long spiel, mostly a lot of blah-blah-blah about justice and taking the wastes back. He's got a radio tower, and the towns love him. He's been gaining a lot of power off to the west of us.'

'The western wastes?' I ask incredulously. 'He wants to take back the *western* wastes?' I doubt that's even possible, but more importantly ... 'What the hell does this have to do with me?' Alex can go over-the-top with the theatrics sometimes, and I'm painfully aware of every passing minute, another minute that Jedediah's crew could be coming for me.

'Well,' Alex says. 'His whole deal is that he's capturing sharks. Er, getting other people to capture them, really – the townies and such bring them to him, and he gives out rewards in return. The idea is to clean up his area of the wastes, but I'm sure he wouldn't complain about getting a famous raider from over here either.'

'Huh,' I say, processing the information. Sounds like the same idea as bounties, but on a larger scale. Jedediah probably isn't the type of person this Saint guy is expecting to get. He and his crew aren't like raiders in the rest of the wastes. They were once the same – loose cannons making a living off raiding towns, killing and looting, preying on the weak. Now Jedediah and his men have moved on to organized tyranny. No point in random raids when the towns are all under the thumb of the self-proclaimed ruler. But, though the west has never seen anything like him, Jedediah *is* a shark, and a raider, and most definitely a menace. If Saint is really trying to do some good for the wastes, surely he won't turn me away.

'What does he do with the sharks?' I ask.

'Supposedly, he holds trials, and executes the ones he finds guilty.'

I let out a huff of air.

'Trials,' I say. 'What's the point?'

Alex shrugs, setting the paper down on his desk.

'Dunno, but that isn't your problem, is it? You hand over Jedediah, you get a nice reward, and the business is over with.'

I rub my thumb over the handle of my gun, considering. The reward would have to be a pretty damn sizeable one to make it worth a trip to the western wastes. Things are shitty here, with a madman in charge demanding monthly tithes, and public executions of everyone who defies him, and his crew doing whatever the hell they want. But at least we have safe trade routes, and a reasonable attempt at a currency system, and rules – even if those rules are defined by a dictator. When people are killed, it's usually for a purpose: profit, or punishment, or power. The townies get the roughest of it, but for someone like me who's skilled enough to live outside of the rules, life isn't so bad.

From what I've heard, the west has none of the structure we have out here. They say it's completely out of control, a cluster-fuck of mindless violence. It's so overrun with raiders and crazies that whenever a bounty runs that way, we usually just check them off as dead and gone. Still, I've always admired the place. It may be utter chaos, but it's also utter freedom. A place where you have a chance to be anything you want. Where you fight tooth and nail to survive, but at least you have a chance to fight.

A place without the tyranny of Jedediah ... yet also without any aspect of the life I've always known. Things may not be great here, but at least they're familiar. Without bounties to hunt and towns I know, who would I become? Part of me has always wanted to find out, and part of me has always feared it. Either way, there's always been too much work to be done over here. Bounties to collect, raiders to hunt, townies to save. Since I lost everything five years ago, I've let my life revolve around my job. Hatred and hunger are enough to keep me pushing forward. I've tried to keep everything else at bay, including that distant but nagging desire to be something more than an outsider again.

But now ... if I could save the eastern wastes *and* take a shot at someplace new, all in one ... there's so much possibility. And maybe the west could be better for me. Maybe it's a place I'd actually fit in, a place where people wouldn't stare at me with fear in their eyes. Especially if I show up to hand an infamous dictator over to this Saint man, whom all the towns love ...

'You're sure this is legit?' I ask.

'I've got mostly rumors and word of mouth to go by, but all the news from the west says he's either a good guy, or doing a damn good job of pretending to be.' He shrugs. 'At the very least, you can be confident that you'll get paid.'

I nod, folding my arms over my chest.

'So. Heading west,' I say. 'I'm going to need a map, gasoline, some basic supplies.'

'I've got whatever you need,' Alex says. 'But what will you trade?'

I can see his greedy little eyes light up, probably already imagining one of my precious guns hanging on his wall. The mere thought makes me sick to my stomach, and anyway, my guns and ammo are essentials. You never know how much you're going to need for a trip like this, especially since I'm going to be traveling through the crazy-ass western wastes.

Unfortunately, though, I only have one other thing to give him.

VII
Across the Wastes

The truck is a liability, I tell myself as I hand the keys over to Alex. Anyone looking for me could recognize it, and such a nice vehicle sticks out like a sore thumb in the wastes. I push away memories of years spent behind that wheel, of nights spent sleeping in the backseat, and instead focus on the stash of goods I'm getting in return: a map to Saint, water and canned food, some gasoline, and a new vehicle.

The car I'm downgrading to is a small, shoddy thing, its chipped brown paint barely distinguishable from the rust. It looks like it won't make it five miles, but Alex swears up and down that it will get me where I need to go. I'm not too keen on trusting people, but I don't have much of a choice here. So I transfer my stuff from the truck bed to the trunk of the new car – water, food, bandages, and all of my guns and ammo. Grabbing the last armful of goods, I give my truck a pat on the hood, the only sentimental gesture I allow myself. After I dump the goods into the trunk and slam it shut, I head back inside.

Jedediah is lying on the floor where I left him, now resting on his side and snoring loudly. He looks way more comfortable than he has any right to be. I resist the urge to kick him again, find a spot against the wall for myself, and doze off.

I catch a few hours of sleep on Alex's floor, just enough to keep me going, and wake up automatically at the crack of dawn. I re-gag a still-mostly-asleep Jedediah with my handkerchief, drag him out to the passenger seat of the new car, and start it up.

The engine comes to life with a pitiful whine, and the entire vehicle shakes and shudders and rattles like it's going to come apart at any second. Wind whistles through a crack in the window, and the interior smells faintly of piss. But despite all appearances, the thing *does* run. So, with a wave at Alex's guard, I take to the road.

The first few hours pass without incident. I'm enjoying the feeling of being on the open road, and reveling in the knowledge that every mile of wasteland is a mile between me and Jedediah's crew. I know that I'm heading into lands full of their own danger. Surely though, it'll be different for me. I'm a bounty hunter. A professional. I've spent my whole life killing raiders. There may be more of them in the west, but they can't be any worse than they are here.

For the start of the ride, Jedediah dozes in his seat, head resting against the window. When he finally wakes up, I have a sinking feeling that my peaceful morning is about to be over. He soon proves me right. He starts with some muffled noises and squirming in his seat, which is easy enough to disregard. Then he progresses to kicking the windshield, which I can't afford to ignore. Sighing, I turn sharply – throwing him half out of his seat – and pull over. I get out, march over to his side, and yank his door open. He tumbles into the dirt.

'What's your problem?' I ask, placing a boot on his chest. He lets out a string of words that are entirely unintelligible through the gag. I grimace and grudgingly remove the handkerchief from his mouth.

Jedediah stretches his jaw, licks his lips, and clears his throat.

'I'd like,' he says in a raspy voice, 'a drink of water.'

I roll my eyes, removing my boot from his chest.

'That's it?' I ask. I thought he had finally realized his life was in danger, and intended to do something about it, but this is much better. I leave him in the dirt and grab my canteen from the trunk. Luckily I have a few big jugs of water left – I would never be stupid enough to travel the wastes without them – so I don't have to be *too* frugal.

I'm not entirely sure what the west will bring, or how long it will last, but I'm as prepared as possible. Alex said it would take about two days of travel to get to Saint's tower, but that's assuming I don't hit any major obstacles along the way, like angry townies, or raiders, or crazies. But whatever comes along, I'll be ready. I have enough food and water for more than a week, and plenty of ammo to mow down anyone who gets in my way.

I take a swig of water before walking over to Jedediah and pressing the container to his lips. He takes several big, greedy gulps, and I tear the canteen away.

'A little more?' he asks, licking the remnants off his lips.

'That's more than enough to last you the whole day,' I say, screwing the top onto the canteen and tossing it into my seat. Clearly, this guy has grown accustomed to a life of luxury. He might've once been a raider, but he's had goods hand delivered to him for years now. Guess he's forgotten what it's like to be out in the wastes.

I move to place the gag back in his mouth, but he ducks aside. I smack him upside the head and try to gag him again, but he shifts the other way. I sigh. 'Oh, come on,' I say. 'Don't tell me you decided to be difficult *now*.'

'Is the gag really necessary?' he asks, his neck craned to keep his face as far from me as possible. 'It's gonna be a long ride. We can talk!'

'I have no desire to talk to you.'

'I'd be a lot happier without the gag,' he says.

'I don't c—'

'And a lot more likely to continue cooperating,' he adds. When I scrutinize him, he smiles.

I suppose a drive with Jedediah occasionally speaking *would* be much better than a drive with him trying to escape. I could always tie him up and throw him in the back, but I'd rather keep him in my sight. He may be mostly acting like a cheeky little shit, but I'm not going to underestimate him. There's a mad genius in there, somewhere beneath the smiles and the sass. It's impossible to tell what he's thinking, but at least I can keep an eye on him.

'Fine,' I say. 'But I won't hesitate to knock your ass out again. Got it?'

'Crystal clear.'

Jedediah seems content to look out the window and hum under his breath, occasionally asking a question, which I respond to with short, clipped answers while keeping my eyes on the road. He stretches himself out in his seat, putting his shoes up on the dashboard and leaning his seat back, getting about as comfortable as a man with his wrists bound in front of him can get.

'My crew didn't kill your father or something, did they?' he asks, after staring out the window for a while.

'What?' I ask, startled by the question.

'Brother? Sister? Mother? Oh, jeez, I really hope we didn't kill your mom. That would be awkward,' he says. He pauses while I struggle to process what he's asking me. '...Husband?'

'No,' I lie, keeping my eyes fixed on the road ahead.

'Do you even have a husband to kill? Er...that came out wrong. Ignore everything after "husband."' He pauses, but continues after I open my mouth and shut it again. 'Or wife. Life partner? Anything like—'

'That's really none of your business,' I say once I've finally gathered myself. I catch myself grinding my jaw and force myself to stop. I can't let him get to me.

'Right. Anyway. Very relieved to hear that I haven't killed anyone close to you,' he says, looking out the window again. 'We get a few of those every so often, showing up at the Wormwood mansion. Lots of yelling and tears. "You killed my mother! Prepare to die!" Etcetera. Very dramatic.'

'I think that comes with the territory,' I say dryly.

'What territory?'

'Being a complete fucking psychopath.'

'Hey now,' he says, in a voice like I've offended him terribly. 'You kill people too.'

My back stiffens at the gratingly familiar words. I've seen the way townies look at me, heard the things they say. Sometimes it seems like they don't think I'm any better than the people I'm killing. And they have no idea how many people I choose *not* to kill – how many I'd really like to, if not for my personal rules.

'It's different,' I say eventually.

'How so?'

'I only kill assholes like you,' I say. For a moment I flash back to words my old sheriff once said about me – *She's a weapon. We've just got to make sure she's pointed in the right direction.* But, like I did back then, I tell myself that's not an issue. I know the difference between good people and bad.

'Ah,' he says. 'So it's okay as long as they're a worse person than you are?' He says it almost teasingly. I tighten my grip on the steering wheel.

'I'm not going to discuss morals with a cannibalistic tyrant,' I say. That shuts him up, giving me several seconds of blissful silence. Then he starts mumbling under his breath.

I know I shouldn't ask, but I can't help myself. I take my eyes off the road to glance over, and find him with a deeply thoughtful expression.

'What are you muttering about?'

'Tyrannical cannibal,' he says, answering overly quickly, like he's been waiting impatiently for me to ask. 'You should've gone with that over "cannibalistic tyrant." Sounds a lot better, doesn't it? Tyrannical cannibal. Rolls nicely off the tongue.'

I sigh. Whatever goes on in that fucked-up brain of his, clearly nothing I say is going to get past the layer of crazy. Not that it matters; he'll be dead soon, and I'll be a hero, and these pointless conversations will fade from my mind.

I stay silent while he repeats 'tyrannical cannibal' to himself several more times, in varying tones and pitches, before finally shutting up.

I shoot down his further attempts at conversation, and we drive through the day in silence, aside from the rattling of the car and Jedediah's humming, which comes and goes every couple of minutes. At first, we pass by a town every few hours, which makes it easy to check our progress on the map. These are all the towns under Jedediah's reign, and he perks up at the sight of each one, loudly announcing its name as if I wouldn't know. 'That's Sunrise!' 'Buzzard's Beak!' 'Last Stand!' He's like a little kid seeing his first meal in a week. Then again, I guess the towns *are* pretty much meals to the man who demands a tithe from each one.

As we get farther out, the sky gets darker, and the towns get sparser, and Jedediah gets even more excited to see each new one.

'Hey, there's Old Creek!' he says happily as he sees the latest one – one of the last before we hit the somewhat official border of the eastern wastes, the end of the area claimed by Jedediah and his crew. 'There was never a creek there. I don't know why they named it that.'

The name sends an immediate and involuntary shudder through my body. I don't need to look to know what I'll find, but I do it anyway. There's no town – not anymore. Just the husks of old buildings, melted and blackened by the fire that scorched the place to the ground almost five years ago. As with most tragedies, there was one name whispered in the aftermath. Unlike others, this one I don't need to rely on rumors to know about.

'Shut the fuck up,' I say, struggling to keep my voice level as a wave of revulsion rises inside me. 'Right now.' He looks at me, eyebrows rising as if surprised by the reaction. I turn to glare at him, and in doing so, show the left side of my face again. His eyes land on the burns, and he pauses.

'Oh,' he says.

One of my hands automatically moves from the wheel to my gun, and for a moment I can clearly imagine pulling it out and putting a bullet between Jedediah's eyes. Or maybe in his knees first – something slow and painful, something I could really relish.

But no. I can't. Killing him now would get me nothing; personal satisfaction isn't good enough.

I take a deep breath and slowly remove my hand from the gun, forcing myself to tear my eyes away from the man nonchalantly talking about the town he burned to the ground. At least he has the good sense to be quiet now, watching the burnt remains of Old Creek fade into the distance.

When I look away from him and glance at the mirror to my side, I notice it: a cloud of dust on the horizon. Behind us, and gaining fast. I squint at the rearview mirror, watch it getting closer. It could be a dust storm ... a very fast, very deliberately moving dust storm. But I know it's not.

We're being followed.

'What's that?' Jedediah asks, noticing the approaching cloud at about the same time I do. My pulse rising, I press harder on the pedal. It coaxes a little more speed out of this shitty car, but not enough. Not nearly enough.

'Shut up,' I say. 'Stay low.' I don't check to see if he's obeying, too busy glancing between the road ahead and the road behind. I can't see the vehicle clearly enough yet. Is it Jedediah's crew behind me, on my trail already? But *how*? Surely they couldn't have already determined that I left the area and headed this way. Unless Alex sold me out ...

I grit my teeth and keep driving.

'Bet you're missing your truck right about now,' Jedediah says.

'Shut. Up.'

I press the pedal to the floor. The car shudders violently, rattling every bone in my body, and chugs along at a slightly faster rate. It's enough to pull ahead for just a few moments, so our pursuer disappears from sight. And I see something else that sparks an idea: a heap of junk alongside the road, what looks to be the remains of two cars after a wreck.

I swerve off the road, drawing a startled yelp out of Jedediah, and drive right up alongside the metal carcasses. I kill the engine and yank Jedediah down with me.

Without the grumbling of the engine and the rattling of the car's frame, it's very quiet. I sit, silent, listening. I hold my breath as I hear the vehicle approaching, wondering if the ploy will work. It's a gamble: a gamble that whoever is following me will be looking for my big truck rather than this shitty car, and a gamble that this piece of junk will pass off as a literal piece of junk.

The roar of the engine becomes nearly overwhelming, until I'm sure our pursuer is about to smash into us. My hand seeks the handle of my gun, and I grip it tightly, my eyes fixed on the window though I can see nothing outside. Then comes the blinding shine of headlights, growing brighter and brighter and then – gone. Past us.

I let out a long, slow breath as the roar of the vehicle recedes. Once the sound is completely gone I sit up, releasing my gun.

'Phew,' Jedediah says, struggling to sit up himself. 'That was a close one, huh? Who do you think it was?'

Ignoring him, I drum my fingers on the wheel. I

could keep driving, but I'd run the risk of encountering whomever that was again, and it's definitely not worth the risk of using headlights in the dark now that I know we're not alone out here. Better to stop now, catch a few hours of sleep. Hopefully, by then, that car will be long gone.

Sleeping with a prisoner in tow is a new experience for me. I never hang on to a mark longer than necessary. Usually I'd keep working right through the night, but the journey ahead is too long for that. Which brings up a new issue: what to do with Jedediah overnight.

I could leave him in the passenger seat, but that would run the risk of him escaping his binds and killing me in my sleep. I could throw him outside, but he might try to run. We're in the awkward no-man's-land between the eastern and western towns, so there's nothing but empty wastes for miles all around, but he hasn't shown much of a sense of self-preservation so far. So, I can't let him kill me or get himself killed. That leaves only one option.

After a lot of squirming and pleading, Jedediah is safely tied, gagged, blindfolded, and stuffed into the trunk. I made sure to tie him up even more tightly than before, wrists and arms and ankles, just to make sure he doesn't get any bright ideas. I move my gun bag from the trunk to the backseat to make doubly sure. After I lock him in, there's some jostling and bumping for about ten minutes, but finally he quiets down. I curl up in the backseat, taking my gun out of its holster and cradling it against my chest.

It's unsettling, knowing that an infamous killer will be just a few yards away while I sleep. But it doesn't matter. I'm not afraid, I tell myself. Jedediah Johnson may be a different breed, but he's still a raider, and I'm not afraid of raiders.

VIII
Poachers

A sound wakes me before dawn. My gun is in my hand before I even open my eyes. I swing it one way and then the other, searching for the source of the mysterious thumping, and then realize it's coming from the trunk. Right – Jedediah. Not danger, just an inconvenience. I sigh, placing my gun back in its holster, and rub my eyes. I could've used another hour of sleep, but I'm awake now, so I might as well get an early start.

It's tempting to leave Jedediah in the trunk, where I don't have to deal with the constant stream of shit coming out of his mouth, but I'm sure he'll find some way to get free or injure himself if I continue to leave him unsupervised. In fact, it's possible that he's already done so, so I take out my gun again as I head to the trunk. But Jedediah is still tied up neatly, and looking very unhappy about having spent the night crammed into the small space. I check to make sure the ropes on his wrists haven't loosened, and drag him up to the front seat. I remove the gag to give him a quick drink of water, and put it back again despite his protests.

'Give me an hour to wake up,' I say. 'If you behave yourself, I'll take the gag out then.'

He nods – surprisingly agreeable, but given the dark rings under his eyes, he's probably just too tired to put up much resistance. Pleased with that, I get into my seat and start driving. Jedediah soon nods off, his head lolling against the back of the seat. I resist the petty urge to make him less comfortable, reminding myself that him sleeping means I get peace and quiet.

The road is still dark, but not too dark to see, the wastes tinged with the bluish light of almost-dawn. I relax as I drive, expecting a good few hours of nothingness before we hit the western towns and the day really begins.

That peace is quickly ruined as I see something on the horizon. I slow down, squinting at the column of smoke. My stomach clenches at the thought of fire, but I force myself to move closer. It soon becomes clear that it's not a wildfire, or a burning town, but a small, personal blaze. A campfire. No one in their right mind sets a campfire, unless they're fully confident that they can kill anyone who sees it, so I'm wary as I approach.

I kill the engine and roll to a stop a good distance away, make sure Jedediah is still asleep, and rustle through my bag in the backseat. I fish out a pair of binoculars and study the camp.

There are two figures by the fire. One is stretched out on the ground, likely sleeping. The other is sitting upright, but looks relaxed, not fully alert. I watch them for several long moments, trying to gauge who they are and what they want – and then I spot their vehicle parked nearby. A rusty old truck, that was once green from the look of it. Not black, like the ones Jedediah's raiders drive.

This must be the vehicle that was following me. Very few people have reason to travel on these open roads, the stretch of nothingness between Jedediah's lands and the wild towns in the west. It's rare that anyone has the means or a strong enough reason to travel from one to the other, and there's absolutely nothing of interest in between. The only reason for somebody to be out here is if they're on the run, or looking for someone . . . and I have a sneaking suspicion that these people are looking for me. But if they're not working for Jedediah, why are they after me?

Now is a good opportunity to find out.

I check on Jedediah again – still sleeping – and gather my weapons. My brain is already forming a plan of attack, the old instinct bubbling up: *Kill.* The thought rises to a clamor as I load my guns, making sure my trusty pistol is full of ammo, slinging a rifle over my back, and grabbing an extra pistol just in case.

There are only two of them, not expecting trouble. They must still think they're following me, and won't expect me to come from behind. It would be easy to kill them both, no matter how prepared they think they are. But it's not that simple. I have rules, rules that set me apart from the people I hunt.

My ma and I made them together when I was ten. I had killed five and a half people by that time, and the 'half' was the reason the rules came to be. He was a man who came to town half-dead, begging for water. I couldn't decide if he looked like a raider or not in the sorry state he was in, but he was a stranger looking to take what was ours, so I opted for caution. I beat his head in with a cast-iron pot we used to make stew. When my ma asked why I did that, I said, 'I didn't have my gun on me.'

That night, when they thought I was asleep, I overheard her talking with the sheriff when he stopped by to visit.

'She's a little girl,' my mom said.

'She's not *just* a little girl,' the sheriff said. 'She's a weapon. We've just got to make sure she's pointed in the right direction.'

That miffed me more than anything – the idea that

I didn't know who to kill and who not to kill. Of course I knew. I didn't kill the sheriff when he shouted at me for eating too much, or old lady Brenda when she pinched my cheeks, though I couldn't say the idea hadn't occurred to me once or twice. I only killed the bad people. Raiders. Men and women who made a living preying on townies like us, who would come into town waving big guns and take whatever food and water they could find. That's what made me a hero. Everyone in town said so.

The next day, my ma sat me down with a pencil and dirty scrap of napkin and said, 'Let's make a list.'

I was never much good at reading and writing, but I was excited to practice back then, so it seemed like a good exercise. I asked what kind of list it would be, and my ma said it was a 'No-Kill List.' A list of people I would never kill, she explained. Even though I was good at killing people, and I never seemed to feel too bad about it, there had to be some people I didn't want to kill ever, right?

Right. I wrote 'Ma' immediately. Under it I wrote 'Pa.' But, after a moment's thought, I erased that one.

'What'd you do that for?' Ma asked, her smile growing strained.

'Well,' I said. 'I'd never *want* to kill Pa, but I think I might, if I had to. If it was you or him, or me or him, I'd probably have to do it.'

It seemed reasonable to me, so I smiled and handed back the paper with only one name, but my ma seemed concerned. So, she tore up the list and proposed a new plan: We would make rules about killing, just to make sure I didn't kill the wrong people by accident. I would only kill for necessity, and for profit.

It took me a lot of time, and one very big mistake, to realize why the rules were so important. After that, I vowed to never break them again.

Which is why, despite all my instincts screaming at me to do so, I don't ram my car into the camp, or snipe them from a distance, or charge in with my guns blazing. Instead, I approach the camp with the intention to talk.

Of course, I approach it as quietly and stealthily as possible, because getting shot on sight isn't conducive to having a decent conversation. And I'm not a goddamn idiot, so I still pull out my two pistols as I approach, keeping one leveled at each of their heads. By the time they notice me, I have them at my mercy.

And I realize, upon getting a better look, that I know exactly who these people are.

There are a lot of *off* folks in my line of work. Loners, weirdos, probably even a few psychopaths. I have no delusions about it, I know I'm definitely at home among them. But these two ... these two are top-of-the-line freaks.

Cat and Bird. I'm sure at one point they must've had real names, but that's all anyone calls them anymore. Cat is tall and willowy, her skin so dark it's nearly black, her hair twisted into tight braids. She has stiff-as-a-board posture, a proud tilt to her chin. Despite a slender build, there's nothing delicate about her; she's all hard angles and lean muscle. Even in the act of standing up when she notices me, each movement is precise and controlled and deliberate, no energy or time wasted. She seems almost normal at first glance – pretty, even – until she smiles, displaying a pair of canines sharpened into points. From what I've heard, she likes to use them.

Bird, on the other hand, does some ungainly flailing and scrambling in the dust before climbing to her feet. She stands stone-still, except for a twitch every few seconds – first a tremble up her arm, then an odd jolt of her head, then a shift in her foot, like a bug is jumping around beneath her skin. Her body is wrapped in cloth, layers and layers of it stacked on top of one another and sewn together haphazardly, with flaps and scraps of fabric hanging off and fluttering around her. The top layer is a tattered, hooded brown cloak. Her patched-together outfit is all in shades of gray and brown, with an occasional deep red stain. She never seems to take off a layer, even when it's filthy or torn. Instead, she just sews up the tears and throws on more clothes to cover it. She wears dirty gloves, at least two scarves wrapped tightly around her neck, and a pair of oversized, bright red rain boots.

But the truly strange thing about her outfit is the mask. It's a gas mask, black and too big for her body. She peers at me now through the darkly tinted goggles, her head jerking one way and then the other.

Of all the people for me to run into, it had to be these creepy motherfuckers. Not only are the two unsettling, but their reputation is questionable at best … even among bounty hunters, which says a lot. Worse than that, we have history.

'Don't touch those guns,' I say.

Cat meets my gaze steadily.

'Hi, Clementine,' she says, staying very still. Out of the corner of my eye I see Bird shift. I turn to her, and she freezes, one hand halfway to a knife strapped to her leg. She jerks her head toward Cat, as if seeking guidance, jerks it back toward me, and flutters a hand at me in an awkward wave.

'Hands up,' I say, and she immediately throws them skyward, her fingers twitching one by one. I keep my eye on her for a few seconds before slowly turning back to Cat. She meets my eyes and runs a tongue across her sharpened teeth.

'What are you doing out here?' I ask. Normally, seeing two fellow bounty hunters wouldn't be such a terrible thing. 'Friendly' would be a stretch, but it's not like we're trying to kill each other . . . without reason.

'Nice to see you too,' Cat says. 'You're not still mad, are you?'

'No,' I say flatly. If I was still mad, I would've gunned them down the moment I recognized them.

'Good,' Cat says. 'Because that was all a terribly unfortunate accident.'

'Accident,' Bird repeats in her muffled, high-pitched voice, mask bobbing up and down in a nod.

'Uh-huh.' A terribly unfortunate accident where they stole a mark I had spent three *weeks* hunting down. While I was cutting through the bounty's men, they yanked her away and claimed the reward for themselves, later arguing that they just happened to be after the same person. 'Now tell me what the fuck you're doing here.'

Silence answers me. I lower my gun to point at Cat's leg.

'We're hunting,' she says quickly. 'Just like you, right? We're on the same side.' She grins at me; it's a grin I don't like, too wide and toothy, made threatening by her sharpened teeth.

'Why are you following me?' I ask, not buying the bullshit excuse. There's no reason for them to be hunting this far out. I guess if anyone would be willing to chase bounties west it'd be these two assholes, but my gut tells

me there's something else going on here. Or maybe I
am still a little resentful about the last time they stole
from me.

'Following you? Like I said, we're chasing a bounty,'
Cat says, with a casual shrug. 'He fled this way.'

I eye her, mentally chewing that answer. It's not completely unreasonable. Sometimes a bounty will run west
if they know there's a price on their head and hunters
on their heels. But still . . .

'Whose bounty?'

'Why should I tell you?' she asks, her eyes narrowing.
'You'll just try to steal him.'

'I'd say you've got bigger things to worry about right
now,' I say, gesturing with my gun. Cat exchanges a long
look with Bird, who stares at her silently.

'Fine,' she says. 'We're after Left-Hand. Heard he fled
this way.'

'Oh,' I say. 'Left-Hand.' I relax, rolling my shoulders
back. 'Well, that's a relief. I was almost worried you were
going to say something feasible, and I'd have to think a
little harder about what to do with you.'

Too bad for her. I saw that name recently – right next
to his famous, freshly severed hand on Alex's shelf. So
I know it's a lie, and I know what a lie means: The only
bounty she's after is the one I'm trying to claim. These
two are damn poachers, trying to take my hard-earned
reward for Jedediah. I don't know why Alex told them,

or why they thought they could get the best of me, but none of that matters right now.

Cat's eyes widen, her mouth opening. I shoot before she gets a word out.

The bullet sinks into her leg, and she goes down with a shout. Bird flings herself at me. She slams into me with a surprising amount of force for her small size, and we both hit the dirt, my back slamming against the ground. I lose my hold on one of my guns, and quickly raise the other, but she pins my arm beneath her knee and renders it useless. I grab at her with my free hand, but my fingers come away with a scrap of filthy fabric. I can't get a good grip, or a good hit, with every inch of her protected by cloth or mask.

Bird grabs the knife off her leg and raises it. She brings it down, and I jerk aside. The blade sinks into the dirt just an inch from my head. She yanks it out and raises it again, and I grab her wrist with my free hand, grappling with her, my hand slipping on rotting cloth. I dig my nails in, trying desperately to get a hold – and when she jerks her hand away, her glove rips.

Bird freezes. She stares down at her hand, at the torn glove and the slivers of pale flesh showing through, as if she can't believe what she's seeing. Then she screams. She leaps off me, clutching her wrist like her hand has been severed. She runs across the camp, emitting a loud, high-pitched wail like a siren.

I climb to my feet, pointing my gun at Cat again. She

has a gun in hand, but lowers it when she sees me aiming at her. She's swaying on her injured leg, a sheen of sweat on her forehead.

'Stop,' I say, trying to hide my own shortness of breath. I wait for her to move her hand away from her gun, then turn to Bird. The masked woman is kneeling in the dirt and has produced a roll of duct tape from her bag. As I watch, she wraps the tape around her hand, again and again and again. She continues until her skin is thoroughly hidden, and keeps going, rocking back and forth as she does it.

I return my aim to Cat, keeping my gun trained on her as I move to retrieve my other pistol from the ground. I keep that one pointed at Bird, though she doesn't even glance up. 'In the spirit of respect among bounty hunters, I'm not going to kill you,' I say. 'But if you keep following me, you'll force my hand. Got it?' I look from one to the other. *'Got it?'* I prompt again, gesturing with both guns. Cat, her teeth bared, nods. Bird clutches her freshly taped-up hand to her chest and trembles.

Guess that's as good an answer as I'm going to get. I back away from the two poachers, keeping my eyes trained on them. Once I'm far enough away, I turn and walk briskly back to my car. I hop in, shut the door, and sigh with satisfaction. Letting people live always makes me feel so benevolent. I pause for a moment, basking in the feeling and listening to Jedediah snore, before starting up the car again.

IX
The Western Wastes

There's not much to see on the ride, just empty wastelands and a seemingly endless road, the monotony
occasionally broken by a broken-down building or car.
There are no signs of life in any of them, nor do I see
anyone traveling on foot. Jedediah dozes in the passenger seat, still recovering from his night in the trunk. By
the end of the day we're far from Jedediah's towns, and
we should arrive at Saint's tower sometime tomorrow.
Just one more day having to deal with this piece of shit.

Just when I'm starting to get excited about how close
we are, we hit a roadblock. I slow as we approach. The
road is covered by junk, heaps of trash and twisted metal
covering the entire width of it, forming an almost-solid
barrier about six feet high. I roll to a stop. These kinds
of blocks can easily be traps. With my truck I would ram

right through, and hopefully take out a couple waiting raiders in the process, but there's no way this shitty little car can handle it.

As I'm thinking, the gunfire starts.

Raiders pour out from behind the barrier, three on each side. Only two of them have guns, which they fire wildly at the car; the rest run straight at us, shouting and swinging blunt weapons. I duck my head, slam on the gas, and turn the wheel sharply. The car rams right into two of the approaching raiders, sending one of them rolling over the windshield and crushing the other beneath my tires. The car whines and shudders, but keeps going. I drive out into the wastes, leaving the raiders and their guns behind.

I'm not sure whether this thing is equipped to handle off-roading, but I don't have a choice. There's no way to know how much of the road those raiders have claimed as theirs, so it's best to avoid it. Luckily, the wastes here are flat and empty. The car rumbles along; it's a bumpy ride, but it holds together, and seems undamaged other than some bullet holes in the windshield.

'Ooh,' Jedediah says, sitting up in the passenger seat with his eyes bright. 'What an adventure.'

I suppress a sigh. As if I didn't have enough to deal with.

Our path is much more difficult to trace without a road to follow on the map. After driving for a couple hours, and taking additional detours to avoid possibly occupied buildings and trash heaps, I find myself uncertain of our location. I keep the map stretched out across the dashboard and continue glancing at it, but there are no landmarks to look for. Just flat, empty wastes, nothing but occasional shells of buildings.

After almost an hour of total uncertainty, I see a town on the horizon. I slow down, tracing a finger across the map. Based on our approximate location, there are two options: This town is either Lefton or Bramble. I gnaw my lower lip, considering my options – but really, there aren't any feasible ones other than stopping. I've heard towns around here can be rough, wary, even worse than the east. But I'm sure it's nothing I can't handle.

'What's this?' Jedediah asks when we stop, craning his neck to look out the window one way and then the other, finally focusing on the town ahead. 'Are we here?'

I ignore him, shutting off the engine.

'We're stopping?' he asks. For the first time, something like alarm crosses his face. 'Here? A town? Are you sure that's a good idea?'

I'm not. I've heard that western towns can be just as dangerous as raider crews. But I need to find out where we are, make sure we're headed in the right direction.

I get out of the car and move around to grab Jedediah. I'm tempted to throw him into the trunk while I'm in town, but I'll probably need to get in there for supplies if the townies want to trade. Bringing him along still tied up could lead to some unwanted attention ... but I definitely don't trust him free. I settle for gagging him again, despite his protests. He digs his heels into the dirt, but I'm more than strong enough to drag him along behind me.

'The townies will stone you to death if they know who you are,' I say as we approach. 'So I'd suggest laying low.'

At the edge of town, we're greeted by three men armed with shotguns. I resist the urge to grab my own gun, though my mind is busily calculating how to survive this if it comes to a gunfight. I could always use Jedediah as a meat shield, though that would make the whole trip here pointless. Better to avoid violence, if possible.

I stop and raise both hands in the air. It's almost physically painful to move my hand away from my gun, but I do it, banking on the bet that the townies won't shoot me unprompted. It's a risky bet, especially in the western wastes, but I don't have many choices.

'Who're you?' one man barks at us. 'What d'you want?'

'We're lost,' I say. 'Want to know where we are.'

The townies look at each other, exchanging shrugs, but nobody lowers their gun.

'Got no business with strangers,' one says, gesturing

with the barrel of his shotgun back at my car. 'Get goin'.'

I sigh, lowering my hands and rolling back my shoulders. I guess townies are the same no matter where you are.

'Tell me one thing and I'll go. Is this Bramble or Lefton?'

They continue scowling at me, not relaxing their holds on their guns.

Goddamn townies and their fear of outsiders. I can't blame them, especially in this area of the wastes, but this is ridiculous. My pride won't allow me to turn and leave without getting *something*. But how can I get them to trust an outsider?

That's when it hits me.

'You guys heard of a man named Saint?' I ask. Hopefully Alex's information was good, and this place isn't too backwater and isolated to know who he is. The three men squint at me, but the one in the middle lowers his gun just a little.

'What about him?' he asks.

'I'm headed his way,' I say. I grab Jedediah by the arm and haul him forward. He tries to scoot backward, but I hold him in place, and his feet scramble uselessly in the sand. 'Following the broadcast. Got a present for him.'

There's a long pause. I wonder if maybe I made a

mistake telling them this. Maybe not all the towns support Saint, or maybe they'll get the notion to take him in themselves. I almost reach for my gun, but one man lowers his weapon to his side, and the other two follow.

'Well, if you're doing Saint's business, you can't be too bad,' the man in the middle says, almost grudgingly. 'You got anything to trade?'

I have to stop myself from scoffing at the idea. As if these townies have anything that would be worth my precious food and water. I've got enough – which is more than a lot of people in the wastes can say – but barely so.

'No,' I say. 'I just wanna know where I am.'

Their scowls are back in an instant, though thankfully their guns stay lowered.

'Surely you've got something to make it worth our while,' one of them says. 'Seeing as you're heading across the wastes to Saint an' all, and got them nice guns.'

Noticing their hungry eyes on the pistol at my hip, it takes all of my resolve not to draw it on them. I take a deep breath and let it out. Goddamn townies . . . I really don't want to hand over any supplies, but I guess I don't have a choice.

'Fine,' I say. 'Might be able to spare a couple cans of food.'

*

Just one more day till Saint, I tell myself as I grudgingly hand two cans of food in exchange for a bottle of dirty water. Once I reach him and claim my reward, I'll have everything I need and plenty more. Still, I hate wasting supplies, and will likely have to throw this water out rather than drink it. But these townies are stubborn as hell about trading. At least they finally give me what I'm really here for: the name 'Lefton.' I dodge the question about where I'm coming from, avoid giving a name, and make *damn* sure not to breathe the name Jedediah Johnson. I'm not so dumb as to think that I'm not recognizable if someone is looking for me, but once I reach the safety of Saint's tower it won't be an issue.

Just one more day. Then Jedediah will be out of my hands, and this whole business will be over and done with. I keep telling myself that as I finish haggling with the townies, letting the conversation drag just long enough that I hopefully won't offend them. Once we reach a deal, I head back toward where I left Jedediah with some townies to watch him, ready to get out of here.

But Jedediah isn't there. I pause, staring at the spot in the dirt where I left him.

Alarm bells ring in my head. Maybe I was right before, in thinking that telling these townies too much was a bad idea. Or maybe one of them had the bright idea of removing Jedediah's gag, and he convinced them to free him . . .

Heat spreads through my chest and simmers there. My hand finds my gun. I grip it tightly and turn to look at the townies. I don't want to hurt these people, but if they've turned against me, I have no choice.

I'll take the armed men first. Then I can use one of the younger women as a hostage. Hopefully, that will minimize the casualties and allow me to get out of here with Jedediah.

'Somethin' wrong?' one of the men asks, nervously eyeing my gun.

'Where,' I ask in a soft, dangerous voice, 'is my prisoner?'

I survey the townies, looking for signs of guilt. One young woman turns an alarming shade of red. I focus on her, taking a step closer so I tower over her.

'He asked for a drink of water,' she says, twirling a strand of hair around her finger and shrinking down. 'So, um, we took him inside to give him some and—'

'*Where?*' I ask. She jumps, and points a finger at the nearest building. I shove her out of the way and step inside. I try to stay calm, but my pulse is racing as I think of all the things Jedediah could have gotten into. I guess these townies haven't intentionally turned against me, but they *are* apparently dumb as rocks, which is almost worse. Clearly they don't know what Jedediah is capable of. This is the man who conquered the eastern wastes, kept an iron grip on the towns there; the man who burned down an entire town for one act of rebellion. He could have gotten free, found a weapon. He could've taken out half the town and been long gone by now. He could've . . .

Been sitting on the floor of a house, surrounded by a ring of children. I stop as I catch sight of him. The first thing I notice is that some idiot *did* have the bright idea of removing his gag, which he's taking full advantage of at the moment, telling some kind of ridiculous story that involves a rocket launcher and mutant bears to the small collection of townie children. He gestures wildly – an impressive feat considering his wrists are, thankfully, still bound – and the kids around him squeal with laughter. Frowning, I make my way closer. A couple of the children turn to me as I approach, and the laughter dies out quickly as they see my scowling, burnt face. Jedediah is the last one to notice me. He pauses midsentence, looks up at me, and grins.

'Oh, hi, Clementine,' he says, using his limited hand motion for a small wave.

'What are you doing?' I ask, folding my arms over my chest and glaring down at him. I'm trying very hard to restrain my temper right now, both at him and at the townies who were dumb enough to let their kids near him. Not that I'm much a fan of children – I find them kind of creepy, really – but still. It's the principle of the matter.

'Telling them a story,' he says, all smiles and innocence. As if he's the kind of person who genuinely enjoys sitting around telling stories to small children.

'The legend of Jedediah Johnson!' a young boy says. I stare at him. Though he's dirty and stick thin, his eyes are wide and sparkling at the moment. 'He's a really famous hero!'

'Really famous,' Jedediah agrees, nodding. 'Also very smart, and strong, and handsome.'

'And born from radio garbage!'

'Radioactive waste, actually, but close,' Jedediah says.

The children all nod excitedly, and I relax a bit. Clearly, they know nothing about the real Jedediah Johnson, only the bullshit that the man is currently spewing about himself.

'Finish telling the story,' a young girl pipes up. 'I wanna hear about how he saved all the towns!'

'We-ell,' Jedediah says. 'First he—'

'Where I come from,' I say, cutting him off, 'they say Jedediah Johnson eats children who trust strangers too much.'

The children all turn away from Jedediah to stare at me, their eyes huge in their little faces, mouths gaping. Jedediah gapes along with them, as if he's also shocked by the news that Jedediah Johnson is a horrible person. I nod, struggling to keep a straight face. 'Then he wears their teeth as a necklace.'

This stuns them all into silence for a solid few seconds. Jedediah is the first to recover, his expression shifting from shocked to affronted.

'*That*,' he says, 'is simply not true. How dare you slander the name of Jedediah Johnson—'

I grab him by the front of his shirt and haul him up before he can continue. I yank him toward the door, but he turns to do one last final wave at the children, many of whom look on the verge of tears now.

'Bye!' he says cheerfully, and I pull him out the door.

'What the hell was that?' I hiss at him, ignoring the goodbyes of the townies as we march back to the car. 'What did I tell you about laying low?'

'Oh, come on,' Jedediah says. 'I was just having a little fun.' He eyes me, still smiling in the face of my wrath. 'Got a lot more fun when you made the kiddos cry, though.'

'I just gave them a dose of reality.'

'Me eating children is *not* a reality!' he says, seeming offended by the notion. 'Not enough meat on them, anyway. I don't see what the point would be . . . '

'More tender, I'd imagine,' I say without thinking about it. Jedediah's head turns sharply in my direction, his eyebrows rising. I open my mouth to say something to defend myself, but before I can, he lets out a delighted laugh.

'Did you actually just make a joke, Clementine?' he

asks. 'Or was it just a creepy slip of the tongue? Either way, I support it.'

I grit my teeth. I shouldn't be engaging with a prisoner. It's a slippery slope, associating with people like him. It's already fucking with the way I think.

Just one more day, I tell myself. One more day, and I'll be rid of him.

X
Saint's Tower

Though I want nothing more than to speed to Saint's radio tower the next day, I force myself to be patient and careful. The area nearby is treacherous; there are some larger towns I'd prefer to avoid, as well as a minefield I need to drive around, according to the map Alex gave me. I'm painstakingly careful to ensure that I'm taking the right roads, heading in the right direction. I'm not going to come all this way just to die thanks to a goddamn mine.

Jedediah is quiet in the passenger seat. Maybe he realizes how close we're getting, how near at hand his judgment is. If this Saint does hold trials, I have no doubt Jedediah will be deemed guilty. Hell, if Saint wants me to, maybe I'll even stay awhile and testify against him myself, and stay to watch him hang too. Jedediah may not be the man I thought he'd be – he's awfully cheerful and *very* talkative for a ruthless dictator – but it changes nothing about what he's done.

Finally, the radio tower appears on the horizon. It's a sight to behold, tall and prominent, shiny metal in a dusty world. Saint's headquarters are in the building beside it, according to the map, but I can't see it from where I currently am, heading up the side of a hill. I jam the pedal, eager to have the end in sight, and the car huffs and puffs its way up the rest of the hill.

Once we reach the top, Saint's headquarters come into sight – and I slam on the brakes. Jedediah yelps as he's thrown forward, but I ignore him, completely fixated on the sight ahead.

Someone drove a fucking truck into Saint's headquarters.

One wall of the building is completely destroyed, a huge semitruck sticking half out of it. Smoke still rises from the wreckage.

'What the fuck?' I ask the air. I reverse down the back side of the hill, stopping the car in a spot where it shouldn't be visible from Saint's headquarters. I reach into the back for one of my bags, grab my binoculars, and climb out of the car. As an afterthought, I drag Jedediah out as well, and haul him behind me as we head for the top of the hill.

There, I fall to a crouch, pulling Jedediah down

beside me, and scope out the building below. I scan it, searching for any signs of what's going on down there. It's easy enough to see that this was an attack. But more importantly, who's winning? Should I get down there and try to help Saint, or will it be suicide?

Soon enough, my question is answered.

They pour out of the building – or rather crash out of it, violent and sudden, like a wave with a grudge against the shore. Raider, after raider, after raider emerges from the doors. They keep coming until it becomes a mob, huge and boisterous and rowdy. I don't think I've ever seen so many people together in one place, let alone *raiders*. I never imagined it would be possible for so many of them to get together without killing each other.

And these aren't the kinds of raiders I'm used to, not the well-equipped, well-trained, purposeful ones that make up Jedediah's crew. These are scarred and pierced and tatted, clothes shredded and bloodstained, armed with rusty knives and baseball bats and iron pipes. They boil and seethe with restless energy. Some are busy – loading up vehicles, arguing with each other, prepping for some kind of journey – while others stand around. But all of them are angry, restless, ready for something, radiating bloodlust. The air brims with the promise of violence. It's only a matter of time before it erupts.

I don't understand what's happening here, why there

are so many raiders or where they came from, but I know a bad situation when I see one. Fuck the Saint plan. Even a huge bounty for Jedediah, and the life-changing effects it could have on my reputation, is *not* worth getting caught in this crossfire. Especially out here in the west, raiders are wild, and ruthlessly violent. I'm sure they'll tear us apart if they find us, just for kicks.

I lower my binoculars and take a deep breath. In, out. Panic surges in my chest, but I force it down. Now is not the time to lose control. I think I'm doing a decent job of covering it up, but Jedediah is looking at me out of the corner of his eye, very still and very quiet, like he expects any sudden motion or sound will make me snap.

'We need to go,' I say after a moment of collecting myself. There's no time to waste. Some of those raiders have vehicles, and vehicles a hell of a lot bigger and more powerful than the piece of shit I'm driving. We need as much of a head start as possible if we want any hope of making it to safety. Thankfully, Jedediah nods and keeps his mouth shut.

I edge backward down the hill before climbing to my feet, and stay crouched even then, moving slowly. When I pull Jedediah off the ground, he follows my lead. He's quiet for once. I'm grateful for that, though it's also concerning. Considering his cheerful, blasé attitude even when he was being kidnapped and had a gun to his head, the fact that he's taking this so seriously means that we're in some real deep shit.

Once we're on our feet and out of sight of the tower, I break into a sprint, dragging a slightly lagging Jedediah with me. He struggles to keep up, nearly tripping several times, but I force him to keep running. Though it looks like I won't be able to turn him in to Saint after all, he's still my bounty, and I'm not going to lose the reason I came all the way to this hellhole. No time to figure the situation out now, but somehow I'll make it work.

I yank open the car door as we reach it, throw Jedediah in, and slam it shut before running to my own seat.

My brain is a blur of thoughts, and my body struggles to keep up with a flurry of actions in response – starting the car, spreading the map across the dashboard, putting on my seatbelt, starting to drive. Behind it all, one thought pushes me: *Get out. Get out. Get out.* I saw those raiders – *so many raiders* – and I need to get the hell out of here before they see me. I drive recklessly, wildly, trying to get as far away from the radio tower as possible. But where do I go? Where the hell can I possibly go, that I'll be safe from that mob?

I glance frantically between my map and the road, knowing the raider vehicles could be bearing down on me with every second. There's no way I'll make it all the way back to the east without getting run down by one of their war machines. I'm not even sure I have the gas to make it. I barely had enough supplies to last the journey here.

Maybe if I can make it to one of the bigger western towns, I could hole up there, wait for this to blow over. But will any of the towns around here actually hold against the onslaught of raiders? *Maybe* Blackfort – I've heard that place is a safe haven, and knows how to kick some raider ass – but I wouldn't gamble on it, and it's too far away for us to reach. We'll never make it there before being overtaken. I don't think we can make it to *any* town in time.

'We've got company,' Jedediah says. Swearing under my breath, I shove the map aside and take a look in the rear-view mirror. The 'company' he refers to is a huge truck, already close enough for me to make out some of the finer details, including spikes on the tires and a grinning skull painted on the front. It's an ugly thing, a killing machine, made of mismatched parts all stuck together. It's massive, and intimidating, and definitely fast enough to catch us. It's too late to hide like we did from the poachers, and there's nothing but empty waste-lands all around us. No room to pull a maneuver or a clever trick; we're out in the open, being run down by an enemy we can't hope to match.

'Untie me,' Jedediah says. 'Give me a gun. I'll shoot while you drive, take out their tires—'

'Not happening.'

'You're going to get us both killed!' he says, his voice rising to a shout. Every bit of his cheerful attitude is gone. 'Let me *go*!'

His plan would make sense, if he wasn't an insane tyrant and I could trust him not to put a bullet in my head the second I gave him half a chance. Unfortunately, that is not the case. Even if we both die, I'm completely willing to let him die tied up and helpless, rather than giving him a chance at taking me down and surviving himself.

I slam my foot on the gas pedal. The car struggles and rattles and whines, gaining a pathetic amount of speed. Despite the vehicle's best efforts, soon the truck is right on our tail.

It hovers behind us for an instant or two, while I swear and Jedediah yells. Then it rams us, slamming hard against our fender. We skid out of control, tires screeching. The truck falls back while I struggle to straighten us out. They're fucking with us, I realize. They could have easily run us off the road, or slammed into us hard enough to send the car rolling, but they don't want to. No need to rush – it's not like we're going anywhere.

I hate being toyed with, and I especially hate that there's nothing I can do about it. I grind my teeth and keep driving, trying to coax more speed out of this god-damn piece of junk car. Jedediah screams something from the passenger seat, over and over again. It takes three times for me to process the word he's shouting at me: 'gun!' I duck my head just as a bullet whizzes past me and through the windshield. I hunch over the steering wheel, while Jedediah shrinks down as far as he can in his seat, eyes shut tightly, letting out a constant stream of swear words.

More bullets pepper the car, none doing any serious damage – just continuing to fuck with us, I'm sure – and then the truck gains speed suddenly, roaring its way up beside us. There it slows again, keeping pace. I look over to see a raider grinning at me. The scarred man hangs half out the window, holding a revolver with both hands, the gun pointed right at me. Heart hammering, I slam on the brakes, and the truck pulls ahead. A moment later it reverses, and I shoot forward again. I stay ahead only for a moment or two before the truck is back at our side.

Desperate, I ram our tiny car sideways, right into their huge truck. The raider nearly topples out the window, and the gun falls from his hands, lost to the road. He scrambles for a handhold, his face utterly shocked. Once the man regains his balance he scowls at me, and shouts something over his shoulder at the driver. Before I can react, the truck rams us back.

We skid sideways, nearly off the road, and I fight to keep control of the car. At least I don't have a gun pointed at my face now ... but unfortunately, I've introduced the raiders to a fun new game. They ram us again, and again. When they're close, I can hear the laughter drifting out of their open window. As soon as I recover, they hit us once more – and this time stay locked to our side, metal grinding against metal, their truck pushing against us.

I grit my teeth and turn the wheel sharply, trying to break away, but the truck sticks to us. It edges us toward the side of the road. The car whines pitifully, engine struggling. I push it harder, harder, knowing I have to get away. I pick up speed, but the truck easily keeps up.

Too late, I see the crumbling building ahead. Too late, I realize the raiders' plan. I jam my heel against the brake in an attempt to slow down, but all it does is make me lose control. With a screech of tires, the raider truck shoves me off the road and the car rams straight into the side of the building.

Car hits wall. Forehead hits steering wheel.

For a moment everything goes black. I fight it. I force my eyes open, will myself to move, to stay conscious. But my brain is hazy, uncooperative. It takes all my effort to lift my head, shaking it in an attempt to clear it while the world spins around me. Jedediah is crumpled in his seat, groaning.

Gradually, my head clears, and adrenaline sparks me into action. I shift the car into reverse and rev the engine. It only makes a horrible screeching noise, producing no actual movement. Judging from the smoke coming from the hood, this poor piece of shit has finally rumbled its final rumble. The good news is that the raiders have rammed their big-ass truck into the building as well, and despite its size it doesn't look like the thing won its battle with the wall.

The bad news is that the raiders are now jumping out of their vehicle and coming for us. I curse, scramble to open the door, and climb out. I stumble in my hurry, my legs shaky beneath me after the crash, but I force myself to keep going. I rush to the trunk, prop it open, and grab the first gun I find: an assault rifle. Jedediah yells at me from the passenger seat, but I ignore him and turn to face the raiders. There are four of them, one with a gun, the others with hand weapons. I immediately release a spray of bullets at the armed one, and he falls with a shout. Before I can aim again, another raider is on me, swinging a knife at my face.

My gunfire goes wild as I jump back to avoid the blade. I try to level my weapon at the man with a knife, but he dives at me, shoving my arm so the barrel of the gun jerks upward. He shoves me back against the same wall my car crashed into.

We struggle. I block his wild swings with my gun, unable to get a shot off as I try to prevent my nose from being sliced in half. He grabs the barrel of the gun with his free hand, yanking it out of my grip; I let go immediately, so his own momentum sends him stumbling.

I grab a loose brick from the wall behind me and launch it at him. It catches him in the side of the head, and he shouts, clutching his ear. I grab another before he can recover and tackle him to the ground. The gun slips out of his hands and clatters into the dust. He holds on to the knife and slashes at me, but I block it with the brick and shove his hand to the side, leaving his face wide open. His eyes widen as he realizes what's about to happen, and his mouth opens, but I bring the brick down before he can say anything. Once, twice, three times, and his face is reduced to a bloody mess. I hold on to the bloody brick, panting.

I have a mere second to recover before I see another raider diving for my fallen gun. I lunge at her, and smash the brick onto her hand as soon as she grips it. She snarls, trying to snatch her hand back, but I keep it pinned. With my free hand, I grab her arm and yank her down into the dirt with me. We tumble on the ground, both losing our weapons and resorting to hits and kicks and bites and scratches. She's smaller than me, scrawnier, and eventually I get a good grip on her hair and pin her facedown in the dirt. I find her companion's fallen knife on the ground nearby, and jam it hilt deep into the back of her exposed neck. She jolts and goes limp, and I slowly pull the blade free.

I climb to my feet with the knife in hand, breathing hard, blood pumping, veins full of the half-fear, half-excitement muddle that a fight always brings out in me. I focus on the last raider still standing. The huge man has dragged Jedediah out of the passenger seat. As I watch, he lifts the wriggling smaller man and slams him down on the hood of the car. Jedediah stops moving.

No. Not my bounty. If he dies here, all of this was pointless.

I run at the raider, a shout tearing out of my throat. He turns toward me, and I sink the blade of the knife deep into his shoulder, just missing his neck. He grunts and grabs me by the arm. He starts to lift me off the ground, but I aim a swift kick at his groin, and he loses his grip. I smash a knee into his face as he leans over, and shove him backward. He stumbles into the car, his back slamming against it, and drops to one knee with a grunt of pain. Before he can recover from the flurry of attacks, I find my gun and release a hail of bullets on both him and the car. Bullets ping against metal, and his body jerks and convulses with the force. Finally the gunfire dies, and the body falls to the ground.

I lower my gun, gasping for breath. My whole body is trembling from the rush. Nearby I can hear at least one of the raiders still groaning, but a quick glance confirms that he's not going to be a threat. I march over to Jedediah instead. He's facedown on the hood of the car, not moving. I nudge him, and when I get no response, flip him over. Blood trickles down the side of his face.

His eyes flutter open and focus on me.

'I'm okay,' he says dazedly. 'I'm good. Don't you worry about me.'

I check him over. The blood looks bad, but the gash on his forehead is superficial. Judging from the look on his face he probably took a couple good slams to the head, but he's still intact enough for my purposes.

'I wasn't,' I say curtly. I leave him there and head to the trunk of the car. We don't have much time to spare, especially since we're on foot now. I glance at the map, noting the towns nearest to where we are, before shoving it into my pocket. I fill a duffel bag with supplies – food, water, bandages, ammo, and as many guns as I can fit. It hurts me to leave any behind, but overburdening myself will slow me down, and slowing down could get me killed, considering there's a fuckload of raiders hot on our trail. I'm not going to die for a couple of guns, no matter how nice they are. With that done, I return to Jedediah and grab him by the arm, hauling him to his feet. He sways, nearly falling over backwards again. I sigh and slip an arm around his midriff to keep him upright.

'You're not very durable for a raider,' I say.

'Well, you're not very … uh … ' He trails off as he notices the scene around us, his head tilting side to side as he surveys the carnage. 'Woah,' he says, blinking.

'You killed them all.' He turns to look at me. I expect him to be frightened, like people normally are when they see what I can do, but instead he breaks into a wide grin. 'Well, damn. Nice work.'

I glance sideways at him, surprised – and, though I'd never admit it, a little bit pleased at the compliment. If he had any lick of sense he'd be terrified after that display, but instead he looks impressed.

'It was necessary,' I say. I half-carry, half-drag Jedediah through the aftermath of the fight, sidestepping bodies and dying men. I put Saint's radio tower behind us, and set off into the wastes.

I wander in the direction of the next town, but my heart tells me there's no way we're going to make it. We have to stop and duck down every time a vehicle passes, though none of them notice us, or if they do, they don't care enough to stop for two pathetic wanderers. Jedediah gradually recovers from the fight, and soon we're walking side by side, though he needs some prodding to keep up.

I'm just trying to put as much distance as possible between us and the raiders, but something unexpected soon looms on the horizon: a town. I frown, slowing down; this is way too soon to hit the place we were heading toward.

'Oh, hell yeah,' Jedediah says, picking up his pace. I let him stumble on ahead as I pause and check the map.

Unless I'm horribly lost, this place isn't on it. Once we get a little closer, it's not hard to see why. The town is tiny, just a cluster of tilted, haphazard buildings that seem like they're drunk and struggling to stay upright. But there are signs of life here and there: blankets covering windows, the faint smell of fire, whispers of conversation carried on the wind. Normally I would never stop here, knowing I'd only find desperate people, and desperate people are likely to do desperate things when they see someone better off than they are. But for now, it's the only thing breaking up the endless emptiness of the wastes, and we need to get out of open ground. I follow Jedediah, checking my guns just in case violence does break out.

As we draw closer, I find that the town is dead silent. There's no movement or sound, nobody around as far as I can see. Maybe I was wrong, and the signs I saw before were just wishful thinking. Maybe it's a ghost town, abandoned or never really occupied. I'm already considering whether it's a smart idea to hide in the abandoned buildings or keep going when I hear conversation nearby. I grab Jedediah's arm and pull him against me, pointing a hand in the direction the noise is coming from. He nods, pressing his lips firmly closed. I draw my gun and we creep around the corner together.

A small cluster of townies gathers in the street we enter. They're dirty, thin people, and all turn to stare at us with wide, reproachful eyes. One man has a gun, but he doesn't raise it as he sees us, just stares with a look of resignation. After a moment I lower my weapon, and the armed man steps forward, holstering his own gun.

'Who're you?' he asks. He's a ragged man with a moustache and a head of scraggly brown hair, eyes squinting out from a wrinkled and sun-spotted face. I holster my gun, keeping my hand on it just in case, but he makes no move to draw on me. The rest of the townsfolk clump together and peer at me fearfully from behind their apparent leader.

'Stranger looking for a place to stay,' I say.

'Friendly?'

'Sure.'

He eyes me for a moment longer, gaze lingering on my burnt face and the gun at my hip, and nods. He must gather that I'm not a raider, based on the fact that I haven't tried to shoot anyone up yet. Either that, or he's accepted his fate already.

'Fine,' he says. 'We've got bigger problems to deal with anyway.' He steps forward and juts out a hand. I shake it firmly. 'I'm the sheriff here,' he says, 'for what it's worth.'

'Place got a name?'

'Nope,' he says. 'We just settled here 'bout a week ago. We were nomads before. When we heard about what Saint was doing, thought it was finally safe enough to settle down. Picked up some stragglers along the way, found a spot nice and close to Saint's tower, and . . . well, here we are now.'

'Shit luck,' I say. He nods shortly, his face grim, and then eyes Jedediah. He takes in the ropes around his wrists and the state of him, as well as the fact that I'm toting several large guns.

'Guess it's shit luck for you too,' he says.

'Yep.' I shrug, as if it doesn't matter. Better to keep a brave face around people like this, not show them that I'm scared shitless just like them. 'You hear what happened? Raiders storm the tower?'

'Oh, no,' he says, his face sagging. 'No word for sure what went down, but those raiders didn't all come from outside the tower. They came from inside.' He folds his arms over his chest. 'People brought him so many raiders . . . he must've not really been killin' them like he said.'

It doesn't surprise me. Not many good men left nowadays, and those that do exist usually don't last long. This isn't a place for good men. Isn't a world for good men.

'Well,' I say. 'No use wasting time chitchatting. You've got a fuckload of raiders coming this way fast. Let's figure out how to survive this.'

XI
The Truth

The sheriff leads us into a building nearby. They seem to have tried very hard to patch it up, and haven't quite succeeded. The windows are boarded up, the door is attached by only one hinge, and the entire place has a very sad, dusty look about it. The interior isn't much better, just a bunch of half-broken furniture scattered in a dim room.

Most of the townsfolk are huddled here. There's a surprising number of them. Every chair and stool is occupied, as well as much of the floor space, making it hard to walk. The atmosphere is grim, the people mostly silent aside from the occasional murmured conversation or person weeping. Clearly these people know what they're up against, and they're not liking their odds. I want to tell the sheriff that it's a bad idea to have everyone clustered in the same building, where they could easily be mowed down by machine gun or a couple grenades, but I don't see the point. These people aren't going to survive.

The first few groups of raiders, the ones with vehicles, will likely pass right by this place; they're not interested in such slim pickings when there are much better things on the horizon. But the straggling groups, the ones who know they won't make it to the real towns before they're already ransacked . . . those are the ones who will see this place as an easy target.

A few of the townspeople perk up as I walk in, likely noting the gun I'm carrying, the absence of the scared-shitless look that everyone else is wearing, and the fact I'm accompanying the sheriff. I'm careful not to meet their eyes. I don't want to give anyone the impression I'm here to save them. I follow the sheriff through the room, struggling not to step on anyone. Jedediah shuffles along behind me, and I hear him consistently bumping into objects and people and muttering apologies.

The sheriff leads us through the room and down an empty hallway to a small supply closet in the back. He shuts the door behind us, and I eye the cramped room. It's full of shelves and wooden crates, most of them empty. These people don't have much other than a couple jugs of water and a handful of cans of food. I grab one of the empty crates, turn it over, and use it as a seat. The sheriff does the same. When Jedediah moves to sit beside me, I shove him to the floor. He sighs and sits cross-legged there instead. The room is dark and dusty, the sole window boarded up, only shreds of sunlight peeking in.

'So,' the sheriff says. 'Who are you, exactly?'

'My name is Clementine,' I say. No point in lying here. It'd be difficult to get in deeper shit than I already am, and this man will be dead tomorrow anyway. 'Bounty hunter. Was taking this to Saint.' I jerk my chin at Jedediah.

'So you worked for Saint?' he asks, eyes narrowing.

'I work for no one. Just heard the broadcast.'

'Ah,' he says, nodding to himself. 'So, then ... this is a raider?' He eyes Jedediah, his eyebrows slightly raised. Jedediah waggles his fingers at him in a wave. I'm ready to kick him if he opens his big mouth, but thankfully he keeps it shut.

'This,' I say, keeping my eyes on Jedediah, who smiles up at me like an idiot, 'is Jedediah Johnson.'

A long silence follows. Jedediah's eyes flick from me to the townsman, and I slowly raise my eyes to him as well when he doesn't answer. I expect him to be startled by the news, or afraid, but instead he just looks very, very confused.

'Do you not know who that is?' I ask, uncertain. These towns are small and unorganized out here. Maybe they have no idea what's happening over in my area of the wastes. 'He's a—'

'I know exactly who he is,' the townsman says, interrupting me. I fall silent, waiting for him to continue. He clears his throat, looking like he's struggling to find the words. 'It's just ... ah ... that's *not* him.'

Now that takes me by surprise. My eyebrows draw together in confusion, and my jaw works for a moment, trying to locate the right words.

I settle on, 'What the fuck are you talking about?'

The townsman turns red. He looks back and forth between me and Jedediah, who is no longer smiling and has assumed a guarded, unreadable expression. The sheriff clears his throat, scratches the back of his head.

'Well,' he says. 'Of course we've heard about Jedediah Johnson. Matter of fact, we've been hearing a lot about him lately. Just got news on the radio this morning that he's headed this way from the east.' He points his thumb in a direction I'm fairly certain is north, and continues. 'Him 'n' his crew just wiped a town called Lefton off the map. Says they're coming to get back one of their crewmates who was stolen.'

We both turn to look at Jedediah – or whoever the hell he really is. He hesitates, looking back and forth between the two of us, and smiles nervously.

'Well, this is awkward,' he says.

I slowly lean back, tapping one hand across my arm.

I stare at Not-Jedediah, and then at the floor, and then at the sheriff.

'Give us a few minutes alone,' I say.

'Or not,' Not-Jedediah says quickly.

'Sure,' the townsman says, ignoring Not-Jedediah. He leaps to his feet, looking more than eager to get away from this conversation. He glances back at us as he shuts the door behind him, leaving just me and Not-Jedediah in the cramped room.

I stay silent for a long moment, which turns into several moments, which turns into minutes. Jedediah says nothing, either, though he keeps opening and closing his mouth like he desperately wants to. After a long deliberation, I sigh, crack my neck, and shove one leg of my pants up above my ankle. Strapped there is my favorite knife, a long, sharp, cruel thing I reserve for especially personal kills. I slide it out of its sheath, let the pant leg fall back down, and toss the knife from hand to hand while staring at the ceiling. My gaze slides to Jedediah, whose eyes are following the movements of the knife.

'Er, so,' he says, clearing his throat, 'clearly we've got a lot to talk about.'

'Not really,' I say. I rise to my feet and move over to where he sits. He scoots frantically away, moving until he bashes into a wooden box. He tries to stand, but can't quite manage to do it with his hands tied together. I stand above him, looking down.

I don't even feel angry. The usual hot rage is missing.
I just feel . . . cold. Purposeful.

'So you're not Jedediah Johnson,' I say slowly.

'You know, technically, I never said I was,' he says, his
eyes flicking from the knife to my face. Whatever he sees
in the latter, he doesn't like it. A drop of sweat paints a
line through the dust on his forehead. 'You just kind of
assumed—'

I crouch down and grab him by the shirt with one
hand, the other bringing my knife up to his face. He
freezes.

'Tell me who you really are,' I say, deadly calm. 'And
the story better make sense, if you want to keep this.' I
press the blade against the back of his ear, just enough
for him to feel the edge. He sucks in a sharp breath,
though he has the good sense not to squirm.

'Okay,' he says quickly. 'Okay, okay. Well. My name
is actually Jedediah Johnson.' I apply more pressure,
enough to draw a thin line of blood, and he squeaks and
shuts his eyes tightly. 'T-the Second, that is!'

I pause and draw the knife back, frowning.

'What?' I ask.

He peeks one eye open.

'Well, they usually call me Jed,' he says. 'Jed the
Second.'

I don't like the sound of that at all.

'So the real Jedediah Johnson is . . .'

'Good ol' Dad,' he says, forcing a weak smile. I stare at him as the words sink in. The son of Jedediah Johnson. I have the son of Jedediah Johnson in my possession. It sounds ridiculous. I've never heard so much as a rumor that Jedediah even has a son ... but then again, it would be in his best interest to keep that hidden, wouldn't it? A son would be a weakness. A vulnerability.

Of course Jedediah would hide his son's existence. And of course he would keep him in a plush room in his headquarters, with an escape tunnel. And of course his son wouldn't look much like a hardened raider, and of course he would be a crazy little fucker ...

The more I think about it, the more it clicks into place. Everything lines up with this explanation ... and it all points to me being in some very, very deep shit right now.

'Fuck,' I say. I sit back on my heels. With his ear no longer at my knife's mercy, Jed relaxes and sits up.

'Yeah,' he says. 'I can imagine this is a bit of a sticky situation for you now.'

'Sticky situation' is an understatement. Not only do I *not* have my hands on Jedediah Johnson, nor any hope of using him to start a new, better life for myself, but now I'm stranded in the western wastes with someone useless, worthless, and yet *very* dangerous on my hands. Nobody's going to be impressed by me capturing Jedediah's son, especially since the world doesn't know he exists. And now I've got the real Jedediah Johnson, who is surely incredibly pissed off, coming for me. Not to mention the fact I went on a wild-goose chase into this godforsaken area of the wastes, and I was never going to get anything out of it in the first place, because this piece of shit isn't the bounty I thought I had.

I've taken all the risk, and I'm not getting any god-damn reward.

'You let me believe you were your father this whole time,' I say in a low, seething voice. 'You wasted my time, you risked your life … *Why*?'

'I didn't know what else to do,' he says, his eyes wide and earnest. 'When you first showed up, I thought you'd probably shoot me if you didn't think I was worth something. And then, once we got all the way out here, I was *sure* you would shoot me if you found out I wasn't who you thought I was, so … ' He shrugs helplessly. 'I didn't want to get shot.'

'So you said nothing,' I say. 'You said nothing and let me come all the way out to this godforsaken hellhole for *nothing*. And now I'm going to die out here, for *nothing*.' My voice gradually rises. I stand and grab him by the collar, dragging him up with me. 'Do you even realize what you've done?'

'Well,' he says hesitantly, like he hasn't fully figured out where the sentence is going yet. His eyes dart around the room. 'As far as I can tell, I've led us on a journey together that has actually, thus far, been pretty—' He cuts off as I shove him against the wall. 'Well, it's n-not the worst thing that's ever happened, right?' he says, forcing a half smile. 'We've had some good times, some good conversations—'

My knife is at his throat in an instant. He tilts his head away from it, wincing.

'You don't have to do this,' he says. His eyes search my face, find it hard and cold. His chest starts to heave a little harder. 'Look, I know—' I pull the knife back, raising it, and he flinches, real fear in his eyes for once. 'Look, I'm sorry I lied. I'm sorry I'm not worth any-thing, but you don't have to—' He cuts off in a yelp, squeezing his eyes shut as I bring the knife down.

He stays with his body braced for a couple seconds, and then slowly opens his eyes and looks down at the severed ropes in a pile at his feet. He looks from them, to the knife, to me, to his chafed-raw but now freed wrists, and flexes his hands wonderingly.

'Oh,' he says. 'Well. This is a nice turn of events.' He looks up at me and smiles, immediately back to his old self. 'All right,' he says cheerfully as I place my knife back in its sheath. 'Now that we've established you're not going to kill me, step two is probably—'

My fist catches him right in the nose, hard, with a sound like I may have broken it. The back of his head smacks the wall behind him, and he gasps sharply. He pauses, his head leaning back, and raises a hand to wipe at the trickle of blood from his nose.

'Um,' he says, his voice coming out thick. He wipes his bloody hand on his shirt. 'Okay. Right. Should have expected that. Anyway, moving on to step three: We make up and figure out what to do next.'

I give him a disgusted look. I can't believe, after everything that's happened, he's expecting us to just *make up*, as he says.

'No,' I say. '*This* is step three.' I grab him by the collar again and pull him out the door. He protests all the way down the hall and through the building full of townies; they all turn to stare at us as we pass by. I ignore them, and drag Jed right out of the building, down the street, and to the outskirts of town. I shove him ahead of me, and he stumbles and falls to the ground on his side. I stay where I am while he struggles in the dust. He rolls onto his back and looks up at me, his expression almost hurt.

'You're free to go,' I say, and turn away. No point in dragging this situation out further. I need to talk to the townsfolk and figure out what the hell I'm going to do about this situation. I only make it a few steps before I hear Jed scrambling to his feet and following me.

'Wait, wait,' he says, running to catch up and falling into step beside me. 'That's it? You're just going to let me go?'

'You're useless to me now,' I say. 'And I only kill when I have to.' I speed up, but he stays beside me, chewing his bottom lip.

'Why can't I stay with you?' he asks, sounding genuinely confused. I stop walking and turn to face him. He has the good sense to back out of punching range. 'Where else am I supposed to go?'

'Go back to your daddy and his crew, dipshit. Or die out in the wastes somewhere. I don't care.' I whirl around and start walking again. No footsteps follow me, and for one blissful moment I think I've lost him. But soon enough he follows again, clinging to my heels like a stray dog hoping for scraps.

'How will I get back to the east?' he asks plaintively.

'I'm sure you'll figure it out,' I say. 'Or you won't, and you'll die. Once again: I. Do. Not. Care.'

'But Clementine, I—'

I pivot to face him again and shove him, hard. He stumbles, barely stops himself from falling, and looks at me with wide eyes.

'Listen up, you fucking dumbass,' I say. 'I'm trying very hard to be nice right now.' My voice is low, anger simmering just under its surface. 'And trying very, very hard to forget that *you* are the reason I'm stranded out in the middle of butt-fucking nowhere, with no car, caught up in a townie-raider war that will probably get me killed. I would suggest getting out of here before I decide to stop trying, and make an exception to my kill-only-for-profit rule.'

He's still looking at me with confused-puppy eyes, making no move to walk away. I growl under my breath and whip my gun out of its holster, pointing it right between his eyes.

'What exactly is hard to understand about this?' I ask, my voice rising. I don't know what it is about this guy that pushes my buttons so hard. Maybe the fact that he can't understand I'm trying to do him a goddamn favor and let him get out of here before shit hits the fan, when by all rights I should be putting a bullet in his head. 'I'm done dealing with you, I'm done being responsible for you, I'm done looking at that stupid goddamn look on your face. Just get out of here, Jed. Fucking *go*.'

Even with a gun in his face, he still just stands there looking at me with that pathetic, dumb-ass expression. I guess I shouldn't be surprised at this point; the man clearly has no sense of self-preservation. The idea of pulling the trigger becomes more and more tempting. After a few seconds, I force myself to lower the barrel. When I walk away this time, Jed doesn't follow.

Back inside, I find the sheriff talking to his people. I must've missed some kind of inspiring speech, because people are smiling and clapping all of a sudden, and he's saying something about defending their home and putting up a fight when no one expects them to. My mood only further sours. I stand apart from the townies, leaning against the wall, and grind my teeth as I watch the sheriff deal out weapons and rations. Townsfolk smile and thank him as they get their share.

Don't these people realize that they don't have a chance? Do they really think these weapons will do anything for them when the raiders get here, or that rationing the food and water will make any difference? As if they need to save it . . . As if any of them will be alive to use it past tomorrow. This level of delusion is pitiful, and the sheriff's cheeriness is only making it worse.

I wait until the sheriff is alone, his people sated, before approaching him. As soon as he sees me coming, he jerks his head at the back room, and I follow him there.

'Surprised you aren't long gone,' he says.

Me too, to be honest. But I'm not going to leave without attempting to get the reality of this situation through the man's thick skull.

'You're going to get your people killed,' I say bluntly. He regards me silently, with no visible reaction. 'I'm being straight up with you because you seem like a decent man,' I continue. 'You and your people will die here. You have no chance. You'd be lucky to handle one raider crew, let alone a dozen of them.'

The sheriff doesn't look surprised at what I say, or defiant, or anything much at all. Instead he just looks weary. Out of the view of his people, he seems suddenly deflated, the shadows around his eyes darker, his shoulders slumping.

'You think I don't know that?' he asks. 'You think I honestly believe we're going to win this fight?' He shakes his head slowly. 'I'm not an idiot. But what else am I supposed to do?'

'Run,' I say. 'Now's not the time for pride, or sentiment about this place, or whatever the fuck is holding you here. Just run.'

He shakes his head again.

'Me and my people have spent less time in this town than we spent walking here,' he says. 'We still haven't recovered from the journey. We're tired. I'm tired. And we have children, and elderly, and sick. We don't have the supplies to make it anywhere in time, and even if we did, we'd be run down before getting there.'

'Leave anyone who can't travel, then,' I say. It seems obvious to me. 'No point in everyone dying. If a few can be saved, then save them.'

'We're a community,' he says, gently, like he doesn't expect me to really understand. 'It doesn't work like that.'

I wish I didn't understand, but I do. It stirs up memories of a time when I had a town to call home, and people who I never would've left behind. As much as I hate to admit it, I know that's something worth fighting for, even if it's stupid to do so. I let out an irritated huff, fold my arms over my chest, and glare at him.

'So what?' I ask. 'You're just going to give up?'

'No. I wasn't completely bullshitting out there. We're going to make a last stand. We're gonna take out as many of the bastards as we can, and we're gonna die with dignity.' He raises his chin, defiant, like he's daring me to tell him that it's pointless. It *is* pointless, but I know that telling him that won't get me anywhere.

'You're lucky if you take out one raider for every three of you,' I grumble. But there's no real venom behind the words, and the sheriff relaxes.

'I'm not asking you to stay, lady,' he says.

'Yeah, yeah,' I say, with a long sigh. 'Tell me what your plan is.'

XII

Defense of the Nameless Town

The sheriff's plan, as it turns out, is a halfway decent one. We do disagree on some points – he thinks the elderly, children, and anyone else unable to fight should hide, while I think that's pointless – but ultimately, the man is sharper than I would've guessed. He and his people construct a wall at the side of town facing Saint's former headquarters. There's plenty of junk lying around town, and the townies drag out all the furniture they have as well. Chairs, beds, all of it – there's no point in keeping any of this stuff, because if the wall falls, they won't have much use for it anyway. I spend some time constructing the wall, meanwhile concocting my own plan in my head. After an idea hits me, I grab the first person in my line of sight: a gangly, awkward-looking teenage boy with a tuft of messy hair. He jumps when I grab his arm, and stares at me all wide-eyed and pale faced.

'You. What's your name?' I ask. He looks around wildly, as if I could be talking to someone else, and gulps.

'Wyatt,' he says, his voice halfway to a whimper.

'Okay, Wyatt.' I toss him my ammo bag, which he barely manages to catch. 'Help me find a good spot to shoot people from.'

Despite all of his stuttering and blushing and struggling to form a coherent sentence, Wyatt ultimately pulls through. He leads me to the roof of a nearby one-story building to set up. I can already see the mob of raiders on the horizon, approaching slowly, all on foot.

I recruit townsfolk to help me drag up the junk they can spare. Some splintered boards, a rusty car door, and a couple blankets become my makeshift barricade. I set it up on the edge of the roof and deposit my supplies behind it. The townsfolk ogle my guns and ammo supply, practically drooling at the sight of how much ammunition I have. Luckily they have the common sense not to ask about using any of it. I may be here to help, but I sure as hell am not sacrificing any of my guns in the process. I fought, sweated, and bled for each and every one of them, and there's no way I'm letting a single piece out of my sight.

From my spot on the roof, I have a good view of both

the townies below and the raiders approaching town. The townies are lined up behind their wall. Every able-bodied man and woman is there, armed with whatever they could find. About half of them have guns – better than I would've expected – while the others are using knives, metal pipes, broken bottles, and a variety of other objects that could potentially kill someone. They all look nervous, as they should. But the sheriff, to his credit, is doing his very best to hold it together. He doesn't cry, doesn't complain, doesn't despair, and does his best to keep his people from doing those things too. I can see the way he bolsters their morale. No wonder these people followed him across the wastes to settle here. He could've been a great leader, and this place a great town, if not for their shit luck. Maybe I could've settled here, if things had been different. Maybe this could've been home. The thought makes a lump rise in my throat, and I clear it, trying to focus my thoughts on the fight to come.

'Your sheriff is a good man,' I murmur, glancing over at Wyatt. The wiry boy is crouched beside me near the makeshift barricade, looking through my ammo bag. I gave him a quick rundown of the basics, and told him to stay up here to hand me ammo and keep me shooting as much as possible. He seemed more than happy to do the job, especially since it meant he didn't have to be down there with the other townies on the front line.

'Yup,' he says. 'Saved all our asses more'n a few

times.' He stands up, peeking around the barricade at the wastes. On the horizon, I can see them coming – a wave of raiders, unhurried but unrelenting. Wyatt looks at them for a long few seconds before turning to me. 'Reckon we can survive this?'

I don't answer. I may be many things, but I'm not a liar.

Chatter from the townsfolk below drifts up to us, but it gradually dies off as the raiders draw closer. My heart sinks as I stare at them. There are so *many* – just over a hundred, I'd guess. Raiders never work in groups this big. Even Jedediah Johnson's crew doesn't have these numbers. But if they were all holed up in that radio tower together, and this was the only direction with towns to loot, I guess they've made some kind of truce.

I had hoped the majority of the mob would be long gone by now, having procured vehicles for themselves or wandered off in other directions, but a good portion of the crowd I saw earlier is coming straight at us. Every time I think the steady stream of them has to stop, more come. They're in small clusters, their own individual crews, but they move together, all toward one target: this little town, too small and fresh to even have a name for itself.

The raiders have to know that this town won't have much for them, but I'm guessing they don't have a choice. The crews with vehicles have the time to skip over this little place in favor of bigger conquests, but the rest of the raiders need to take what they can get as they cross the wastes.

The town is silent. I can hear my heartbeat thudding in my ears, but soon enough that is drowned out by a different sound – the shouting and heckling of the raiders. They're psyching themselves up for the assault, bloodlust rising to a frenzy as they approach.

'Holy shit,' Wyatt says, peering around the barricade beside me. 'There are so many of them.' He looks at me, the whites of his eyes showing. 'We ain't got a chance. We should run.'

'Too late.' I grab my sniper rifle and set the barrel atop the barrier. Once it's steady, I place the first of the raiders in my sights.

'We're gonna die here,' Wyatt says.

'Make it worth something,' I say, and fire.

I take down a dozen raiders before they get close enough to start firing back. When they do get in range, I duck down and ditch the sniper rifle, swapping it out for an assault rifle. I shout out quick instructions to Wyatt, who looks on the verge of puking or pissing himself, but he follows my orders nonetheless. Despite my warnings, he can't seem to help but keep peering around the barricade, watching the approaching raiders with growing panic.

As soon as the new gun is in my hands and loaded, I start firing again. I mow down raiders, but it hardly seems to make a dent in their ranks – there are so *many*, and they never seem to stop coming. Despite my best efforts, the wave of raiders soon crashes against the barrier the townies have set up. With crowbars and pipes and hands, they make short work of tearing it apart, and the battle starts for real.

It's a bloody fight, a desperate one for the townies, and quickly devolves into a free-for-all. I fire into the mess, doing my best to handle the worst of the threats. Any raider with a gun I instantly take out, or anyone who tries to climb up to me. But soon they realize I'm the biggest threat here. More and more of them notice me up above, and anyone with a gun starts shooting my way. Bullets ping against the makeshift barricade, or zing through weak spots – it really is a shoddy thing, not sturdy enough to hold up long in a gunfight. I'm forced to crouch down, keeping myself behind the rusty door, and peek around the side to take shots.

'Need more ammo,' I say, keeping my eyes on the messy fight below. When one raider sets his sights on me, I send my last bullet through his face. 'Now, Wyatt.' I hold my hand out for it, still watching below for any signs of imminent danger. A few seconds pass, but my hand remains empty. I tear my eyes away from the fight with a hiss of frustration. 'Wyatt, what the fuck are you—'

I start, and stop. Wyatt is down, a bullet hole through his throat and a whole lot of blood around him. I didn't even hear him hit the ground.

'Fuck,' I mutter under my breath. 'What a mess.'

I pry the blood-splattered ammo pack out of his stiff fingers and haul it over in front of me, searching through and reloading my gun myself. When I'm not staring down my sights, the battle seems a lot louder, a lot closer, a lot scarier. I'm suddenly aware of all the sounds of people fighting, the cries of the dying. The air smells like gunpowder and death. With adrenaline flooding my body, my senses are all kicked into over-drive, and the battle overwhelms them. But somehow, through everything else, I pick up on one thing: foot-steps behind me.

No time to finish reloading. I turn immediately, swinging my rifle in an arc, and catch the approaching man in the side of the head. He lets out a grunt of pain, stumbles, and lands on his ass.

'Oof,' he says, shaking his head. 'Ouch.'

'*Jed?*' I stare at him. I can hardly believe it, but there he is. 'What the fuck are you doing here?'

'You really ruined my entrance.' He squints up at me, clutching his head. 'But, uh, figured you'd be missing me right about now. And you know me, people pleaser an' all.'

A lot of emotions fight for control of my head and

my heart, pulling me back and forth between anger and relief and utter bewilderment. Jed should be long gone by now. He should be someone else's problem ... or someone else's rescue, or whatever is happening right now.

But there's no time to figure out that mess right now, or argue with Jed about why he didn't hightail it out of town long ago, so I shut off my thoughts. I turn around, finish reloading, and use one foot to shove the ammo bag in his direction.

'You're on ammo duty,' I shout without turning around, and set my sights on a new target.

'Yes, ma'am,' Jed says. Out of the corner of my eye I see him kick Wyatt's body out of the way and grab the ammo bag.

I take raiders down, one after another after another. Each shot is a kill. Jed is quick with the ammo, much quicker than Wyatt, already moving to resupply me before the words are out of my mouth – he must be counting my shots just like I am. He watches the kills, too, shrewd eyes moving over the battlefield. He stays quiet, but every time I glance at his face as he hands me more ammo, he looks more grim.

Despite my best efforts, the town is being overrun. There are too many raiders to handle, and no one other than me is doing much to impede the assault. The townies below go down one at a time. The sheriff is the last to fall. He fights tooth and nail as he goes down, wild and animalistic in his will to live, but he goes down nonetheless. With no one left to stop them, the raiders swarm into town, right into the buildings where the townies who couldn't fight sought shelter.

Then the screaming begins.

I lower my gun, taking a deep breath. With the frontline gone, there's no hope of defending this place. The battle is lost. I let that sink in for a few moments, and then raise my gun and resume firing.

'Give me a gun,' Jed says from beside me.

'No,' I say. 'No point, we're leaving.'

'You know as well as I do that we're going to fight our way out,' he says. 'Give me a *gun*.' His voice is edging on desperate now.

'So you can shoot me in the back? I don't think so!' I shout without looking at him, too busy taking out as many raiders as I can. When I run out of ammo, I drop the rifle into the bag and grab one of my pistols. I have a feeling this fight is about to become very short-range; the raiders are flooding the town, and soon they'll find a way to me. Sure enough, I hear footsteps on the back stairs. I turn to face them, steadying the barrel of my gun.

'You try to fight this on your own, you're dead anyway,' Jed shouts at me. 'At least together we have a chance!'

Even if there were five more people with guns, or ten,

or twenty, 'we have a chance' would be a long shot. But at this point, he's right – we're probably both going to die here anyway. I stare at him for a moment, studying his face. When it comes down to it, really, I don't know much about who this man is at all. I spent most of our journey assuming he was the man who burned down my home and killed my family. It was an easy thing, a simple thing, to hate him. But now, things are a lot less simple. He's the son of one of the worst raiders the wastes have ever seen … but does that mean he inherited his father's character? His father's guilt? I don't know. But I do know that a gun in his hand could slightly up our chances of survival.

'Are you even a good shot?' I ask.

He grins. With chaos all around us and very probably impending death, he grins.

Part of me is certain that this is a bad decision, but even so, I grit my teeth and force myself to hand over a pistol. He takes it and turns to face the stairs just as three raiders burst onto the roof.

With a gun in his hand, Jed transforms. It's like the weapon becomes an extension of his arm, and the rest of his body shapes itself around it. My eyes suddenly find taut muscles in his arm, a hard set in his jaw, a shrewd gleam in his eye, things I swear weren't there a few minutes ago. When he raises the gun, it's easy to see the raider in him, the bloodline of a devilish tyrant, the instincts of a killer. For a moment, I'm certain I made a grave mistake putting that gun in his hand.

His first shot rings out a half second before mine, his second shot just afterward. All three raiders topple over lifelessly. Jed lets out a whoop of excitement, and in that moment returns to the ridiculous human being I became acquainted with on our journey here, the one who hums when he's being kidnapped and tells absurd stories to townie children. I guess I can add 'smiling while shooting people' to that list of hobbies now.

'Right in the nose! Did you see that? That was disgusting!' he says happily, firing another two shots in the time it takes him to get the words out. I'm about to tell him to shut up and focus, but when I see a body on the ground for each bullet he's loosed, I figure I'll let him do his thing.

People have a tendency to surprise me, but it's almost never in a good way. Jed is different. He's a damn good shot – almost as good as me – and we fall into a surprisingly easy rhythm. Between the two of us, we take raiders down as fast as they swarm us. I've fought side by side with others before, and I've always found it uncomfortable. I can never focus knowing there's another person so close, with a gun they could turn and fire at me at any instant.

But this feels almost natural. There's a wordless synergy between us – choosing different targets without calling them out, unconsciously planning our timing so we don't need to reload at the same time, covering each other without needing to ask. It feels like we're a two-man army, shooting down raiders as fast as they come, and I find myself smiling amidst the bloodshed. This is what I'm good at, the only time I feel *right*, like I'm exactly where I need to be – blood pumping in my veins, heartbeat thudding in my ears, bullets flying from my gun, walking that fine line between fear and joy, danger and triumph.

And Jed smiles too – smiles and laughs. He feels the rush just like I do; has the same ability to thrive in the chaos rather than surviving it.

Then, as I pause to reload, he turns his gun on me.

I stare at him, my eyes going wide and time slowing around me as I realize there's no way for me to react before he can get a shot off. His smile vanishes, his mouth becoming a tight line as he fires.

I gasp and jerk as the bullet flies right past my head. After a moment's pause, I turn to glance behind me, and see the body of a raider facedown just a few feet away, a crowbar still clutched in his dead hand. I blink at the body and look back at Jed.

'Whew, that was close,' he says, an easy grin splitting his face again.

'Guess they found a way up on that side,' I mutter, not sure what else to say. Without another word, we place our backs to each other so we cover all directions.

We manage to keep the raiders at bay for longer than I would've thought possible, taking out each one as they come up the stairs – three at a time, and then four, and then more, and then ... too many. The buzz of a good fight fades as I remember this is still a losing battle. We've held our ground, but the raiders keep coming, and we're steadily running out of ammo. Next time I pause to reload and look into the bag, my heart sinks.

'Jed,' I say, finishing reloading and covering for him as he does the same. 'We have to go.'

'What?' he asks, moments before peering into the ammo bag. 'Oh.' He looks like a kid whose dog just died, being told the fight is over, but he heaves a sigh and slings the ammo bag over his shoulder. He jerks his head at the side of the building. 'Follow me,' he says, and takes off before I can voice my disagreement.

I hesitate. He may not have shot me the second he got a gun in his hands, but that doesn't mean I trust him. He's not the man who burned down my home and killed my family, but I don't have a damn clue who he really is either. But there's no time to figure it out right now. Jed is already gone with my guns and ammo, so I don't have any choice except to follow. I fire off one last shot, directly through the eye of a man running at me, before following Jed.

I have to sprint to keep up, dashing across the rooftop and following as he shimmies down a rusty pipe on the side of the building. He's running again the moment he hits the ground. I rush to match his pace, my steps quickened by the roar of the mob behind me. Thankfully not all of the raiders are on our heels. Most are too preoccupied picking off the last of the townies and pillaging the town. Still, a few stragglers hunt us. I catch glimpses of them as I follow Jed through the ruined buildings.

He dashes through alleyways, climbs through windows, smashes through flimsy barriers. The town isn't even very large, so we must be backtracking and running in circles, but he seems determined to follow this nonsensical path. I want to shout at him to hold up, but I can't spare the breath, so all I can do is follow. Twice I'm afraid that I've lost him, but I always manage to catch him at the last moment, a glimpse of my ammo bag disappearing around a corner or a straggling shoe disappearing through a window.

Finally, we emerge into open ground on the other side of town. I glance behind us, but we've lost the raiders who were chasing us – apparently Jed knew what he was doing with his ridiculous path.

Out in the wastes, I turn to take one last look at the nameless town we've left behind. It's quiet now; without Jed and me, it seems there's no one left to shoot or be shot. Smoke rises from one building, blackening the sky above. I give it one last, searching look, and then harden my heart and turn my back on it – to find Jed standing with his hands up and a gun pointed at his head, and another gun aimed right at me.

'Well, well,' Cat says, smiling her sharpened smile from behind the gun. 'Look who we have here.'

XIII
The Capture

They subdue Jed and take my weapons. Bird pats me down roughly while her companion keeps a gun trained on my head. Cat glares at me, and I glare back, while Bird removes my gun from my holster, and my knife from its strap on my leg, and my other knife from inside my boot. She takes the bag from Jed as well, and lets out a low whistle after a peek inside, slinging it over her shoulder.

'You followed me all the way here,' I say, still not really believing it. I don't fight as they take my weapons, knowing it'll just make things worse.

'For *him*, we'd follow you anywhere,' Cat says, jerking her thumb at Jed and looking immensely pleased with herself.

'He's worthless,' I say.

'I think you mean priceless.'

Clearly, they're still under the impression that this man is the real raider king. I hesitate, unsure if I should correct them.

'You can't even claim the bounty,' I say. 'No one will take him.'

'No one sane, nope,' Cat says. 'Luckily, we have several less-than-sane contacts who will gladly pay out for him.'

It could be bullshit, greed, or plain old wishful thinking, but she's not going to believe anything I say; she'll just think I'm trying to scam her out of the reward. I know because I'd think the same in her position. I take a deep breath and change tactics.

'You don't have to do this,' I say, trying to keep my voice calm. 'There are bigger issues than a bounty here. There's an angry mob of raiders right behind us.'

'Oh, we saw 'em. And they'll spend at least a few hours combing that town and deciding where to go next,' Cat says. 'We'll be long gone by the time they get moving.'

I flex my hands, resisting the urge to take a swing at her. If I want any hope of getting out of this situation alive, I have to get on her good side somehow.

'You're really going to kill a fellow bounty hunter?' I ask. 'Won't do good things to your reputation.' An already-shitty reputation, but I keep that to myself.

'Who's gonna tell?' Bird asks in her high voice.

'Anyway,' Cat says, 'we're not going to kill you.'

I turn to look at her.

'You're not?' I ask warily, sure there must be a trick.

'Oh, no.' I don't like the way she smiles at me at all. It's playful in a nasty way, like she's toying with her food. 'You were *kind* enough not to kill us when you had us at your mercy. So, we're going to return the favor. But like you said, there's a lot of angry raiders around here, and we've got a long journey back home.' She shrugs. 'So I'm afraid we're going to need to take your guns, your ammo, and, uh . . . just about everything else, really. I'm sure you understand.'

'I see,' I say, my voice deadly calm. 'So you're not going to kill me, you're just going to leave me to die.'

'Bingo!' Bird says.

My eyes flick to Jed, who has been absolutely silent this entire time. He's staring at me, his eyes wide and troubled, and hasn't moved an inch from his original position. There's only one other card I can pull here – the fact that Jed isn't who I thought he was, and who they still think he is. I could tell them that taking him is useless, because there's no bounty to claim. Maybe they'd just leave us both here to rot, then . . . or maybe they'd shoot him in the head for causing all this trouble. Considering how vindictive these two seem, I'd guess the latter.

And I find, to my immense surprise and puzzlement, that I'd rather Jed stay alive. So I say nothing.

'Okay, well, I think we're done here,' Cat says. 'You're going to stay right here, and not lift a single finger, or we're going to shoot you. Got it?'

I stay still and silent as Cat grabs Jed and drags him along, Bird walks away with my weapons, and the three of them head to their truck. Jed looks back at me twice, as if waiting for me to do something, but I stand and watch and do nothing. The truck starts up with a roar and takes off, leaving me alone in the wastes.

I take a deep breath, and then another one, trying to force back the tightness in my chest and the panic buzzing in my ears. Now is not the time for panic. Now is the time to figure out how to survive.

First things first: I take stock of what I have, searching myself just in case Bird missed one of the weapons hidden on my body. She didn't. Nor was I smart enough to store any food or water somewhere clever in case I got myself into a situation like this. So, in short, I have absolutely fucking nothing other than the clothes on my back and the boots on my feet. I suppose they could have taken the latter if they were really feeling cruel, so maybe I should be grateful, but mostly I'm just feeling thoroughly, utterly fucked. I don't even have my map, though I've looked at it enough times that I have a shaky sketch of it in my head, just enough to know that there are zero towns close enough for me to reach without any rations.

Still, I'm not the type to sit and accept my fate. I'm not going to wait for raiders to catch up to me, or for the thirst to take me. I force my feet to start moving, walking in the direction that I saw the poachers take Jed, because I have no other goal to aim for.

It's almost strange, being alone now. I was used to it before, but over the days with Jed, I must've gotten accustomed to his constant chatter and inane questions. He always had something to say, questions to ask. I found it ... interesting, if I'm being honest. If nothing else, it kept me distracted. Now there's nothing to keep my mind off the tired aches of my body and the reality of this awful situation. At one point I catch myself humming under my breath to fill the silence and stop myself.

The wastelands are silent, hot, and utterly unhelpful, stretching out all around me with nothing to break the monotony. Perhaps I should be grateful that there's nothing to see, because whatever it is would probably try to kill me. But a slow, passive death is much worse. At this point, there's nothing I can do except keep walking. And walking. And walking.

After a while, my brain shuts down.

One by one, I tune things out: the sun bearing down from overheard, the blisters forming on my feet, the sense that I can feel my skin frying. Soon, all that's left is walking.

One foot forward, then the other, then the first again. I do it mechanically, unthinkingly, because that's the only way I can keep going. I'm especially careful to tune out any thoughts about how long I've been walking, or how much farther I have to go, or how long I can possibly go on like this.

I stop when it gets dark, sleep curled up in the dirt with shivers racking my body. When the sun rises, I walk again. More tired, more thirsty, more hopeless than yesterday, but I walk, because the only other option is to stop and wait to die.

I tell myself lies to keep going. I've only been walking for an hour. I only have another hour until I'm done. I know where I am going. There is someone waiting for me there.

When driving, I sometimes forget just how *huge* the wastes are. In a car, with a destination in mind, the flat expanse of wasteland is just something to tolerate for a brief while. But out here, on foot, alone, not knowing where I'm headed, the wastes are everything: vast, empty, and unchanging. I travel all day, and see nothing but sand. Then suddenly, just before sunset, I do find something: a broken-down truck.

And it's not just any truck, I realize as I draw closer. It's the very same truck that was driven by the poachers who took Jed and left me for dead. I'm incredulous at first, certain that I'm hallucinating at this point. I reach out to touch the vehicle, and immediately pull back my finger with a hiss as the hot metal burns me. It's real. And it's easy to see why the truck stopped when it did: A tire's been slashed. Nearby, the cracked earth is splashed with blood. Not too much of it – not a lethal amount – but definitely blood, dried to a muddy red brown. I stare at it for a moment, and then search through the car, every inch, hoping for a forgotten scrap of *anything* left behind for me. But there's nothing; the poachers made sure not to leave anything potentially helpful for whomever found this. I wonder if they suspect I'm on their trail.

I spend the night in the backseat. It may not be my own truck, but it's still a familiar place to sleep, and warmer than the ground. When I wake, my body is more tired than ever, but my mind is invigorated.

I walk briskly now, and with purpose, despite the fact that I can feel my body wasting away.

After a couple hours, I make a new discovery: the sun glinting off metal, which turns out to be a few aluminum cans lying in the dirt. I pick up each one and check for scraps. To my surprise, one still has a few mouthfuls left. Cold beans, mixed with a not-inconsiderable amount of dust, but I scarf them down anyway. Only afterward do I realize it may have been a trap, because what idiot would possibly leave actual, edible food lying out in the wastes?

At least one idiot, it seems, after I've walked another couple hours without dying. I think I know exactly who that idiot is . . . and how this move might not actually be so idiotic, if he knows that I'm following in his footsteps.

Humming under my breath, I keep walking, with a new energy to my steps. The sun may still be hot, my skin still burning, my feet still aching, but that all seems much less important than before. I have it now: a destination. Someone counting on me. Something to aim for.

As I walk, I alternate between thinking of my guns and fantasizing about my hands around the poachers' throats, slowly squeezing the breath out of both of them in turn. I may have spared them once, but that was before they stole my guns and my bounty and left me to die. Now, it's personal. I want to hear them beg for their lives.

After another hour of brisk walking and thinking about that begging, I think I'm imagining it when I catch a whisper of voices carried on the wind. I stop and look around. Nothing to see yet, but after another moment, I'm *sure* I hear a snatch of conversation. My heart jumps as I recognize Jed's voice – and then Cat's. My hand moves to my gun, only to grasp at empty air. A good reminder that I need to be cautious, no matter how badly I want to sprint toward the voices and smash my fist into someone's face until I feel better. I move carefully, crouching low, sweeping my eyes over the wastes around me. There's nowhere to hide out here, and nowhere to run. It's very important that I see the poachers before they see me.

But after a few minutes of walking and straining to hear, I have yet to see them or hear more voices. I pick up my pace, frowning, wondering if they managed to lose me somehow or if I really did imagine it. After a couple more minutes and still no sign of them, I walk even more briskly. I should've caught up with them by this point, but there's nothing but the wastes.

Just when I start to panic, I see a lone building ahead. It barely stands, missing its roof and one wall, but it will provide some shelter. I half-jog toward it, and to my relief, catch a snippet of voices as I approach. I press myself against one of the walls.

'But I'm *tired*,' Jed's distinctive voice complains just on the other side. 'Can't we rest for ten more minutes? And can I get some more water?'

I grin, and a surge of something dangerously close to affection rises inside of me. The truck's slashed tire, the food left behind, and now this. Jed must have orchestrated it all, giving me the time I needed to catch up to the poachers. I would never have made it without him helping. Thanks to him, both of us have a chance.

'We've wasted enough time,' Cat snaps. Judging by

the tone, I'm guessing she's had more than enough of Jed's shit at this point. 'And keep it down. We don't know who else is out here.'

'Ten more minutes,' Jed insists, followed by the sound of a scuffle.

'No, you—' Cat says. 'Don't lie down! We're leaving!' A long pause, and then a sigh. 'I *know* you're not sleeping. Closing your eyes isn't going to fool me. Get the fuck up.'

It's far too easy to imagine the irritated look on Cat's face, listening to her exasperated groans as she presumably tries to get Jed off the ground. No wonder I was able to catch up to them, if he's being this difficult. He may be completely out of his mind, and damn lucky that the poachers haven't given up and shot him, but I have to admit I'm impressed.

'Fucking hell,' Cat says finally. 'We're going to have to drag him.'

The sound of more scuffling comes toward me. I duck to the side and crouch down. After a few moments, the trio emerges. The poachers are dragging Jed along the ground behind them, each holding one of his arms. He's lying completely limp with his eyes shut, making it as difficult as possible for them.

I follow from a distance. I have to stay quite a ways back in order to stay hidden. Luckily, they make it easy enough to follow. Jed's dragging body leaves distinct marks in the dirt, and he complains loudly every few minutes, his voice carrying across the empty wastes. Honestly, I'm surprised they haven't attracted more attention than just me. The raiders must have stayed in the Nameless Town for a little while, like Cat guessed they would, but they can't be too far behind.

As I follow the poachers, my brain works to come up with a plan. Finding them was the easy part. Now I have to take them out and get my guns back. If I had even a single weapon, it'd be easy. But without one, I can't stand up against two armed hunters. Maybe I can sneak into their camp at night . . . but even then, it's risky.

I keep following, turning the situation over in my mind. No matter which angle I approach it from, I can't see a way to win this fight, even if I have Jed on my side. He's tied up, I'm running on fumes, and we have zero weapons between us. The only advantage I have is the element of surprise, since they don't even know I'm still alive, but that can only do so much.

My excitement over stumbling upon the group gradually fades. I can follow them all I want, and Jed can do his damnedest to slow them down, but there's not much either of us can do aside from that. Even with the scraps of food that Jed left for me, my body is running down, each step harder than the last. I'm weak, definitely not in any state to fight. While there may be a goal in sight, it's starting to seem like an unobtainable one, and I'm not sure how much longer I can carry on like this.

I find myself lagging farther and farther behind the poachers and Jed. *Maybe this is foolish*, I think. Maybe I should give up on this chase and try to find a town to resupply in. Cut my losses, focus on staying alive. Jed's efforts could be enough to help me survive the journey, and maybe that's the best I can hope for.

When I first hear the voices, I'm too distracted to process them. I'm used to catching snippets of conversation from the poachers. But eventually, it dawns on me that the voices I'm hearing are not familiar ones, nor are they coming from ahead. I stop, turn, and squint at the wastes behind me. I can't see anyone – but there, again, voices. The words are unintelligible, but they're definitely men's voices, coming from behind me.

My fingers once again grasp at the air where my gun should be. My pulse quickens. I force myself to take a deep breath, let it out, and resume walking. I'm in a delicate situation now; I can't walk too slowly and let whomever is following catch up, and I can't walk too quickly and stumble into the poachers. At this point, I have to assume that running into either party will result in a bullet in my brain. As I keep walking, with nothing but empty wastes all around, panic creeps up on me. How long can I keep this up? How long until I get too tired to continue, or at least too tired to keep this pace? How long until one of them realizes I'm here? So many ways this could all go to shit.

But soon comes a reprieve in the form of a small cluster of buildings. It's not a town; these buildings are falling apart, long abandoned. There are no signs that anyone tried to make the place livable, not even any attempts at patching up the holes in the walls. Still, the buildings provide shelter, and I gratefully duck into the closest one. Using crumbling walls and narrow alleys to stay hidden, I can relax my pace. The poachers and Jed are up ahead, still noisy and easy to follow. If I'm bold enough, I realize, I can even wait and see who's behind me.

And with swiftly waning strength and no end to this journey in sight, I don't have much to lose. I find a perch atop a wall, with a good view of the streets between buildings. It's a risky move, but I can't resist the urge to get a look at whomever is coming. If I'm lucky, it could be a group of townies, fleeing the onslaught of raiders; possibly even a group I could join up with.

The approaching voices get louder and louder, and I fight with the urge to run. Finally, the group comes into sight as they walk between two buildings on the edge of town.

Raiders. It's obvious at a glance. They're big and bulky, wielding rusty, bloodstained weapons. I don't see any guns, but their shitty pipes and knives are still more than I have. They're a small group, only six of them. They must have split off from the rest of the army.

Either they fell behind those who went ahead in vehicles, or they pulled ahead of the mob behind, leaving them isolated. I could probably handle them myself, if I had my guns. Since I don't, I jump down to the ground and quickly, quietly move to the edge of the ghost town, taking great care not to be spotted.

Defenseless or not, I think I know a way to deal with those raiders. Slowly, carefully, I begin to construct a plan.

When night falls, I'm ready. I follow the poachers until they make camp. They're smart enough to go without a fire now, and stay quiet in the darkness, but I make sure I know exactly where they are.

I leave them and head for the raider camp. Contrary to the poachers, the raiders are loud and rowdy, with a crackling fire much larger than necessary. They have no fear of the wastes surrounding them – and why should they? They're bigger and meaner than anyone in the area, myself included. Well, they're bigger at least, and I'm not much of a threat without my guns.

Yet here I am, creeping closer to their camp, using darkness as my cover. Clutched in my hand is a tin can – left behind by Jed, licked clean by me, and now the only weapon I have.

My heart pounds as I approach, but I won't let myself panic. *I have a plan*, I tell myself. *This isn't suicide.*

The raiders don't even check the surrounding area for threats. They're drowning in overconfidence, and currently wrapped up in a meal: meat, judging by the smell. They eat and talk among themselves, completely at ease.

I get as close as I dare, and push myself to get even closer, so close that my mouth waters at the smell of meat and I can hear one of them chewing with his mouth open. Close enough that, if he were quick enough, one could grab me if he noticed me – but lucky for me, none of them do. I take a deep breath and slowly stand. Still, no one notices me in the darkness. I wind back my arm, and send the can flying.

It smacks right into the side of a man's head. He grunts and drops his hunk of meat in the dirt.

'What the fuck?!' the raider shouts, rising to his feet. He turns to glower at his companions. 'Which one of you idiots did that?' The others match his confusion, staring at the can on the ground. After a few moments something clicks, and the man's gaze travels from the fallen can, to the edge of camp, to me, probably barely visible by their fire. The raider's eyes widen. 'Who the hell are *you*?'

I run. Shouts and footsteps follow me. *Good.* If they were a little smarter, they might be more wary about following a lone stranger into the darkness. Then again, they probably think I'm just a desperate scavenger trying to steal some food. Either way, their pride won't let them sit back and wait for me to escape. So, they follow.

I run as hard as I can, but my body is weak from lack of food and water, and soon I'm stumbling and panting for breath. If any of the raiders had guns, I'd be dead right now, but luckily they don't. I just have to stay a few paces ahead, far enough that they can't reach me with their fists or weapons. I force my shaking legs to keep moving – just a little farther. A little farther. I'm almost there.

As I see my target I gain a final burst of adrenaline, and hurtle right into the heart of the poachers' camp.

They turn their guns on me in an instant. Cat bares her teeth in a snarl. Bird turns her head one way and another, scrutinizing me through her goggles like she doesn't quite believe what she's seeing. Jed, tied up on the ground and looking like he just woke up from a nap, smiles.

'Clementine!' he says cheerfully, apparently unconcerned by the fact I now have two very big guns pointed at me.

'What the *fuck* are you doing here?' Cat shouts, while I pant for breath. 'Guess you really do have a death wish. And I'm more than happy to—'

She cuts off as a half dozen raiders charge in behind me.

For a moment there's a pause – a long pause, as the

raiders and the poachers stare at one another across the camp, mirroring the others' bewilderment. As they stare, I drop to the ground. A moment later, the shooting begins.

I crawl on my hands and knees across the camp while the fight rages. I flinch and duck at every gunshot and clang of metal and thud of flesh, but none of it is aimed at me. The raiders are more concerned about the ones with guns, the poachers too busy handling three angry raiders each to pay attention to me, but Jed's eyes never leave me.

'I knew you'd come for me,' he says, grinning, as I draw closer.

I crawl right past him, my eyes homing in on one thing: my bag of guns. I scoop it up and unzip it, quickly sifting through to verify my guns and ammo are inside. I check that my pistol is loaded, take that, and sling the bag over my shoulder. I find two bottles of water as well, tossing those in with my weapons. Unfortunately, there's no food to be found. But despite that, a deep calm settles over me. With a gun in my hand, it feels like I just might make it through this alive.

'Clementine,' Jed says, attempting to wriggle in my direction. 'Hey! You *are* here for me, right?'

I pause, glancing over the fight still raging between the poachers and raiders. As much as I'd love to be the one who kills those damn poachers, I don't think it's worth getting involved.

'C'mon! I left that food for you. I saved your life!' Jed is saying. I finally look at him. He's a bit battered, with a split lip and a swollen eye. His good eye is very wide and locked on me. 'You know I can be useful. We're better off together.'

'Yeah, yeah,' I mutter, crouching beside him. Getting my guns was more important, but I never planned on leaving him here either. He's right that he's saved my life more than once now: first in the Nameless Town, and later when he left food behind. And while he's probably going to run back to his father as soon as he gets a chance, for now, we are better off together. Can't say that I'm not eager for companionship out here in the wastes, either, as much as the realization of that surprises me. The long days of wandering alone have changed my perspective a little, and given how weak I am right now, it won't hurt to have someone else around.

I work at the bindings around his ankles first, and then those around his wrists. I glance over him as I do so. Aside from the minor wounds on his face, he seems mostly unharmed. Considering the way he was acting, he's pretty damn lucky to still be in one piece.

We're going to need a little more of that luck to get out of here alive. The raiders and poachers may be too busy dealing with one another to pay much attention to us, but there are still bullets and limbs flying every-where. Cat stumbles right toward us, entangled with a raider twice her size. Jed sticks out a leg to trip the man and they both go down. Cat's pinned beneath the man, trapped – but a moment later, the raider screams as her sharpened teeth rip into his throat.

I keep one eye on the fight as I finish untying Jed's wrists. Right now it's a total bloodbath, and it's hard to tell who's winning. We need to get out of here before that changes and they suddenly remember we exist. Once I get Jed free, I stand and yank him to his feet beside me.

Nearby, Cat is grappling with two men now, a third lifeless nearby, blood still spurting from his torn throat. Bird has another raider on the ground, and is currently straddling his chest and driving a knife repeatedly into his face. Her head jerks up as Jed and I stand, her mask whipping toward me, goggles shining in the darkness. Another raider tackles her to the ground before she can do anything about it.

'Whew,' Jed says. 'Like I said. Knew you'd come for me.'

I glance sideways at him, suppressing a smile.

'Oh, shut up,' I say. 'Let's get out of here.'

Together, we run into the wastes.

XIV
The Council of Fort Cain

We run until we can't hear the sounds of shouting or gunfire any longer, and then slow to a walk, side by side. Neither of us talks. Not enough breath, and nothing to say, at least on my part. We're back together, for better or for worse.

After a while, it feels like we've put some good distance between us and the poachers. My weakened body is exhausted, and stumbling around blindly in the dark becomes more trouble than it's worth. I point out a cluster of rocks nearby, which seems like the best shelter we're going to get, and we curl up against the biggest one. I down most of a bottle of water, rest my hand on my gun, and drift into sleep beside Jed.

*

We wake up at the crack of dawn and start walking again. I'm more tired than ever, my body wearing down quickly from the lack of food, but I force myself to keep moving. The wastes are quiet around us. No poachers, no raiders. Maybe they killed each other off, though I doubt we're that lucky. I'd be willing to bet that Bird and Cat made it through. It's more likely that they just don't know where we are, or have temporarily pulled back to lick their wounds. Either way, we're safe for now. Better yet, Jed says the poachers spoke of a town while he was with them, and he knows what direction to head in, though he doesn't know how far it is. It's possible we'll run into the two assholes on the way there, but it's still our best bet.

'Wait,' Jed says, jerking to such a sudden stop that I quickly look around for some kind of threat. There's nothing but empty wastes around us, so I turn back to Jed, who is staring off into the distance and frowning. 'Wrong way,' he says, turns to the left, and starts walking again.

Within the next hour, he does the same thing twice more. I have to admit I was relieved to be reunited with him and have some decent company out here, but that relief dwindles as my stomach growls. We may have gotten enough water to keep me from collapsing, but I'm still weak from exhaustion and hunger.

'Do you actually know where we're going or not?' I

ask, grinding my teeth and trying to refrain from snapping at him. Jed stops walking again, placing his hands on his hips and tapping one foot.

'Good question,' he says. He pauses, gnawing his bottom lip while he thinks, and then his eyes light up. 'Wait – got it!' He licks one of his fingers and thrusts it up in the air above him. He holds it there, the rest of his body stock-still.

'What the fuck are you doing?' I ask, after several seconds of this.

'Checking the wind,' he says without moving. I stare at him, bewildered. A solid thirty seconds pass without any change. Finally, he lowers his finger. 'There's no wind,' he says, regretfully.

'Yeah, no shit,' I say. 'This isn't the time to fuck around, Jed.' I know at this point that he's certainly no idiot, but he *is* wasting our time right now, and we don't have much to spare. My legs feel like they're going to give out at any second.

'Just trying to lighten the mood,' he says, shrugging. 'It's getting kind of grim around here.'

I sigh and resume walking in the latest direction he's chosen, beginning to wonder how the hell Jed has survived this far, and how I could've ever missed having him around. After a few moments, he trudges after me.

After seeing nothing but empty wastes for a few hours, I start to think Jed might have no idea what he's talking about. Even if there's a town somewhere around here, I'm not sure if I can make it. My legs are starting to shake, threatening to give out every few steps, and my head feels light. Progress is agonizingly slow, and I can feel my already-paltry strength waning by the minute. My throat and eyes burn, every blink and breath harder than the last one. Soon Jed ends up walking ahead of me, while I lag behind. Jed shoots worried glances over his shoulder and stops humming and making his stupid jokes.

'Can't be much longer,' he says. His voice is quieter than normal, almost coaxing, his face etched with a frown that makes him look older.

Of course it can be, I think, half-delirious, looking out at the expanse of endless wastelands around us. It could be forever. The town we're looking for might not even exist anymore. It could've been swallowed by the wastes, and soon we will be too. But I say nothing, and force myself to keep moving.

And against all odds, after a second hour passes, a town emerges on the horizon.

'There it is,' Jed yells, pointing toward the looming buildings and turning to me, as if there's any way I could possibly have missed them. 'I told you so!'

'Quiet down,' I say, eyeing the place. 'We don't know if they're friendly.'

'Well, it's not like we're gonna sneak up on them,' Jed says. Still, he quiets as we draw closer.

This place is certainly bigger than the Nameless Town. It may not have been on the map I had, but it's clearly an established town nonetheless, not something shoddily thrown together. A wall constructed of scrap metal and spare car parts surrounds the place, topped with barbed wire. The only break in the fence is the front gate, a huge and impenetrable-looking sheet of rusty metal. Jed and I stop a few feet away from it. I scrutinize the gate, searching for a way to open it.

'Move along, strangers,' a voice calls from above. I lean back and look up to see a woman scowling down at me from a lookout perch. It sticks out just above the wall and is tilted slightly, as if it's on the verge of falling over. The woman wears a helmet and wields an impressive sniper rifle. I raise both my hands, and elbow Jed in the side, prompting him to do the same.

'We mean no harm,' I shout up to the woman. 'Just need a place to stay for a night or two.'

She says nothing, but gestures with her gun for us to leave. My gut tightens. If this town turns us away, I'm done for. I need food badly. Without it, I don't think I'll be able to get up tomorrow. But talking to people has never been a strong point of mine, and it's harder still with my head swimming from fatigue and hunger.

'Do something,' I whisper to Jed.

He blinks at me, and looks up at the guard above.

'Please,' he says, with as much desperation as he can

channel into a shout. 'We've got nowhere else to go. We won't make it to the next town.'

'Not my problem,' she says, and leans back in her perch, a clear dismissal. Jed and I exchange another glance, and I shrug.

'All right, strategy number two,' Jed mumbles under his breath, and clears his throat. 'We've got guns to trade,' he shouts up to her. 'And ammo.'

'I don't—'

'You're gonna need 'em,' he adds, 'for what's coming this way.'

She leans forward, looking down at us.

'The raiders?' she asks. 'We got word from out there, but . . . '

'We've faced it ourselves,' I shout up to her. 'Barely made it out.'

She stares down at us, clearly thinking about something. I have no idea what it could be, but Jed's face sharpens with realization.

'Let us in and we'll tell you all about it,' he says. 'We faced them once and lived. We'll help you do the same.'

She pauses for a long moment. Then she stands up, looks down at the other side of the gate, and gestures to someone. A moment later, with a screech of metal, the gate starts to rise. It does so slowly, full of creaking complaints, like it's tired of doing its job and wants the world to know.

'Nice job,' I say to Jed, glancing sideways at him.

'Told you I could be useful,' he says, grinning.

Jed and I stay where we are with our hands in the air. Gradually, the rising gate reveals the town within, including a man manually working the crank, and a half dozen armed townies waiting on the other side. I resist the urge to grab my gun. When they gesture at us to enter, we step inside, and the gate slams shut behind our backs.

The townies welcome us by shoving guns in our faces and shouting commands.

'Get on the ground!' one man yells, at the same time another says, 'Don't fucking move!'

Jed and I look at each other in confusion.

'Uh,' Jed says. 'Which do you want us to—'

One man circles around to Jed's back and jabs him forward with the gun, and another promptly shoves him back. He stumbles, struggling to stay on his feet. It takes all my willpower to keep my hands in the air.

'Give us your weapons,' a man in front of us says. I reach for my pistol, and immediately another townie screams at me not to touch my gun. I stop moving and take a deep breath, desperately trying to keep my shit together, while the townies push us this way and that, shouting a variety of commands.

Jed keeps his hands held skyward. I very slowly pluck my gun out of its holster, lower it to the ground, and raise my hands again. Thankfully none of the idiot townies mistake that for aggression, and once it becomes clear we're not going to resist, the shouting gradually dies down. Despite our cooperation, they still insist on holding us at gunpoint while others pat us down, removing each and every thing that could remotely constitute a weapon from our bodies. I force myself to bite my tongue as they take my guns, no matter how much I hate it. I just got the damn things back, and already they're gone.

Despite the treatment, part of me is glad to see that the townies are so wary. It means they haven't given up yet. They are, however, very afraid. They're tightly wound and jerky in their movements, eyes skittering around, three lookouts keeping an eye on the wastes outside like they expect us to have armed friends charging in behind us. I'm half-certain they're going to take our weapons and throw us out in the wastes again, which would be a death sentence. But thankfully, after we've made a great show of being cooperative and peaceful, they relax a bit – though they keep our weapons.

The town looked imposing and organized from the outside, but on the other side of the wall, we're merely the newest addition to a cluster-fuck of activity. Townspeople are running everywhere, carrying personal belongings and supplies to and fro, arguing over what belongs to whom, fighting over what should be saved and what should be left behind. We pass two men playing tug-of-war with a half-broken chair, yelling about whether it's better to burn it for cooking or add it to the defenses. If there's someone in charge here, they're not showing their face. I guess they have bigger things to worry about than a tussle over furniture.

A group of five of the men and women who were guarding the front wall escort us through town, completely ignoring the chaos around us, guns pointed at our heads the whole time. Jed lowers his hands and walks at a leisurely pace, glancing around at the various ridiculous scenes around us. He looks like he's trying very hard not to smile. I shoot him a glare for that. We're already walking on thin ice; the townies don't need to see him being amused by their trouble. Thankfully, none of the townies notice his mirth.

They lead us to a building in the back, away from the chaos at the heart of town. After muttering among themselves, the group accompanying us disperses, leaving only the woman from the lookout perch behind. She silently escorts us into the building.

The room we enter is quiet. It holds only a run-down, stained wooden table, with two women and a man seated at it. Spread across the surface between them is a frayed, yellowed piece of paper with curled edges. As soon as we enter, the three grab it and turn it facedown, hiding its contents from our sight. I catch only a glimpse of what seems to be a diagram of the town.

'What's this?' one of the women asks sharply. She's middle-aged, with pinched lips and olive skin. She scrutinizes Jed and me and glares at the guard accompanying us. 'I thought we agreed not to let any strangers into town. We've got enough to worry about already.'

'I know, I know,' the guard says. She takes off her helmet, runs a hand through her sweaty hair, and shrugs. 'But these two say they've seen the raiders. Thought we should hear what they have to say.'

The woman at the table looks back at us, her eyes narrowing.

'They've been disarmed, at least?'

'Of course,' the guard says. 'And I gotta say, there was a lot of disarming to be done. The two were packing. Her especially.' She jerks her chin at me. I keep my face neutral, meeting the eyes of the woman at the table. Her lips twist to one side, and she nods at the guard.

'Got it. You can go now.'

The guard leaves us. When the door shuts behind her, the room is quiet. The three townies at the table eye us warily. Jed, beside me, shifts from foot to foot and clears his throat. I shoot him a warning glare, just to make sure he doesn't get any stupid ideas, but he stays quiet.

'So which of you is in charge here?' I ask finally, looking from one to another.

'All of us,' the single man says. He has hard eyes and a scruffy black goatee. 'We're the council of Fort Cain.' He says it with a proudly raised chin, like I should recognize the name of their backwater little western town. I look at Jed, wondering if I should have heard of the place, but he shrugs back at me, as lost as I am.

'All right,' I say. 'Well, we—'

'So you saw the raiders?' the woman who spoke before asks. 'We've had a few people fleeing this way, talking about some massive army coming this way, but no details. You actually saw them?'

I take a deep breath, trying to stifle my annoyance at being interrupted, reminding myself that we're currently at these people's mercy.

'We did,' I say. 'They overtook the last town we stayed in.'

'How many of them were there?' the man asks. I know what he's really asking: *Do we have a chance?* I don't think he really wants to know the answer, but is it really better to lie to him, set up false hopes? I exchange another look with Jed.

'A lot of them,' I say. 'It's hard to get an exact number.' It's the best I can do, I figure, without causing a panic. But the council, of course, isn't pleased with that response – or maybe the implied answer behind it: *Too many.*

'It's possible some of them have split off from the main group by now,' Jed adds, finally speaking up. 'But yeah, last time we saw, I'd say ... about a hundred of them, at least.'

Clearly he hasn't taken the hint to be vague. The council members murmur among themselves, their expressions troubled. I stay silent, waiting for them to speak again. Whatever damage Jed has done with the truth, it can't be undone at this point.

'We appreciate the honesty,' the third council member says, speaking for the first time. She has a plain and open face, lined with age and experience. 'Is there anything else you can tell us?'

I pause, considering. I know what she wants to hear is good news, something that will help them, or at least boost morale, but there's not much to give. There isn't some big secret that's going to change the fact that they're completely fucked. But I'm not going to be the person to tell them that, especially not when I'm looking to stay here for a night or two, utilize their shelter and supplies for as long as they last.

'They don't have any vehicles,' I say after a moment. 'The ones who did already went ahead. These are ... the strays, I guess. They don't have the best weapons, and they're disorganized. Not a singular army, but a bunch of crews who happen to be headed the same way. They'll work together, but only to a certain extent.'

Of course, the council looks disappointed. I know they wanted more, but I can't give anything else without lying blatantly to their faces.

'Thank you,' the older woman says. While the

other two are sullen, she at least seems to be holding it together. 'I have one last question. Is it true the raiders came from Saint's tower?'

I hesitate for a long moment. I don't want to break these people, but so far this woman, at least, seems to have genuinely appreciated the honesty.

'Yes,' I say finally. 'That's what it seems like. The sheriff of a nearby town said most of them came from inside the tower, that they'd been there all along.'

I've barely finished speaking when the other woman suddenly slams a fist on the table. The man and the elderly woman turn to face her with startled expressions.

'He fucked us,' she says through gritted teeth. 'Do you know how many raiders we brought to him? And this whole time, he was lying about killing them. Jesus *fuck*. He's no better than that Jedediah Johnson in the east.'

'Jedediah Johnson would've been better,' the man mutters. 'At least he's upfront about what he's doing.'

I try to suppress my reaction, and refuse to look at Jed, though I see him glance at me. I clear my throat, collecting myself before speaking.

'You know of Jedediah Johnson?' I ask, very carefully.

'Heard of him recently,' the older woman says, speaking before the other two have a chance to. She's still maintaining her composure. I respect that. 'Other towns sent warning that he's headed this way, stopping at each and every town, looking for someone. I guess a couple of them have sworn their loyalty to him already, hoping he'll protect them from the raider army. Word is he'll be here within the week.'

I feel a cold prickle of fear at that. Within the week? As if we didn't have enough to worry about with the raider army. Even if this town miraculously holds against that onslaught, I still won't be safe from Jed's father here. There's no way the town can keep him out, especially not when they'll be worn down from their encounter with the raiders.

'Dunno why he's bothering with this area,' the other woman says. 'It's enough of a shitfest already.'

'Maybe that's the point,' the man says with a shrug. 'This place is ripe for the picking, ain't it? And maybe it wouldn't be so bad. Maybe we should consider swearing to him when he gets here. *If* we make it that long.'

'Jedediah Johnson is a monster,' I spit out, unable to help myself. The council turns to me, surprised by the interjection, and I take a breath to calm myself. 'I've been to the eastern wastes. People live awful lives. Whatever you may have heard, he's nothing but a dictator. And not a benevolent one.'

Beside me, Jed shifts and makes some noise that sounds almost like protest under his breath. I shoot him a dark look, and he presses his lips together, saying nothing.

'Well, at least they live,' the man says. 'Better to be

under his control than to be wiped out by raiders, ain't it?'

The two women exchange a glance, drop their eyes, and say nothing. I keep my mouth shut as well and, to my own shock, feel a glimmer of uncertainty about whether he's right.

The conversation may not have gone too smoothly, but in the end the council agrees to let us stay in town. They let us loose without a guard, though I suspect that's less of a sign of trust and more of a sign that they can't spare anyone to babysit us. They do, however, refuse to give us our guns back, which leaves me feeling itchy and vulnerable.

This place is certainly better equipped than the Nameless Town. They have real defenses set up, real guns to arm their townies with, real plans on how to hold out against the flood of raiders headed this way. If I hadn't witnessed the massacre at the Nameless Town, I might've let myself have a shred of hope. I might've thought they could at least hold well enough that the raiders would get bored and move on to an easier target. But as it is, all I can think of is the march of raiders on the Nameless Town, the seemingly endless amount of them, the sheer viciousness of the mob as they tore their way through the people there. Plus, by now the raiders will be hungry. I can't help but feel that, no matter what defenses and plans they have, these people don't understand what's coming for them. It's all too easy to imagine the wall coming down and these people being slaughtered.

But Jed and I are in no position to be on the run again so soon. We need this time to rest, prepare ourselves for more travel ahead. We have little choice but to stay here – for as long as we can, at least. I'll be happy if we get one good night's sleep under a roof instead of out in the open wastes. I know better than to expect more than that. After Jed speaks to the townies and gets us a tiny serving of water and canned food to share, I keep to myself in town, sitting quietly in the shade of a building and watching the townies go about their defensive preparations.

Jed, apparently, is not on the same page as I am. He's unnaturally quiet for the first hour or so, probably exhausted and shell-shocked from our bumpy journey here. But after a brief nap – during which I keep watch, because I don't fully trust these people – he's back to his old self again, but in hyperdrive. I have no idea where he finds the energy or the spirit, but soon he's flitting around and chatting up just about anyone who will listen. I sit by myself and watch him, half-annoyed and half-puzzled, as he talks the ear off every townie he can find.

It's easy to write him and his constant chatter off

as ridiculous, but he's remarkably skilled at getting on people's good sides. The townies seem mistrustful of him at first, but soon he's earning himself smiles, and then laughs, and soon enough they're treating him like one of their own. Meanwhile, I sit alone, and townies shoot me nervous glances and give me a wide berth as they pass by. I don't understand how he does it ... but I have to admit that I respect his ability to earn people's trust. Not just respect – part of me envies it. No one has looked at me the way people look at him since Old Creek burned.

Still, I don't see the point of getting to know these townies when they're basically dead already. This is not the time or the place to get friendly with the locals, and it irritates me that Jed is wasting time working his charms on them right now.

'Hi,' a quiet voice says. I look up to find a townie girl standing a couple feet away. She's young, barely a teen-ager from the look of her, with mousy hair pulled back in a ragged braid and a pair of buck teeth.

'What do you want?' I ask, a little more harshly than I intended, and the girl blushes.

'Um, well, I heard that you and your partner got into a scrape with some raiders,' she says, and I suppress an eye roll at the word 'partner.' Goddamn Jed. 'I thought you might be hurt, so I brought some bandages.' She holds up a bag for me to see, gauze poking out from within.

'I'm fine,' I say. Again, the words come out

unnecessarily hard, but the girl doesn't back away like I'm half-hoping she will. I glance around for Jed. He's busy talking with a small crowd of men nearby, and doesn't notice me looking.

'Are you sure?' the girl asks, her forehead creasing. 'You've got a cut on your cheek, and—'

'I said I'm fine, girl.' My voice is intentionally sharp this time. 'Now shoo.'

The girl's eyes widen, and she scurries away without another word. Sighing, I let my head fall back against the cool bricks behind me. My brain flashes an unwanted image of that townie kid, Wyatt, who helped me in the Nameless Town, and I grimace. I don't need any more faces haunting my thoughts. If things were different, maybe I could make an effort, try to settle down here. But this place is practically dust and ash already. While I want to find a new home, I don't think I can take losing one again.

After a few minutes, footsteps approach. I raise my head again, bristling, ready to tell off whatever townie is disturbing me this time, but it's only Jed. He looks down at me with his head tilted to one side, and then drops to a seat beside me. He hands over a bottle of water. It's much more than the townies initially gave us; at least Jed's socializing has gained us that benefit.

'What are you up to over here?' he asks, while I take several greedy gulps.

'Keeping my distance,' I say, lowering the bottle and wiping my mouth with the back of my hand. I eye him as I hand the bottle back. 'What are *you* doing?'

'Well, I was over there telling Dan and Bert about our journey here, but Mary came by and said—'

'Stop it,' I snap. 'For fuck's sake, Jed. I don't want to know these people's names.'

'Why's that?' he asks, frowning.

'Don't play dumb,' I say. 'You know as well as I do that these people will be dead come tomorrow. This stay is *very* temporary.'

He's quiet for a moment.

'Yeah, I know,' he says finally, without any of the casual joviality from before. 'Still, can't hurt to figure out how many people are in town, how many will be armed when the raiders come, what kind of defenses they're setting up . . . '

I stare wordlessly at him. I never would have expected that, with all of his joking around and casual chatting with the townies, he's getting important information. Once again, it seems I've underestimated him. I give him an appraising look. He's a damn good shot, charming as all hell, clearly much smarter than his constant joking suggests . . . What else lurks beneath that ridiculous exterior?

'I'm getting a feel for our options,' he says, when I don't comment.

'What's that supposed to mean?'

He smiles. After one more sip of water, he hands me the last of it and stands up.

'Don't worry about it,' he says, brushing dust off his pants. 'Just ... y'know, you do you, and I'll do me.'

With that he's gone, back to talking with the townies and helping with the hustle and bustle around town. I watch him, frowning, still trying to puzzle him out and decide whether I trust him. He may not be the infamous raider I thought he was, but he's still a raider, and his father's infamous blood flows through his veins. I have yet to figure out how I feel about him, but I do know that I don't understand him at all.

Plus, I think, watching him dramatically reenact our journey here for a group of townies, *I'm still not convinced he's entirely sane*.

As night falls, the townies retreat into their saloon. Despite its worn appearance and half-broken door, it isn't too bad inside. The floorboards are scuffed up but mostly intact, and there's even some makeshift furniture: tables and mismatched chairs, a bar with a couple of rickety stools. The bar doesn't actually serve anything other than water, but still. A few townies stay outside on the wall to keep watch, and the rest crowd inside of the small building.

I stand in a corner, waiting to grab the attention of

someone important and ask where Jed and I can spend the night, but anyone with any semblance of authority seems to be dealing with a steady stream of worried townies. As I wait, Jed brings me a warm can of beans. I slurp it down, and he leans against the wall beside me, looking out at the townies with an oddly shrewd face. I stay quiet, watching alongside him.

'Wait a second,' he says, his face lighting up as his eyes find something in the corner. 'Is that what I think it is?'

'Oh, no,' I say under my breath, following his gaze. I reach out to grab his arm and stop him, but he's already weaving his way through the crowd on the way over.

What he finds, stuffed into the corner of the room and half-covered with a ragged blanket, is a piano. He drags the blanket off, revealing a dusty and cobwebbed but still mostly intact instrument. The townies make room for him on the bench without him even asking. He slides onto it between two townie women and brushes his fingertips over the keys. He blows off some dust, cleans a spot of grime with his shirt, and prods a few keys to test it out, his head tilted to one side and his expression deeply thoughtful. A satisfied smile spreads across his face, and he starts to play.

'You've got to be fucking kidding me,' I mutter to myself, still leaning against the wall where he left me. Of course Jed actually knows how to play a goddamn piano. There are some missing keys and the thing is clearly not in the best state of repair, but he still manages to play a song that sounds almost correct. I recognize it as the one he hums all the time – and he hums still as he plays, fingers dancing over the keys. The townies are absolutely delighted by the unexpected entertainment, their faces lighting up, gathering around Jed as he plays. Some attempt to clap along, though it's clear none of them actually know the tune.

'Of all the useless skills to have,' I mutter to myself, shaking my head. What person nowadays actually knows how to play an instrument? Who would spend their time learning *that*, of all things? And how would someone even manage it? It's absurd. Then again, I suppose if anyone had the time and resources to learn a useless skill, it would be the son of a crazy dictator. I guess when you don't have to constantly worry about how to survive, you can spend your time on other things.

The 'why' of the matter is a bit harder to grasp, but it always seems to be with Jed. Spending time with him is basically a long series of me repeatedly wondering *why*. I don't think he even knows the answer half the time.

Though the 'why' of learning the piano is hard to gauge, the 'why' of playing it now is evident: the townies absolutely adore him for it. The tension melts away, and the townies treat him like an old friend, laughing and joking and clapping him on the back. Jed invites me to join him on the bench a few times, but I shake my head and keep my distance.

It's strange, watching how easily Jed interacts with people. I've never had his easy charm and way of speaking to strangers like they're friends. Actually, I seem to have the opposite effect on most people. People respect me, fear me, occasionally trust me, but I'm well aware that most people don't particularly *like* me. Nobody has, ever since Old Creek. Except . . . Jed, perhaps.

But people look at Jed like he's a torch in the darkness. They listen to every word he says, laugh at every joke out of his mouth – some of which are *definitely* not funny. The men trust him easily, and the women blush when he looks at them. It's puzzling, and a bit aggravating, especially when I know his father's legacy. Jed's skills with both guns and people must have come from him, I realize. It's a disquieting thought. And I think I'm beginning to see how Jedediah Johnson came into power.

Later, when most of the townies have dispersed and we've finally managed to get someone's attention for long enough to ask about a place to stay, we leave the saloon. Jed is cheerful, still humming his song under his breath, though I don't understand how he has any energy at all left after the events of today. He follows as I trudge ahead, finding the building on the outskirts of town. It must be the living quarters for the townies as well, because we pass several others headed to bed, many of whom greet Jed as they recognize him. I ignore them and follow the directions we were given to a room in the back corner.

We step inside, shutting the door behind us – and thankfully it has an actual, functional door – and Jed raises the lantern we were given to get a better look at the place. It's a dim room, with a single window that's been boarded up, bare except for a single cot in one corner.

'Wow,' I say. 'They actually gave us a cot. With a blanket and everything.' It's more generosity than I'm used to getting, though I'm sure it has more to do with Jed than with me. Still, Jed immediately finds a spot against the wall near the foot of the cot, leaving it to me without a moment's hesitation.

I inspect the cot for any overly concerning stains or marks and, finding nothing, lower myself onto it. My body creaks as I stretch out, and I sigh with relief, pulling the blanket over me.

I know I should just try to get some sleep, but while my body is exhausted, my mind is a-whir with the events of the day. After a few minutes of tossing and turning and attempting to sleep, curiosity gets the better of me.

'So where did you learn that?' I ask, staring up at the ceiling.

'What?' Jed asks from the foot of the cot, his voice groggy and half-asleep.

'Music,' I say. 'I've only known a couple of people who could play it, and they learned it before.' Before the bombs, when people had all the time in the world to spend on silly things like that.

There's a moment's pause. Jed sits up and scoots closer, all hints of sleepiness gone.

'Clementine?' he asks, his voice *far* too excited. 'You're asking about me? A personal question? You want to get to know me?'

'Jed—'

'This is it,' he gushes, his eyes sparkling. 'A bonding moment. It's finally happening. You. And me. Forming a lasting friendship.'

Noticing that he's scooting a little too close for comfort, I sit up and shove him. He falls back with a thud and immediately scrambles up again, sitting cross-legged just beyond the foot of the cot.

'Forget I asked,' I say, rolling my eyes, and fighting back embarrassment because he's right – I *did* want to know more about him. Because, while Jed is strange and difficult to understand and frequently irritating, I can't help but find him interesting. I want to figure him out, though I'd be hard-pressed to explain why that is.

But, as earnest as he seems, I'm guessing that obnoxious response was his own crazy way of derailing the conversation and brushing me off. I guess he doesn't want to tell me the truth, which is fine. It was probably a mistake to bring it up. We're together out of necessity, not anything else; I can't let myself forget that. Jed may be friendly toward me, but he's friendly to anyone. It was stupid to think there was any other reason for it. I pull my blanket tighter around myself and try to get comfortable again. But just when I think Jed is about to go back to sleep, he speaks up again.

'My mom taught me,' he says. He speaks quietly now, the over-the-top excited act totally gone. I pause, letting the words sink in, and resume curling myself up in a nest on my cot. Clearly, the question was even more personal than I intended it to be. 'She taught me when I was a kid. Before she, uh, died.'

'I see.' No point in expressing condolences. It sounds like it happened a long time ago, and anyway, it isn't anything special to lose one's parents. Pretty much everyone's parents are dead at this point; it's just a fact of life. The wastelands aren't a place where people lead long, healthy lives.

'Was killed, I mean,' Jed says. 'By my dad. My dad killed her. When I was a kid.'

'Oh.' Now that is a more unique scenario, and I'm feeling even more deeply uncomfortable. It's been years since I had a conversation this personal, and I don't think I ever really mastered how to handle them. Again, speaking condolences seems wrong, but what else can I say? We both fall silent, the only sound our breathing in the dark room. After a moment, barely even knowing what I'm doing, I sit up and reach out to him. My hand finds one of his, and I squeeze it briefly. When I try to pull back, Jed holds on to me.

'Clementine,' he says quietly.

'Yeah?'

'I have to confess something,' he says. I stay silent, still gripping his hand, all too aware of the small amount of space between us. 'I got caught on purpose.'

'What?' It takes me a few moments to realize what he's talking about. We've been through so much at this point that the start of our journey seems impossibly long ago.

'I could've called for a guard. There was one right down the hall,' he says. 'And I could've told you I wasn't who you thought I was too. But I didn't.'

'Why?' Again, with him, the eternal 'why.' Why would he do that? Why is he telling me? Why now?

'Because I couldn't stand being there any longer,' he says. 'And I don't want to go back now.' He loops his fingers through mine, squeezes more tightly. 'Can I stay with you?'

It's been a long time since I've been asked something like that. A long time since I kept company that wasn't for necessity or profit. I was half-convinced nobody ever would again after I lost my home. I'm not sure how to react to it now. I open and shut my mouth a couple times, trying to come up with an answer, and de-tangle my fingers from his.

'Let's just worry about surviving for now,' I say finally. 'We'll work the rest out later.'

'Okay,' he says, his tone hard to read. He curls up on the floor again, his head resting on the edge of the cot now. I sigh quietly, and after a moment, I lie back and try to sleep.

XV
Preparations

I wake to the sound of shouting. I jolt upright, untangling myself from my blanket and standing up. The commotion is coming from outside, not within our room, so the danger isn't immediate ... and it's lucky that's the case, because Jed hasn't moved an inch. I stare down at him, still fast asleep despite my movement and all the noise outside, and wonder how the hell he's managed to survive for this long.

He finally wakes up when I kick him, and blinks at me from the floor.

'What is ... What? Is something happening?' he asks, rubbing at his eyes with one hand. I ignore him and go to grab my gun from its holster, only to realize that it's empty. No guns, not even a knife; the townies stripped us bare and helpless when we walked into town.

'Damn it,' I say, looking down at a still-groggy Jed. For a moment I feel a flicker of discomfort, remembering our way-too-personal conversation last night, but I stifle it. There's no time to dwell on that. I grab him by the arm and haul him to his feet, pulling him toward the door without giving him a chance to protest. 'C'mon, Jed. Time to be useful again.'

By the time we've left our room, the chaos has died down somewhat. A handful of townies are still running around, moving supplies and checking defenses, but the majority of them have already taken their places on the wall. From the way they're talking and moving, it's easy to guess what caused the ruckus: The raiders are coming.

Despite the still-obvious fear, the townies seem to know what they're doing. They have a strong front line, some good vantage points, even a couple snipers set up on the rooftops. The elderly and children hover just behind the fighting folk, carrying ammo, water, and first aid supplies. They're preparing themselves for a long siege.

It's far more organized than I would've expected from a shitty little western town. Jed and I exchange a glance as we head to the wall, and I imagine he's thinking the same thing I am: *Is it possible these townies actually stand a chance?*

As much as I want to charge in and demand my

guns, I hang back as Jed goes to talk to one of the town's council members. After a few minutes of conversation, Jed shoots me an overly enthusiastic thumbs-up before disappearing with the man. A few minutes later, he returns with our weapons.

The moment I see the bag, I'm itching to have my hands on it and fill the hole its absence left. I suppress the urge to run over and rip it out of Jed's grasp. The townies already eye me like they think I might be a mass murderer on the verge of snapping. It won't help my case if I act like a psycho who's in love with her guns, whether or not that may be true. Still, when Jed hands over the bag, and I find my pistol sitting right on top, I hold it to my chest like a long-lost child.

'Gee, thanks, Jed,' Jed says, after a moment or two of me cradling the gun. 'Good work, buddy. I like you at least half as much as I like my guns. Maybe one day it will be three-quarters as much.'

I smirk and tuck the gun into its holster.

'Never gonna happen,' I say, grabbing my knife and slipping it into its strap on my leg. I'm about to sling the assault rifle over my shoulder, but pause, hesitating briefly before handing it to Jed. His jaw drops.

'You're giving me the big gun?' he asks, hugging the weapon against him. I eye it in his hands, wondering if I've made a mistake.

'You know how to use it?'

'Of course I do!' He shifts the gun so he's holding it properly, and turns in a quick half circle, making sound effects under his breath as he pretends to fire at invisible enemies. I watch him warily, but despite the ridiculous attitude, it does look like he knows what he's doing. I nod at him, sling the now-mostly-empty weapons bag over my shoulder, and head to the wall. I find one of the council members nearby, the older woman. Relief flickers across her face when she sees us. Guess she thought we were going to take off, which isn't an unreasonable concern. I'm still not convinced that staying is the best option, but it's a little late now.

'Glad to see you two,' she says, and gestures to the wall. 'You can take a place on any of the towers, or wherever else. I'll trust your judgment.'

I nod to the councilwoman, Jed shoots her an obnoxiously over-the-top salute, and the two of us head to a nearby watchtower. From there, we should have a good view of the front gate, the direction the raiders will be coming from. I climb the ladder propped up to allow access, and Jed follows close on my heels.

The townies already waiting in the tower are all smiles once they see us and the guns in our hands. Jed strikes up a conversation with the man to our left, but I stay silent, busying myself with checking my ammo supply. It's wearing thin. I'll have to make sure every bullet is worth it.

I look up again only when I hear a gasp beside me – a gasp quickly joined by a surge of murmurs and whispers from the townies, which then dies down to a total, complete silence. My eyes find the horizon.

They're here.

XVI
The Fight for Fort Cain

The raider mob is even bigger than I remember. For one moment of pure terror I wonder if their numbers have grown — but that's impossible. If anything they must have lost men, between the assaults on previous towns, the long trek across the wastes, and the fights that surely broke out among them, but it doesn't seem that way.

They don't shout and jeer and tussle among themselves as they approach the town. They're not treating it like a game this time. I wonder if they've grown, become more organized . . . But when I get a better look at them, it's easy to see the truth: They're getting desperate. They can't have looted much of value from the Nameless Town, or any other small groups they came across. After traveling all this way, they must be tired, hungry, thirsty. I'm not sure if the raids before were out of necessity, or fun, or just a general sense of sticking with their vicious way of life, but now they need supplies if they're going to survive. They've already come so far, and it's a long journey to the next town worth looting.

I steal a glance at the townies on either side of me, wondering how they'll fare now that they've seen what they're up against. Their faces are grim, but not terrified. This isn't like the Nameless Town. These people may be afraid, but they're not helpless, and they certainly haven't given up. I can feel their determination, even the most nervous of the townies steeling themselves as they see the raiders approaching. They stay in position along the wall, weapons at the ready. Not a single one of them turns and flees in the face of the approaching enemies. No one breaks down or breaks rank. They're ready to fight, no matter what the odds may be.

A townie fires off the first bullet, the sound of a gunshot ringing across the quiet space between the raiders and the town. It goes wild, sinking into the sand, but the sound of gunfire incites both sides to a frenzy. More shots ring out, and a shout goes up from the raiders. The mob breaks into a run, swiftly closing the distance to the wall. Hands and weapons batter at the front gate. The metal shudders and screeches but holds firm, not showing any sign of weakening. Other raiders, seeing the futility, start hoisting one another up to scale the wall.

The council members, spread out along the wall, shout out orders and targets, prioritizing the biggest threats: raiders with guns, or those nearing the top of the wall. Most of the townies are pretty shit with their weapons, but each target goes down eventually. I follow orders as well, taking down raiders as I'm told, counting down bullets in my head.

Amazingly, the townies actually seem to have the advantage here. The wall is holding, and so is the front gate, and between the two, the raiders have no way of getting inside. Townies fall here and there, taken down by well-placed shots, but most of the raiders don't have guns, and anyone who doesn't is entirely useless in this fight. Soon enough, the raiders are forced to retreat. They seem baffled by the turn of events, looking at one another with uncertainty. There's no organization among them, no one shouting orders for anyone other than their individual crews. They're starting to fall apart. Some crews fall back, and others run forward, indecision ripping their ranks apart.

Maybe this place really can win, or at least hold out long enough that the raiders will lose interest and find easier prey. I turn, opening my mouth to comment to Jed, and pause. He's gone.

'Jed?' I ask, looking one way and the other, unable to find him anywhere. 'What the hell?' Frowning, I holster my gun and head for the ladder, dropping down to the ground below. Where the hell could he have gotten to? Why would he have left without telling me?

The ground level of town is quiet and mostly empty, and Jed is still nowhere to be found. I search the area with a growing confusion. Finally, I spot him running toward me from the heart of town. He skids to a stop in front of me, panting for breath and red in the face.

'Where the fuck were you?' I snap, my worry quickly turning to annoyance now that I see him safe. He leans over with his hands on his knees, trying to catch his breath.

'Danger,' he says between gasps for air. 'I saw some raiders sneaking around back and ... We need to move ... Need to—'

'What are you talking about?' I ask, frowning. Of course there's danger, but as far as I could tell, the townies are holding up pretty well. 'What's—'

Then I smell the smoke.

My head whips up, searching the town behind Jed for the source. The mere smell is enough to send my senses into overdrive; the sight of the cloud rising above town freezes me in place. My eyes follow it down to the source, and find flames flickering over a building in the back end of town. With the dryness of the air and the already shoddy structure of the house, the place is ablaze in seconds, fire hungrily eating its way up the building and spreading to the next one.

As I stare in silent horror, a townie screams.

'Fire!'

The shout ignites a panic that spreads as quickly as the flames. The townies' attention shifts immediately from the raiders to the threat inside their town. One of the council members shouts to throw sand on the fire, but everyone is already busily scrambling to escape from the blaze. The townies abandon their posts all at once, flooding down from their watchtowers and rushing toward the front gate.

The fear is palpable, all consuming. In the wastes, fire means total destruction. With so little water to spare, it's practically impossible to contain. It can easily eat through entire towns. And here, we're trapped with it. The wall surrounds us, and there's only one entrance, an entrance that's currently shut, with raiders waiting just on the other side. The panicked townies will just clog it up on this side, making it impossible for anyone to get either in or out. And all the while the fire blazes closer, *closer*—

It takes me a few seconds to realize Jed is shaking me. I forcibly tear my gaze away from the fire and focus on his pale, alarmed face. He's shouting my name. I only know because I can read his lips; the sound is swallowed by the growing chaos around us. For a moment my mind flashes to another fire, another town – to the skin on my hands blistering as I tried to clear a path into the bonfire that used to be Old Creek, desperately trying to reach the screams inside; and the crack of the building collapsing, flaming wood falling right on top of me—

I wrench my thoughts away and force myself to breathe deeply, in through the nose, out through the mouth. This isn't the time to panic, especially not with everyone around me already panicking. The town's defense is crumbling, and the fire is still spreading, buildings falling one by one to the flames.

The only thing not catching is the wall, huge and metal and imposing. Suddenly it seems that it's not keeping the raiders out, but keeping us in, trapped with the fire.

'Clementine,' Jed shouts in my ear. 'Snap out of it!'

I pull out of his grip and shake my head to clear it. Jed looks from me to the growing blaze behind him, his face lit by the flames. Unlike everyone around him, he doesn't look afraid. His face is sharp and calculating. For a moment, I think of Old Creek, the town burned to the ground, and wonder if his father looked at the fire there in the same way. I banish the thought from my mind.

'This place is done for,' I say. Jed's attention snaps back to me.

'Well,' he says, 'I think it's about time to try things my way.'

'What?' I ask, frowning – but he turns and takes off without answering, pushing through the flood of townies

around us. I cast one last look at the growing fire and
follow him. I keep pace with him as he runs, thankfully
away from the fire and toward the front gate. 'What do
you mean? Where are we going?'

'Well, Clem, so far on this little escapade we've done
things your way,' he says, half-shouting to be heard
above the terror and confusion all around us. 'By "your
way" I mean mostly shooting people and making everyone hate us. And, no offense, but your way kind of sucks
and has nearly gotten us killed several times now.'

That successfully renders me speechless. My first
instinct is to punch him, but I manage to restrain that
and consider what he's saying. Ever since I lost my home,
my way has been the only option for staying alive. But
Jed is different. He's good with people. He proved it by
getting us into this town in the first place, which I'm not
sure I could've managed on my own. Maybe he sees an
option I don't. Because between this town crumbling,
the mob of raiders outside, Jed's father and his crew
coming for us, and the poachers likely still on our trail,
I'm not really seeing a way out of this.

'So your plan is what, exactly?' I ask, slowing as we
approach the front gate – and the heart of the chaos.
Some townies are trying to raise the gate to escape from
the fire, while others staunchly defend it, wanting to
keep the raiders out. I tighten my grip on my gun. This
situation is right on the verge of boiling over. I'm sure

Jed sees it too, but instead of backing off, he turns and grins at me.

'The plan is ... we make some friends!' he says, splaying his hands wide and looking far too pleased with himself. I stare at him, so baffled by the words that I momentarily forget everything else going on around us.

'What the fuck are you talking about?' I ask, but a moment later, he walks into the mob of townies at the front gate.

Swearing under my breath, I shove my way through right behind him. A half circle of terrified townies has formed around the crank for the front gate. Amazingly, the gate still holds. I have to get closer before I can tell why: The crank is being guarded by a councilwoman. It's the elderly woman, the one who seemed to truly be in charge, and even in the midst of this uproar she seems level-headed. By her side is the guard woman who initially let us into town. She stands with a gun in her hand, not actually firing, but swinging it around whenever anyone gets too close. The mere threat of it seems to be enough to keep the townies at bay. Her face is pale, her hand shaking, but she manages to keep everyone away from the crank.

'We need to stay calm,' the councilwoman yells, her voice barely audible above the other noise. There's shouting from the townies, gunfire from the watchtowers, banging on the metal gate from the raiders outside. Even I'm barely able to keep my cool in this situation. My senses are all wrought out and singed, and my trigger finger itches, especially with a noisy mob pressed in so close around me and the constant threat of the fire. I want to shoot, to kill, to escape from here – but I hold my bullets, for now.

Jed stands beside me, one hand gripping my arm to make sure neither of us is pulled away by the movement of the mob around us.

'I know things are bad in here,' the councilwoman says, 'but if we open the gate we'll be slaughtered. If we wait for the guards to thin out the mob, then—'

'If we wait we die!' a woman wails from beside me.

The townies shout and press inward in response. But the councilwoman stays where she is, planting her feet and setting her jaw. She shows no sign of being intimidated, and that seems to give the townies pause. Despite the chaos and panic, they still recognize this woman as their leader.

'Give us a chance to fight!'

It takes me a moment to realize that shout came from Jed. It's followed by more shouts and cheers of agreement. Encouraged by the support of the townies, Jed presses forward, moving through the mob and over to the councilwoman. I follow in his wake, elbowing and shoving townies aside. I don't know what he's trying to do right now, but I have no choice but to trust him. I stop on the edge of the crowd, but he moves farther still, until he's just a couple feet from the woman, face-to-face, eye-to-eye.

'I'd rather die fighting than helpless in here,' Jed continues, with the support of the mob at his back.

'We can handle the fire,' the woman says. Her voice is composed despite the situation, and she meets Jed's eyes with her own level gaze. 'We just need to stay calm. If we let panic take hold—'

'*Handle* it?' Jed asks, cutting her off. 'Have you *seen* the fire? A blaze like this will destroy the whole town. It's out of control.'

'We have precautions for—'

'For what? A simultaneous raider attack and fire in the town? I don't fucking think so!' Jed says. The mob is eating his words up, their energy hardly contained. They still don't move forward, not yet ready to commit a total uprising against their leader, but they're clearly on the verge of doing so. 'Let us out before it's too late! Let us out!'

The mob roars in response. But the woman seems to hardly notice them. Instead, her eyes search Jed's face, her expression growing puzzled.

'What are you doing?' she asks. Her voice is softer now, so I doubt many people other than Jed and me can hear her. 'You're not this dumb. You know you're advocating suicide.'

'Nope,' Jed says, very cheerfully. 'I'm not dumb at all.'

The woman's eyes widen suddenly.

'Traitor,' she says in a harsh, low voice, and my skin prickles with alarm. Whatever Jed is trying to do, if this woman announces that he's a traitor, the townies aren't too far gone to listen to her. The councilwoman raises her voice to a shout. 'This man is trying to—'

In one smooth motion, I un-holster my gun, raise it, and fire a bullet right between her eyes.

Jed turns to face me, his mouth forming an 'o' of surprise, as the woman's body falls. For a moment it seems there's only him and me, our eyes locked. He looks at me – a long, searching look – the same way he looked at the fire as it consumed the town. I stare back at him, utterly shocked at myself for what I just did, and how easy the decision felt in the moment.

Then the townies surge around us, full of noise and movement. For a moment I think they'll come for me, but instead they swarm over the body of the councilwoman, overtake her guard, and fight for control of the crank. Jed pushes past them, and they let him take hold of it. I stop beside him. My hands are shaking, my heart pounding in my chest, as I replay that bullet sinking into the townie woman's forehead again and again. *Necessary,* I tell myself. I have to believe that.

'This is your idea of making friends?' I ask Jed, still unsure what he's trying to do. I don't see how opening this gate can do anything good – but nonetheless, I don't stop him. 'That woman was right. You just ruined whatever chance this place had left.'

'I didn't say we were making friends with the townies,' Jed says, and pulls the crank.

Slowly, haltingly, the front gate begins to rise. I find myself holding my breath. The townies push toward it before it's even high enough for anyone to get through, rushing the gate in a mad frenzy to escape. As soon as it rises high enough, they surge forward – and surge back as they find the raiders waiting right on the other side.

Complete madness follows. Both sides fight – one to get in, one to get out. People fall, crawl, get trampled; they fight and die; they struggle against the flow, one way or another. The raiders and the townies are soon one indistinguishable mob of people tearing and clawing at one another, most quickly becoming too immersed in the flood of people to remember which way they're trying to go. I grab Jed's arm and yank him back, away from the thick of the mob. We stare at it wordlessly. I feel sick to my stomach.

Next to me, Jed lets out a low whistle.

'Well,' he says, 'this is a shitfest.'

'Were you planning on turning on the townies the whole time?' I ask, dreading the answer.

'No,' he says quickly, and I suppress a sigh of relief. 'This was the backup plan, in case the town's fall seemed inevitable. Which it did, with that fire adding to the confusion.' He glances over at me, tensing slightly as he searches my face for a reaction. After a moment, I nod, and he relaxes. 'I'm sorry I didn't tell you before,' he says. 'I just ... I didn't really want to do this, unless we had to. It was our only option.'

I nod again. Part of me is still angry at him; he's the one who pushed me to kill that townie woman, which is something I know will haunt me. But as long as this is part of some plan that will help us survive, I think I can call it necessary and live with myself.

'So what do we do now?' I ask, assuming there's a next step to this 'making friends' idea.

'Let's find somewhere safe to talk,' he says. 'This place is going to hell real fast.'

He's right. I can't believe how quickly the town fell apart when it came down to it, and this was a place I almost believed had a real chance against the raiders. The fire certainly made things worse – but that must've been something the raiders planned somehow, proving their army is more capable than I thought. And Jed's little plan to 'make friends' may have helped with Fort Cain's destruction, but like he said, it was inevitable at that point.

I'm still feeling queasy about our part in this, and about the fact that Jed sprung it on me without warning, but I keep telling myself that all he did was speed it along and prevent us from being swallowed by the madness. And now I know the truth: No one can stand against the raiders. The western wastes as we knew them are done for.

Still, I hesitate. Part of me wants to stay here and try to help, to rage against this raider army even if it costs my life, but I know my death will ultimately do nothing. The best thing to do now is just survive, and hope that later I'll have a chance to make up for turning my back on these people who took us in and kept us alive.

I find a cellar nearby, an old bomb shelter that won't be in any danger of catching fire. We head inside and down a flight of stairs, finding the cellar empty but for a few empty wooden crates and some broken pieces of furniture. Jed attempts to keep a wooden stool with a broken leg upright, fails miserably, and sits cross-legged on the floor instead. I lean against a wall, staring at the floor and listening to the fight rage on above us.

'So what's the plan, exactly?' I ask, after several moments of silence. I'm still reeling from what I've done, and what I've allowed Jed to do in the opening of that gate. I need to focus, figure out where we go from here.

'Like I said, we make friends,' Jed says. 'This time with the winning side. We'll pretend to be raiders – well, you'll pretend, I mean. Seems like the crews have some kind of truce right now, so as long as they think we're just fellow raiders, we should be safe.'

'So then, what, we travel with the army?' I ask, raising my eyebrows. 'That's insane.' The mere thought of surrounding myself with my hated enemies makes my stomach flip.

'No, it's not,' Jed says, all too confident. 'It's our best bet. You heard the council. My dad and his crew are coming for us. Even if we escape from the raider mob now, we've still got that to deal with. But they won't think to look for us with the raiders. Neither will the poachers, if they're still alive and on our trail. This solves all our problems.'

I tap my fingers against the butt of my gun, processing his words. It's definitely a risky plan, but it does make sense. The only problem is whether I can pull off fitting in with the raiders. If they realize I'm really a bounty hunter who makes a living off killing their kind, they'll shoot me in a second. And if I *am* going to pull off the ruse, how far will I have to go?

'I'm not going to become one of them,' I say. 'I can't. I won't.'

'No, no, of course not,' Jed says. 'It's just until we get out of this bind. When it's safe, we'll escape.'

I chew my lip, looking down at my feet.

'I'm sure they lost a lot of raiders in this assault,' I say. 'They should keep thinning out. By the time they reach somewhere like Blackfort, the townies will have a chance. We can turn on them then.'

'There we go!' Jed says, snapping his fingers and grinning. 'We've got our plan.'

I still think it's tenuous at best, but I keep my mouth shut. No matter how crazy it is, it's the only plan we've got. Another brief silence stretches out, and I try to stay calm and composed. *This is the only way to stay alive*, I tell myself.

'Anyway, you okay?' Jed asks.

'Hmm?' I look down at myself, unsure if the adrenaline surge made me oblivious to some injury, but I find none.

'I mean the fire,' he says. 'You looked kind of . . . ' He trails off.

Right. That. My nerves still feel jagged and raw after the rush of terror I felt before, and bad memories stir uneasily in the back of my mind. The flames, the screams – they were a little too close to when Old Creek burned. But I'm calmer now, down here in the shelter and away from the chaos.

'I feel better here,' I say, and mean it. The shelter feels safe, secure, isolated from everything going on up above. I can still hear it distantly, but it feels very far away.

'Really?' Jed asks. 'Being trapped like this makes me feel caged.'

'In the early days, when trouble came to Old Creek, we'd hide in one of these under our sheriff's house,' I say, remembering. The shelter was dark and cold, and a couple times we spent a full night or longer there before we were sure the danger had passed. I'm not sure why I'm telling Jed. Maybe home is just too fresh in my mind right now, but at least this memory isn't of the town burning.

'Ugh,' Jed says. 'Weren't you scared in there?'

'No,' I say honestly.

'Fearless Clementine,' Jed says, smiling. I don't offer up the truth: that I felt safe because my parents told me we were untouchable there, and I blindly believed them. Better to let him think I'm fearless.

All this dredging up of old memories makes me uncomfortable – but it also makes me curious. Jed and I have been stuck together for a while now, but we've barely spoken about our pasts. To my surprise, I find myself wanting to know more about his.

'What was it like growing up with … your father?' I ask, stopping myself from using less kind words. He blinks at me, startled by the question, and then smiles.

'We were always on the road,' he says. 'He never tried to hide what he was – what *we* were – even when I was young. He explained that this was what the world was like, that raiding was the best way to survive in the wastes. I started getting in on raids when I was about twelve.'

No wonder Jed thrives in chaos; he was born and raised in it. He was killing and looting when he was just a child. He must've believed in his dad the same way I believed in my parents when they told me we were safe in our shelter. If I had grown up like he did, who would I be now? The thought makes me shudder.

'How old were you when you first killed someone?' I ask, the question popping out before I've fully decided to ask it. It's one of those questions you just don't ask people, but I have a sudden, desperate need to hear the answer. I've never been close enough to anyone to ask; I was afraid to ask my parents and my old sheriff. Somehow, in all of this, Jed has become the closest thing I've had to a friend – and I have to know. Is it possible he's just as fucked up as me? That I'm not the only one who took to killing so easily?

Jed hesitates. Before he can answer, a sound comes from above. Not from the town, but closer. Someone is in the building above us. Several someones, actually, judging from the cluster of heavy footsteps.

Jed and I turn toward the stairs in anticipation of company. I move away from the wall, pulling out my gun. Jed stays seated on the floor, but pulls his assault rifle off his back and places it in his lap.

A few moments later, a group of townies comes down the stairs. There's a good dozen of them, wielding pipes and bats and other blunt weapons. They're all looking pretty worse for wear after the fight above, coated in dust and soot and blood. One of them is being carried by two of the others. After a moment, I recognize him as the councilman.

My eyes shift quickly from one townie to another, sizing each of them up. Individually, they're not a threat, but all of them together is a different story.

The townies stop when they see us, fanning out at the bottom of the stairs and neatly cutting us off from the only exit. They set the councilman down, and he looks at us with a puckered expression, like he's thinking very hard about something and doesn't like where his train of thought is headed.

'Well, fancy seeing you here,' Jed says, cracking a grin. With all eyes on him, he slowly, lazily rises to his feet and stretches out his arms, his rifle still clutched in one hand.

'What are you two doing down here?' the councilman asks, his voice sharp and accusatory. He's leaning against the shoulder of one of the other men, keeping his weight off one leg. 'Shouldn't you be out fighting?'

'Well, yeah, about that,' Jed says. 'Clementine is, uh ... She's injured,' he says, gesturing to me.

The councilman looks at me, and I look back. After a moment I realize Jed probably meant for me to fake an injury ... but I'm not much one for faking, and it's too late now.

'She looks fine to me,' the councilman says.

'Yeah, she's a trooper,' Jed says, with an awkward half laugh.

'Must be,' the townie says. 'Because clearly you two wouldn't be hiding out down here, abandoning the people who took you in, right?' His eyes shift back and forth between Jed and me. Jed says nothing, and I tighten my grip on my gun. One of the townies adjusts his hold on his baseball bat, his eyes locked on Jed.

'Well, of course not!' Jed says in an affronted tone. 'We would never do such a thing. We're just, uh.'

In an instant, Jed's gun is pointed right at the man's face. The townie barely has a moment to open his mouth in shock before Jed pulls the trigger and—

Nothing happens.

I'm not sure which of the men is more surprised that the townie's face remains intact. They stare at each other. Jed jams the trigger a few more times – still nothing.

'Well, shit,' Jed says, and the townies lunge toward him.

XVII
Making Friends

I take out two townies before they can reach Jed. It's an automatic response, a thoughtless one, and only afterward do I realize those were my last two bullets ... and firing them has drawn attention to myself. Three townies quickly prove more than enough to take down Jed, which leaves plenty to focus on me.

I throw my gun at the first man who comes at me, and reach into my weapon bag for a replacement. Two townies grab ahold of the bag before I can get one. We struggle with it briefly, and the bag rips, sending ammo scattering across the floor. Cursing, I look around frantically for another weapon. My gaze finds an empty wooden crate on the floor. I grab it and smash it over the head of the next townie. She hits the floor, but the box shatters into splintered boards. I grab two of them.

The rough wood digs into my hands, but I only tighten my grip, swinging one at a woman coming from my left, and the other at a man coming from my right.

'Clementine!'

Jed's voice cuts through the rest of the noise, and my head instinctively jerks toward the sound. The moment my attention shifts, a townie's fist strikes the side of my head and sends me stumbling. Before I can recover, another swings a metal bar at me. I block it with one of my wooden boards, which shatters when the bar hits it. I drop the useless splinters and swing the remaining board at the townies in an attempt to fend them off, the blow finding no one within striking distance. I'm forced to back up, which only puts more distance between Jed and me – a distance that is quickly filled with more townies. I curse, eyeing the circle of them around me and digging my fingers into the barely useful wooden board.

'Clementine, *help*!'

I wish the growing panic in Jed's voice didn't affect me as much as it does. Normally he's more than capable of handling himself in a fight, so something must be wrong; he must be in serious danger. Adrenaline floods my veins, and a deadly murmur in the back of my head grows to a clamor. All thoughts of my rules, and of morals, and of being a hero fade from my mind. As a townie swings a bat at me, my instincts shift from *defend* to *kill*.

I raise my arms and twist, so the blow glances off my forearms. It should hurt like a motherfucker, but I barely feel the sting through my adrenaline spike. The townie is taken off guard by my choice to take the hit, and I take full advantage of it by bringing my wooden board down on his head. He crumples to the floor. I grab the bat from his hands as he goes limp, and swing it at the next townie with a satisfying *crack*. Something hits one of my legs, and I fall to one knee, but keep swinging.

I send another townie to the floor with a hit to the knees, and the next stumbling backward with a blow to the stomach. The successes barely register through the sound of Jed screaming from across the room. I rise to my feet, half-dragging my injured leg, and swing my way through the crowd of townies toward him.

Finally, I'm able to get a glimpse of Jed – on the floor, crawling on his hands and knees away from a townie woman with a knife. As I watch, one of the men grabs him and hauls him back, dragging him to his feet and pinning his hands behind his back as he struggles. The townies close in like a noose around him, and the woman steps forward, raising the knife. A moment later I'm on top of her, digging a thumb into one of her eye sockets. She's screaming – and then she's not, as I slam her head against the concrete. I grab her knife, slash at the first hand that grabs at me, and lurch to my feet, toward the man still holding Jed. Eyes going wide, the townie jerks the smaller man in front of him like a shield.

I don't hesitate, stepping forward and thrusting my knife right through the narrow space between Jed's arm and torso. He lets out a rather undignified squeal as the blade grazes his side, just before it sinks deep into the gut of the townie. The man releases Jed, who scoots quickly aside, and I rip the knife back out. The townie falls to his knees.

I take a deep breath, and turn to see a crowbar swinging toward the back of Jed's oblivious head. I yank him toward me, and the bar *swoosh*es right through the space where his head was a moment before. I slash the throat of the townie holding it, spraying blood out in a wide arc. Jed promptly slips in the resulting puddle and crashes to the floor, nearly taking me down with him. My own feet slip and slide. When I finally catch my balance, I plant myself there, standing over the ungainly pile of limbs as he tries – and fails – to get up. I lash and hack at every townie that comes near us – slashing at an arm, cutting off a finger, slicing through an ear. One by one, I cut them down.

And finally, they stop coming.

I stay braced, knife held ready, my body tense. I look around, taking in the room and the bodies strewn across the floor. It's a bloody mess. Nothing moves, except for me and Jed, who's still on the floor, his chest heaving.

It's over.

I force myself to relax, consciously loosening each muscle, letting my arms fall to my side and the knife clatter to the floor. It's hard to make myself stop after a fight like that, to let the adrenaline and rage drain out of me. I shut my eyes, breathing deeply, and the roar of blood in my ears gradually fades. When I open my eyes again and look down at myself, I realize that I'm utterly drenched in blood. My hair has come loose from its ponytail and hangs in messy waves around my shoulders. I push it out of my face with a bloody hand, and look down at Jed again.

He's staring up at me like he's never seen me before, his eyes very wide in a blood-splattered face. I reach out a hand to help him up. He hesitates a moment before taking it, and carefully climbs to his feet again. We study each other; me trying to gauge his reaction to what he just witnessed, him presumably deciding that I'm a complete psychopath.

I'm starting to feel sick to my stomach now that I see what I've done. These were townies . . . just townies. I've never killed townies before today. A lump rises in my throat, and I swallow hard.

Jed's spent his whole life around ruthless raiders, and even he looks shocked after that display. I'm all too aware of his gaze traveling from my face to my blood-soaked clothes to the utter mess of my hair. He's silent for a few seconds.

'My hero,' he says softly, and smiles.

The words sent a jolt of shock through me. I stare at him, my mouth opening slightly, some warm and unfamiliar feeling bursting in my chest. I never thought anyone could ever look at me like—

Someone clears their throat.

I automatically step between Jed and the intruder and grab my gun off the floor, holding it tight despite the lack of ammo.

Standing at the bottom of the stairs is a girl, wielding a shotgun that looks far too big for her. She looks from us, to the bloody mess surrounding us, and back to us, her eyebrows slowly rising.

'What the fuck?' the raider says, each word punctuated with an incredulous pause. At least, I think she's a raider. She's dressed like a raider, and carries herself like a raider. She's just a very small raider, fresh faced and knobby-kneed, who would not be intimidating at all if not for the shotgun in her hands, which is currently aimed right at my face.

'Woah, relax,' Jed says. 'We're on the same side, here.'

The girl immediately turns her gun to him, and then back at me when she realizes I still have my gun trained on her, and then back to Jed as she realizes he too has a gun.

'You two are with the raiders?' she asks, forehead creasing.

'Of course we are,' Jed says. 'I mean, do we *look* like townies?' I hear him move closer, almost beside me at this point, but I don't take my eyes off the girl and her gun. She frowns, probably processing the fact we're both drenched in blood and surrounded by dead townies.

'Dunno,' she says after a few seconds. 'I'm not much in the habit of judging people based on looks.'

'Smart,' Jed says. 'But I can assure you, we're not townies. About as far from townies as you can get, really.'

She narrows her eyes, sizing him up. Jed is usually good at talking to people, but right now his charm doesn't seem to have its intended effect. Quite the opposite, in fact. Seems like the more he talks, the more this girl suspects something is wrong.

'Our crew came from the eastern wastes,' I say, before Jed can speak again. I ignore his questioning glance and think back to the plan he laid out earlier. 'We got brought in to Saint, and then ... well ... you know how that whole fiasco went.'

The girl eyes me up and down.

'So where's the rest of your crew?' she asks. Still wary, but not with the open distaste she treated Jed with.

'Dead, probably,' I say. 'We got separated. It's just me and this jackass now.'

'*Hey*,' Jed protests, but the girl's expression softens just a bit. Taking a gamble, I lower my gun. After a moment's hesitation, she does the same.

'Sorry you lost your crew,' she says. 'Maybe you can come along with mine.'

'Thanks,' I say. 'I'm Cl—' I pause, realizing abruptly that I don't have a fake name at the ready. 'Uh . . . Cled,' I say. 'And this is . . . Jem.'

I groan inwardly, but try to look confident. I've never been much of a liar. The little raider's face wrinkles at my words, and she shakes her head.

'They've got some real ugly names in the eastern towns,' she mutters, half under her breath. 'But that's okay. We don't use real names around here anyway.'

'So what should we call you?' Jed asks. I don't miss the slight twist of her mouth when he speaks; for some reason, he really rubs this girl the wrong way. She turns her back to us, heading for the door.

'I'm Kid,' she says over her shoulder. 'Come meet the others.'

XVIII
The Crew

The town is completely overrun by raiders. They swarm unimpeded through the streets, ransacking every building and every box for anything useful. As I walk through town, raiders are everywhere, causing trouble wherever I look. They fight over objects I'm sure none of them really need, smash windows for fun, throw townies' bodies aside like they're garbage. My body is a tightly wound spring; I jump at every shout and every gunshot. The fire still rages, but nobody pays attention to the blaze. They're much more concerned about clearing out the remaining buildings before the fire reaches them.

Every time I make eye contact with a raider, or pass too close to one, I'm sure they're about to call me out. Surely one of them must recognize me by my burns, or at least catch the scent of an outsider. I feel like every movement screams that I don't belong here, like my face is broadcasting all of my fear and disgust and hatred. Especially the hatred, which seems to fill me to the brim and leak out of every pore – a hatred so intense my chest feels like it's filled with fire, each breath singeing my lungs.

'All right,' Jed whispers to me, and I nearly jump out of my skin. 'You remember the plan?'

I glance ahead at the tiny raider, who is too preoccupied with finding her crew to pay much attention to us.

'Yes,' I say quietly. The plan is that I pretend to be one of them. We blend in until it's safe to leave. 'But I don't know if I can do it. I have no idea how to act like one of them.' My chest feels tight. There are raiders everywhere – raiders looting, killing, celebrating their victory. My gun hand is twitching, my pistol seeming to burn a hole in its holster. I have only a handful of ammo left, salvaged from the floor of the bomb shelter and tucked into my now-tattered duffel bag. But if I could take out a raider with each bullet, perhaps it would be worth it.

'You'll be fine,' Jed says, and I force myself to look at him instead of planning a suicidal attack on the raiders. 'The best lies have a little bit of truth in them. So, just ... be yourself. Kind of. But more raider-y.'

I put my hand on my gun.

'But not too much yourself,' he says hastily, glancing around at the raiders we're passing to make sure they're not watching us. 'Actually, scratch that idea. Just act like you think a raider should act. But, uh, don't try *too* hard. If you're exactly what they expect you to be, they'll be suspicious.'

'Jed,' I say through gritted teeth, 'this isn't helpful at all.'

Jed sighs and runs a hand through his tangle of hair, flecked with blood from the fight. He looks tense, but a moment later he shines his usual grin.

'Just stay quiet and look tough,' he says. 'I'll do the rest. Trust me.'

Trust me, he says, as if I have any choice at this point. He's the closest thing I have to an ally in the middle of a mob of raiders.

Raiders. They've been the enemy since I was old enough to know there was evil in the world. Since they threatened my home, they were the people I was allowed to kill – the people I was *encouraged* to kill – and so I did. By now, it's basically a trained response: See raider, kill raider. To see so many of them, so close and yet so untouchable, makes me want to rip out my own hair. I need to fight. Hurt. Kill.

I imagine gunning them down, or slicing their throats, or bashing their faces in with my fists. I imagine a bitter, violent end for each and every raider I see, my mental body count piling higher and higher as I walk. I start calculating how many of them I could take out before their numbers would overwhelm me. And how is it possible that none of them see that written on my face? Surely someone must suspect that every time I look at them, I'm imagining a brutal death.

I clench my fists at my sides, my breath quickening. It's almost physically painful to refrain from drawing a weapon, especially when every step feels like a step further into danger, a step further past enemy lines. Surely someone will see through the ruse ... And yet, they don't. Most of them don't even spare me a second glance.

Jed saunters along behind me, humming cheerfully, completely unconcerned. But of course, he doesn't have anything to be concerned about. He has nothing to fake. He may be a different breed of raider from this lot, but he *is* a raider, and a son of a raider, and has been around raiders his whole life. He probably feels more at home here than he did with me. It's not a reassuring thought.

Almost as if he can sense what's going through my head, Jed steps up beside me, reaches out, and squeezes my arm. Just the briefest touch, but in that moment it seems to imply a lot. *I'm here*, it seems to say. And I find myself relaxing my tightened shoulders, letting my hands go slack at my sides. When Jed falls back, I take a deep breath and hold my head high. Nobody knows. Nobody will find out. I have to keep believing that. I'm more concerned about keeping a lid on my anger, which simmers like an itch beneath my skin.

I steel myself as Kid leads us through town – and then back the way we came, muttering under her breath. She searches for several more minutes, peeking into buildings and apologizing when other raiders glare and shout at her to butt out of their 'looting turf.' It seems ridiculous to me, that they could claim certain areas of a town they all worked to take down, but apparently that's the way of things. Kid doesn't seem to be looking for a fight, anyway, and briskly moves on to check other places. We search building after building after building, but whoever she's looking for isn't anywhere to be found.

I'm starting to wonder if we made a poor choice of a 'friend'; this girl doesn't seem to have a clue what's going on, and I'm getting impatient. After all this buildup, I'm getting real tired of waiting to see if we can pull off our ruse, and convince these people that we're raiders just like them.

'Fucking *shit*!'

The shout cuts through the quiet on the edge of town we've wandered to, an abandoned area dangerously close to the still-smoldering fire. Kid breaks into a grin.

'Oh! There they are,' she says, and heads right toward the noise. I exchange a glance with Jed, who shrugs back at me, and we follow the girl. She leads us right into a building that seems to be partially on fire, and *very* on the verge of collapsing. Kid walks in without any apparent concern. Jed hesitates at the doorway, but follows.

Like hell am I going to be the one too scared to go in.
I swallow my fear, brace my shoulders, and walk into
the building.

Inside, a small cluster of people is waiting. Aside from
Kid and Jed, there are three others: a stoic Asian woman
with bright red hair; a huge, scarred black man; and a
white man with long dreadlocks who is currently swearing up a storm for no apparent reason. Kid is looking
to the latter, so I look at him as well. He's a lean man
with a pair of goggles pushed up on his forehead and a
mouth full of absolutely disgusting teeth. There's a bandage wrapped around his torso, with a bit of red leaking
through on one side, though the injury isn't holding him
back from a lot of animate swearing and hand gesturing. Only when he's finished spitting out curses does he
finally turn to scrutinize Jed and me. He stares at us for
a few moments, then wordlessly gestures toward me and
looks at Kid.

'Found them killing some townies,' she says with a
shrug. 'They lost their crew. Told them they could travel
with us for a while.'

'Oh, is it your fucking job to recruit new members
now?' he asks. The ferocious tone takes me aback, but
Kid just shrugs again, completely unbothered. Getting
no response from her, the man grumbles and eyes me
up and down.

'You look like a woman who knows how to use a gun,'

he says. I nod. His gaze shifts to Jed, who smiles. 'And you look fucking useless,' he says dismissively. While Jed makes a startled noise of protest, the man looks back at me. I hesitate, and then nod again, and he grins. 'Well, whatever. Maybe bigger numbers will keep those bigger crews from trying to fuck with us.' He looks at the large man, who nods his agreement, and the red-haired woman, who stares at me with an unreadable expression. He seems to take that as agreement. 'Alright, fine. You can keep with us for a while. But do anything shady, and I won't hesitate to blow your fucking heads off, got it?'

'Right,' I say, since Jed seems at a loss for words for once. I clear my throat, and pointedly glance around the room. 'Well, now that that's settled . . . you do realize this building is on fire, right?' This floor seems fine for now, but I can hear the building creak and groan above us. Everyone looks up at the ceiling as if they just noticed the danger.

'I'm not a goddamn idiot,' the dreadlocked man says. 'I picked this one specifically.'

'You picked the one that's . . . on fire?'

'Yeah,' he says without hesitation. ''Cause none of the other assholes are gonna be crazy enough to loot this one, yeah? So I figured we'd grab some good shit.'

'Huh,' I say, and leave it at that. I guess he has a point . . . a crazy, barely understandable one that puts all of our lives at serious risk.

'Unfortunately,' he says, 'this place doesn't have shit.'

'At least these townies are partially cooked already,' Kid offers.

'At least there's that,' he says. 'Anyway, on to the next one.'

He walks out, and the rest of the crew follows. Jed and I linger behind in the slowly burning building. I glance at him, raising my eyebrows, wondering what the fuck we've gotten ourselves into. Jed grins back, and we both trudge after the bickering raiders ahead of us.

XIX
Fitting In

We trail after the odd crew until sundown. By that time, the town has quieted down as raiders retreat with their prizes. Over the hours, the fire has mostly died out, though it still smolders quietly here and there, grudging embers that refuse to admit defeat. We pick through the burnt buildings, following our new crew's leader – Wolf – as he grumbles and curses and shouts that 'The good shit has gotta be around here somewhere.'

As it turns out, the 'good shit' was either taken by other raiders, lost in the fire, or never was here in the first place. I'm not sure what they were expecting, really. These western towns are small and poor. I'm sure one town's loot would be plenty for a single crew of raiders to live on, but a horde of them? No way there's going to be enough to go around. Then again, Kid seems to carry an unlikely amount of optimism with her, and maybe it's enough to infect the rest of the crew as well.

Optimistic or not, by the time the sun is setting, we're forced to retire for the night. Not even this madman raider is crazy enough to keep searching through questionably stable buildings without light to guide us. We've collected a small, pathetic pile of loot: tattered blankets, some ammo, a few bottles of murky water. It's a sad haul, especially considering we put in a few hours of work after most of the other crews retreated for the night. Nobody is happy with it, but nobody seems willing to say anything. Instead, the group seethes quietly as we leave town.

The remnants of town are unstable and ripe with death, so we head out into the wastes to make camp. Most of the other crews are already set up. Small fires dot the wastes surrounding the thoroughly looted town. The raiders seem to be celebrating, the camps lively and rowdy, full of shouting and singing. The air is thick with the smell of cooking flesh and the occasional whiff of alcohol. None of them pay much attention to us as we pass through, keeping to whatever temporary truce is holding this mob together.

I keep shooting Jed long, angry looks. I know it isn't really his fault, but I need someone to direct my frustration toward, and I'm not going to take the chance of pissing off any raiders. Of all the goddamn raider crews, we just had to pick this bunch of misfits, the only ones who seem to have gotten nothing of worth.

Aside from the bodies, of course. The big man carries one over each shoulder, looking quite cheerful about the task, and Wolf drags one with much greater difficulty through the dirt behind us. He huffs and puffs with the effort, hampered by his injury, but snaps at anyone who offers help. The two women of the group carry the loot that isn't dead flesh, while Jed and I trail behind, carrying armfuls of blankets, since that's all they would trust us with.

Throughout the day, I worked on picking up the names they use for one another. They were difficult to distinguish from the insults Wolf throws around, but I got them eventually. The girl, as we already learned, is Kid. The odd, quiet woman is Dolly, the big guy is Tank, and, of course, their foul-mouthed leader is Wolf. It's all very western-wastes in nature, not having real names, but I try to accustom myself to it. After all, we could be stuck with these people for a while. Thinking about exactly *how* long puts a knot in my stomach. How long will it be until I have to raid with them? How long until I get hungry enough to become a shark? How much will I have to sacrifice in order to survive?

In the midst of the revelry all around us, Wolf and the others quietly make camp and start their own fire. I sit beside it – but not too close, the sight of the flames devouring Fort Cain still vivid in my mind, mixing with my memories of Old Creek burning to the ground – and sift through my duffel bag. On the edge of camp I hear Wolf and Tank hacking up the bodies we brought out with us. I try very hard not to look, but the sound of knives hitting flesh is evocative enough without the visual. It reminds me of death, and violence, and I feel like I'm going to be sick. I force myself to breathe deeply and calmly, keep my face cold and stone-like, and force my attention onto cleaning my guns.

I've always known there was cannibalism in the wastes. It's the final taboo, the hard line drawn between sharks and other wastelanders. The thought has always sickened me, always brought up my burning hatred for the raiders and made me feel justified in it. Everyone in the wastes does horrible things to live. We all kill, we all make sacrifices. But this? This is too much. This is the one thing that truly separates them from the rest of mankind. They're not people anymore; they're just sharks.

And now, for the first time, I have to sit here and face it.

I may have imagined these things, but it's a different matter entirely to watch them reduce a human being to meat. At least it doesn't look so obviously human by the time they've put it over the fire to cook, but the sizzle of skin still makes my stomach roll. It smells deceptively like real food, like any other meat, but nonetheless revulsion rises in my throat. It's even worse how *casual* they are about it. There's no grim recognition of how horrible this is, no solemnity about the process. They're even cheerful, talking unabashedly about how hungry they are and how good it smells, no shame in their eagerness to consume what was a living person just earlier today.

At least I feel a little safer with a gun in my hands. It quiets my wailing nerves and the vengeful murmuring of my mind. Being here, in the middle of a raider camp, surrounded by enemies and doing nothing about it, is a betrayal of everything I've ever said and done. I'm a coward. I'm a traitor. My head feels hot, my hands tremble, my vision blurs. I need to hit something. To *kill* something.

As I busy myself cleaning guns and counting ammo, I gradually settle my nerves to a tolerable level. *I'm just doing what I need to do*, I tell myself. Just tolerating this to stay alive. Now is not the time to be a hero.

After prowling around and chatting with the others for a while, Jed sits beside me. He's quiet for once. I wonder if he's concerned for me. I glance at him, but he's staring into the fire, his face impossible to read. I should know better than to attempt guessing at his thoughts. I may have grown closer to him, even to the point where I trust him to some extent, but that doesn't mean I understand what happens inside that weird head of his. He remains an enigma to me. I hope I'm the same to him.

I manage to avoid attention from the rest of the crew for a while. They're busy with their own tasks, and tired from the raid. But once the meat is done cooking and they start doling it out, I can't remain overlooked anymore.

When Tank offers me a slice of meat, my stomach clenches. If they think I'm a raider, they'll expect me to eat it. It's normal for them. If I turn it down, I'll stick out like a sore thumb. But can I go so far? I raise a hand, reaching for the meat – and then draw it back. Tank's forehead creases, still extending the meat like he expects me to grab it at any moment.

'Not eating?' he asks. 'Plenty to go around. It's not charity or anything; you're with us now.'

'I'm not—' I start, and hesitate. No way are they going to believe I'm not hungry. As Jed said, the best lies have a bit of truth hidden in them. But what can I say that won't completely give me away? 'I don't eat meat.'

'Eh?' If possible, Tank looks more confused than before. 'You serious? A raider who doesn't eat meat?' He looks at Wolf. The leader of the crew scrutinizes me.

'You don't seem like the squeamish type,' he says. 'What kind of half-ass raider doesn't eat meat?'

'They're not from around here,' Kid volunteers. 'Maybe it's different where they come from.'

I almost nod, but notice everyone's eyes shift. I follow their looks to see Jed eagerly digging into a piece of

meat, so gleefully invested that he's totally oblivious
to the conversation. It takes him a couple seconds to
notice the stares. He pauses, hunk of meat halfway to his
slightly open mouth. He tentatively takes another bite,
chews it, and swallows. 'What?' he asks, finally, his eyes
locking with mine.

I swallow hard, disturbed by the image of him eating
human flesh just like the others. Before we met up with
these raiders, it was easy to forget who he was. Now I'm
suddenly finding myself wondering if he's really still on
my side, or if it was just convenient. He could throw me
to the raiders right now, and carry on his way.

'Looks like you're wrong,' Wolf says to Kid. 'Surprising no one.'

And then everyone's looking back at me, awaiting
explanation. I clear my throat, trying desperately to
think of something reasonable to say and finding nothing. The tension rises with every silent second. I'm
itching to grab my gun just for the comfort of having
it in my hand, but I have a feeling that would incite an
all-out brawl right now, and I'd rather avoid that if I can
help it. I keep my eyes on Wolf, assuming the others will
take their cues from him.

If he reaches for a weapon, it's over.

'She's a vegetarian,' Jed says, abruptly breaking the
silence. Everyone, including me, turns to stare at him.

'*What?*' Wolf says incredulously, while I try to wipe

the dumbfounded look off my face before anyone sees it.

'Weak stomach. She's actually allergic to meat,' Jed says. Though I'm grateful that he's trying to argue for me, I bite back a groan. *That's* the best explanation he can come up with? But he keeps a straight face, nodding solemnly.

'Is that a real thing?' Kid asks, looking over at Wolf, who seems about as baffled as she is. She frowns. 'It doesn't sound like a real thing.'

'Oh, it's real, all right,' Jed says in a very grave voice. 'I've seen it in action. Real ugly. She'll break out in hives if she even touches the stuff.'

As the crew turns back to me, I fold my arms over my chest and force myself to nod. The moment they turn away, I give Jed the most intense glare I can muster up. His lips twist to hide a smile.

'Oh, not to mention she gets the shits,' he adds. 'You don't even wanna hear about *those*.'

There's a pause. Then Wolf and Tank burst into laughter, while Kid turns red and Dolly looks on, unruffled.

'Shut the fuck up,' I say.

'Sorry. Didn't mean to embarrass you,' Jed says, chuckling.

'Idiot,' I mutter, dropping my eyes to my boots. But, despite my words, I know better than to think Jed is anything close to an idiot at this point. Embarrassing as that exchange was, he did successfully de-escalate the situation. The crew doesn't question it again, and Kid is happy to hand over a can of beans.

I pry it open with my knife and inhale the food in seconds. I notice the big guy – Tank – staring at me, and glare at him out of habit, but he looks more impressed than anything. Still, I maintain the scowl. I'm not going to let my guard down around these people, and definitely don't plan on being friendly.

Once I've finished my meal, I toss the can aside and make myself comfortable by the fire. I try not to think about the fact that I'm surrounded by raiders, or the sound of Jed gnawing the last of the meat off a bone. The rest of the crew chats idly among themselves, and Jed is more than eager to join in, but I stay quiet and tune it out. I catch occasional bits of conversation, mostly about where they're going and what their plan is, which all seems up in the air right now.

Honestly, I'm not sure how this crew made it this far. I haven't seen them in action yet, but they already seem barely competent. They have hardly any loot from this raid, and hardly any idea where they're headed. Perhaps my standards for raiders are too high. Crews like Jedediah Johnson's don't exist out here; if they did, the western wastes wouldn't be the way they are. Still, I expected better than *this*.

'You guys aren't worried about Jedediah Johnson?'

Jed asks out of nowhere, jerking me away from my thoughts and into the conversation. I shoot him a warning look. Surely it's better to stay away from subjects like that, which could lead to hints that we're not who we say we are, but apparently Jed has other ideas.

'Who the fuck is Jedediah Johnson?' Wolf asks without looking up from his meal. Jed lets out an exaggerated gasp of surprise, pressing a hand to his chest.

'You don't know?' he asks, appalled. I sneak a glance at the crew, but luckily they don't seem suspicious about how personally he takes the lack of knowledge. Instead, they're just giving him blank stares. 'The *legend* of Jedediah Johnson? The one, the only?' He pauses, as if expecting that to ring any bells, and sighs loudly. 'They say he was the son of an assassin and a whore – his father being the whore, that is, and also the source of his overwhelming charm and good looks—'

'Skip to the important part,' Wolf says, while I resist the urge to roll my eyes at Jed's ridiculous dramatization of his own father.

'Well, it's all important, but yeah, okay. He's a famous raider, king of the eastern wastes—'

'Oh,' Wolf says. 'Well, that explains that. I don't give a single fuck about the eastern wastes.'

Jed, shocked into silence, only stares at him.

'Well, you should,' I say. 'The eastern wastes are what happen when you let a psychopath take charge.' Jed certainly isn't doing the story justice, so I guess I have to step up. 'He's a tyrant. You westerners are lucky you killed Saint before he got a chance to do that here.'

'I don't know if that's fair,' Jed says. I look at him, eyebrows rising. I know Jedediah Johnson is his father and all, but I can't believe that he'd suggest his rule is anything but tyrannical. 'You really think life is better here than there?' he asks. I open my mouth to answer, but before I can, he continues, 'Not for people like you – people like *us*.' He gestures not just at himself, but also at Wolf's crew. 'People like you and I are fine out here, obviously. But for other people? Normal people?'

His usual playfulness is all gone, his tone serious and his stare intent. I open my mouth again, ready to argue, but falter. I don't think I realized it until this very moment, but he could be right. People like me, and Jed, and these raiders thrive in the chaos of the wastes, but other people – townies like Wyatt, or that girl who tried to help bandage my wounds in Fort Cain – don't stand a chance on their own. All the townies we've met out here are dead. Under Jedediah Johnson's rule, they'd probably still be alive right now.

'Everyone hates Jedediah Johnson,' I say, well aware that it's not an answer to his question.

'Sure, but they're safe,' he says. 'They're alive. Probably leading longer, fuller lives than the townies out here.'

I open my mouth and shut it again, unable to come up with an answer. I'm left feeling shaken. Jed glances around at the raiders, as if suddenly reminded that we have an audience.

'I mean, it's shitty for people like us out in the east,' he says. 'Just saying, I can respect the guy for what he's doing. Begrudgingly.'

There's a long pause, and I look around, worried that he might have ignited suspicion in the raiders. Tank and Dolly have clearly stopped following the conversation, though Kid is giving Jed an oddly piercing look, and Wolf looks thoughtful.

'Fucking eastern wastes,' the crew leader says, shaking his head. 'Who knew anything interesting was happening out there?'

'Uh,' Jed says. 'Mostly everybody.'

'Next you're gonna tell me shit's going down in the southern wastes or somethin'.'

'Wait,' Jed says. 'You don't know about the southern wastes? Are you serious? They're—'

'No, no, no,' Wolf says, waving a hand at him. 'I don't wanna know. Got enough shit to worry about already.'

Jed sighs, but says nothing.

'You know, I think I have actually heard the name,' Tank says, scratching his chin. 'Some of the other crews were talking about some guy coming from the east. Some famous raider king, yeah, I remember now. They say he's getting real close to us. We could cross paths with his crew any day now, and no one is sure what will happen.'

'Well, he sounds like an asshole to me, calling himself a king,' Wolf says. 'If we run into the guy, I say we kill him.'

I bite back a curse. I knew Jedediah's crew was drawing near to this area, but I didn't know he was quite that close, and didn't think the raiders might intentionally start shit with him. If that happens, our plan of hiding among the army will fall apart. And if it comes down to that, I wonder, will Jed side with me, or his father? I glance at him, trying to gauge his reaction to Wolf's words, but he shows none except for a small twist of his mouth.

'Anyway,' Tank says, 'if I can make a suggestion to lighten the mood . . .' He reaches into his bag, pulls out a plastic bottle, and holds it up triumphantly. 'Got a surprise in town.'

'Oh, damn,' Wolf says. 'Is that what I think it is?'

'Pretty sure it's vodka,' Tank says, squinting at the unlabeled bottle. 'Or moonshine. I dunno. Something that smells like rubbing alcohol. I bashed a guy's head in to grab it.'

Wolf whistles under his breath and holds out his hands. Tank tosses the bottle to him.

'Ugh,' Kid says, her nose wrinkling. 'I'm not touching that stuff again.'

'Suit yourself, kiddo,' Wolf says, unscrewing the top. 'More for me.'

What he should've said is 'more for Jed,' as it turns out. Soon enough, my companion is unsteady in his seat and talking much too loudly, with plenty of over-the-top hand gestures that throw him further off-balance. He spouts off story after story, spinning some ridiculous yarn about how we ended up here. The crew doesn't seem to suspect it's a lie, or if they do, they don't care. Tank and Wolf laugh uproariously at each of his stories, and he even earns himself one small smile from Dolly, though Kid still seems wary of him.

As for me, I keep a careful eye on Jed. I didn't expect him to actually get drunk. I haven't taken a sip myself. I'm not usually one to turn down a drink or two if the opportunity arises, but it seems too risky in this situation, surrounded by people who would kill both of us if they knew the truth. But Jed seems to have no reservations, taking eager swigs every time he gets ahold of the bottle, getting progressively drunker and messier. I don't like the way he's letting his guard down, or the way he's talking so much as a result. It seems like it's only a matter of time before some little lie causes suspicion – or even worse, he lets out something true.

I try to act like I'm just relaxing by the fire, but I listen very carefully to every word out of his mouth. More than anything I want to knock the bottle out of his hands, or drag him away to shut him up, but I know that will only arouse suspicion. We have to keep acting like we have nothing to hide. And Jed's constant chatter does do that job . . . as long as he can keep pulling it off.

'Really, though,' he says, holding his hands up to get everyone's attention, which he clearly already has. 'Let's talk about Jedediah Johnson. The man, the king, the *legend*—'

'All right, well, I think my partner here has had more than enough,' I say, cutting him off. He's spewed out a lot of bullshit tonight, but we definitely don't need another conversation along those lines. I grab Jed's arm and haul him upright. He sways on his feet, murmuring slurred protests. 'It's time for bed,' I tell him firmly. He pouts at me, but he shuts up, and doesn't resist as I pull him away from the fire. I grab the blankets we looted from Fort Cain and throw them over my shoulder as we head for the edge of camp.

'Not gonna sleep by the fire?' Tank shouts after us.

'Nope,' I yell back. My skin is still crawling from the blaze earlier, and I have no desire to sleep anywhere near flames. Plus, it's risky being around the crew with Jed like this. As we leave the warm glow of the fire he pulls back, digging his heels into the sand.

'But it's cold out there!'

'Should've thought of that before you downed half a

bottle of moonshine and started running your mouth,' I say. 'I knew your scrawny ass couldn't handle the liquor.'

'I'm handling it fine,' he protests, right before tripping on a rock. I turn and grab him with both arms to yank him back upright, and we end up face-to-face. It's dark now that we're not by the fire, too dark to see him clearly. He sways toward me, and I place a hand on his chest. The plan was to push him away, but instead I end up resting it there.

We stand still in the darkness for a few moments, breathing quietly, and eventually something dawns on me. I frown and pull Jed closer by the shirt; he initially leans in, and then back when I give a loud sniff.

'Uh, Clementine? What the hell?' he asks, startled. I scowl at him, and release the handful of shirt I was clutching. He stumbles back and falls to the ground.

'Woah there,' he says. 'Be kind to the poor drunk man.'

I fold my arms over my chest and glare down at him.

'You're not drunk,' I say.

'What?'

'Not a whiff of alcohol on you.' With the amount he supposedly drank, he should've reeked of the stuff. Yet just a few inches away from him, I couldn't smell even a hint of it on his breath.

Jed throws back his head and laughs.

'All right, you caught me,' he says, holding up his hands to admit surrender. 'I had you fooled for a while though, didn't I?'

'Hmph.' I silently watch him climb to his feet. Once upright, he spreads his arms and bows, gesturing with one hand as if to encourage applause. But the only audience he has is me, standing with my arms folded and a scowl on my face. After a moment he peeks up at me, grins, and straightens back to his full height.

'I can't tell if that's your genuinely-pissed-off scowl or your I'm-secretly-pleased scowl,' he says thoughtfully, squinting at me. 'It's a little too dark.'

'I only have one. It's my shut-the-fuck-up-Jed scowl.'

He laughs, and I roll my eyes and turn away from him, spreading a blanket on the ground. I toss three of them to Jed and arrange my own two into a makeshift bed. I have a sinking suspicion even two blankets won't do much to ward off the cold. I'm still not used to sleeping out in the open ... but even knowing that Jed isn't drunk, I refuse to sleep near the fire, surrounded by raiders. Just the distant crackle of their fire and murmur of conversation is enough to make me feel uncomfortably vulnerable.

I settle into my blankets, and turn to see Jed setting up his own several feet away on the ground.

'What are you doing over there?' I ask, my brow furrowing. He pauses, looking up at me with a blanket clutched in his hands.

'Huh?' he asks. I sigh, and point at the ground beside my own nest of bedding.

'Get over here,' I say. He stares at me for a moment longer, and slowly his face splits in a grin.

'Oh,' he says, dragging the sound out with a ridiculous waggle of his hips. 'What's this, hmm? I thought you'd never a—'

'Don't be an idiot,' I say, cutting him off. 'I'd just rather not freeze my ass off. We need the body heat.' Before this trip to the west, it had been a long time since I slept outdoors. The blistering heat of the wastes can make it easy to forget how bitterly cold it gets when it's dark, but the nights where I was trailing the poachers were a good reminder. I'm not planning on spending another night racked by shivers.

'Oh, right,' Jed says, his obnoxious grin fading. But it doesn't faze him for long; soon enough, he's right at my side.

He pulls his blankets on top of us both and burrows himself snugly against me. I grumble at the touch of cold skin and the uncomfortable closeness, attempting to find a comfortable position. It doesn't prove easy, especially since Jed seems to be made of pointy elbows and knees. The worst, though, is his face, looming up way too close. His breath is warm on my cheek.

'Turn around,' I say gruffly.

Jed laughs.

'No need to be shy.'

'I'm *not* being shy,' I say. 'I just don't want you breathing on my face.'

I firmly grab him by the shoulders and turn him over. He doesn't fight it. I pull him against me, curving my body around his, one arm ending up wrapped around his torso because it doesn't make sense to put it anywhere else. We finally settle into a position that doesn't involve being awkwardly tangled in each other, or elbowing each other in the stomach. Finally, I admit to myself that this *is* actually pretty comfortable, and definitely warmer. I relax, listening to the sound of our quiet breathing, glad that the crackling of the fire is far away.

'Knew you'd wanna be the big spoon,' Jed mutters, and I jab him in the side.

'Shut up, I'm sleeping,' I mumble against his ear.

'Good night, Clementine.'

'Good night, Jed.'

XX
Crewmates

In the morning, Jed and I sleepily untangle ourselves from the blankets and each other at first light. We pack up camp quickly and quietly with the raiders, and set off.

We move with the horde.

Wolf's crew keeps their distance from the others, but they keep pace with them and move in the same direction. I wonder if there's a plan, a reason they're headed this way, or if they all just follow the first crew to move.

Alone, the wastes always seem endless, empty of anything but a huge and vaguely threatening silence. Alone, it's easy to remember that this isn't what the world is supposed to be like; this is what happens after the world ends. We're merely survivors who weren't meant to be, clinging to life when we rightly shouldn't. Maybe this world is so harsh because it's trying to get rid of us, the last of the infestation. Those are the kinds of thoughts that creep up on you when you're by yourself. They're the kind of thoughts that can kill.

With company it's different. The wastes seem much less empty, much less dead, much less threatening. But perhaps that's because I'm surrounded by much louder and more immediate threats.

Jed certainly seems at ease among the raiders, talking and humming as he walks, once even breaking into song, though that's quickly silenced by a chorus of groans and boos and a smack to the head from Wolf. After that he quiets down for a few minutes, but he's back to his cheerful self soon enough. It all seems so easy for him. Maybe that's just the way he is. He adapts, and charms, and weasels his way into peoples' hearts with his smiles and disarming small talk.

Talk that never seems to end, especially with an audience. After last night, I'm not worried about him slipping up and revealing that we're lying to them. Despite his antics, he's not an idiot, and I trust him now to handle himself. I'm content to tune out his chatter and retreat to my own thoughts.

But my thoughts aren't exactly a welcome retreat right now. Surrounded by raiders, hatred still seethes and boils at the back of my mind – and I know that's the real enemy to our façade, not Jed's chatter. I just have to hope that I can keep myself from snapping until we reach safety.

Now that I think about it, maybe it won't be quite so long after all. The close proximity of Jedediah Johnson's crew could be a blessing in disguise. If we pass each other soon *without* violence erupting, Jed and I will be free to go wherever we please, with his father still searching for us closer to Saint's tower. We could steal some supplies, sneak away at night – maybe even head back east, if Jedediah's crew is busy over here.

Stewing on that, I glance around at the other raider crews around us. Though Wolf doesn't seem concerned, I'm not so stupid as to believe there's any real honor code among raiders. Cat and Bird proved there's sure as hell not one among bounty hunters, and raiders are even less scrupulous. Though they seem peaceful for now, I know any of them could turn on us the moment we show weakness. There's a particularly nasty-looking group of men about a dozen yards to our left. They don't seem to be paying attention to us, but I catch occasional snippets of their conversation, usually revolving around their dwindling food supplies. I keep an eye on them, just in case.

I'm so focused on the nearby crew that it takes me several seconds to realize someone is walking beside me. When I do I jolt to attention, my hand moves to my gun. Her hand does the same, and we end up staring at each other, both on the verge of drawing. It's Dolly, with the red hair and the strange staring. After a tense moment, I slowly remove my hand from my weapon. She does the same, and keeps on staring at me.

'Nice gun,' she says, her eyes wandering there. I scowl automatically, unsure if the statement is some kind of threat, but she says nothing else.

'Yeah,' I say. I eye her. The pistol on her belt is nothing special, but the sniper rifle she carries on her back – which I've seen her holding like a child – is possibly the nicest gun I've seen aside from my own. I'm almost jealous of the thing. I nod my head toward it and let my scowl soften. 'Yours too.'

She nods.

'You're a good shot?' she asks. At least, I think it's a question; it's hard to tell, sometimes, with the monotony of her voice.

'Yeah,' I say.

'Me too,' she says.

I hesitate. That statement could be a brag, a threat, or a simple attempt to build rapport. Her face gives no hints. I decide to say nothing in response. We walk next to each other for a couple minutes, both silent after the quick exchange, before she pulls forward to walk alongside their leader. I watch them, trying to see if she's saying something to him, but she's as silent as usual.

Jed pulls back from the rest of the crew to walk along-side me.

'She's a weird one, for sure,' he says quietly, jerking his head at Dolly. She glances back at us, as if she could hear the comment, and Jed gives her a bright smile that she doesn't return.

'I dunno,' I say, watching her and half-smiling myself. 'I think I like her.'

After a long day of travel, we make camp again. It's a much quieter affair than last night, with none of the yelling and post-raid revelry from the mob. There wasn't much to loot from the half-burnt Fort Cain, so the dwindling water supply leaves little to celebrate. At least there's plenty of food to go around – for anyone but a 'vegetarian' like me, that is. There's only one can of normal food left. They reluctantly hand it over to me, and I make myself eat slowly for once. I'm not sure when I'll eat again. And I wonder, if it comes to starvation, how long will I be able to keep turning down the meat? Honestly, I don't want to find out.

After eating, I'm content to sit cross-legged beside the fire, my shoulders sagging, letting weariness overtake me. I'm thirsty, dusty, and worn-out, but it feels good to rest my bones for a while, as the heat of the day grad-ually wanes.

I'm not aware that I've dozed off until a loud sound

wakes me again. I sit up, reaching for my gun, my heart racing – but it's only a disgruntled-looking Wolf dropping a bag on the ground near me. I shake off my grogginess, mentally kicking myself for letting my guard down.

'Well,' Wolf says. 'The bad news is that nobody wants to trade for meat, 'cause everyone's already got plenty.'

'What a surprise,' I mutter under my breath.

'The good news,' he continues, 'is that everyone's sayin' we're gonna hit the next town tomorrow.'

My stomach flips.

'So that means—' Kid starts.

'That means it's raiding time!' Wolf says, cutting her off. His formerly somber attitude disappears in favor of a fierce grin. 'And we're gonna do better this time. Gonna get some good loot, not be the poor stragglers pickin' up scraps. You got that?' He points at Kid, who nods, and Tank, who gives him a thumbs-up. He seems content to see Dolly cleaning one of her guns, and then looks at Jed and me. 'Are you two in?'

'Of course we are,' Jed says – thankfully, since my own tongue seems to be tied up in my thoughts. I swallow, and muster up a nod and a stoic expression when Wolf glances my way.

'Fuck yeah,' he says. 'Two more bodies will be nice to have.'

'Bodies?' Jed repeats.

'He doesn't mean it like that,' Kid says, though Wolf ignores him. 'Two more guns. That's what he means. Right, Wolf?'

'Meant what I said,' he says, grabbing a hunk of meat for himself.

'Well, that's slightly concerning,' Jed says. He does a double take upon seeing my face, and scrutinizes me. 'What's wrong?'

My insides are a mess of feelings right now – fear, anger, nausea. These people are talking so nonchalantly about raiding a town tomorrow. Do they understand that they're destroying peoples' homes? Their lives? And they talk about it with such *excitement*. Not that I don't feel the same urges – every wastelander knows those urges, that drive to steal, fight, kill, do *anything* to stay alive another day – but at least I try to control them.

Our little hero, I think, and suppress the harsh, manic laughter that bubbles up inside me at the thought. What would my townspeople say if they could see me here with these raiders?

'Clementine?' Jed asks, reaching for my arm. I flinch away from the touch.

'Nothing,' I say. When Jed opens his mouth, getting ready to argue, I grit my teeth. 'Later.'

He nods and drops it.

I spend the rest of the evening stewing in my thoughts. After a couple attempts to draw me into the conversation, the crew gets the message that I'm not in the mood to talk. Jed keeps glancing at me, but he leaves me alone as well.

Eventually, the conversation dies down and the others prepare for bed. Like last night, Jed and I grab our blankets and leave camp to find our own spot out in the wastes.

'You nervous about the raid tomorrow?' Jed asks, once we're a fair distance away. I glance back at the others, just to make sure they're not within hearing range.

'No,' I say.

'Well, you don't need to be,' Jed says, in a soothing voice, as if my answer was the opposite. I glare at him, but he blathers on. 'I'll be with you the whole time, and anyway, should be a piece of cake for you. They're just a bunch of dumb townies.'

I stay quiet for a few moments. I want badly to agree with or just ignore him, yet instead I find a confession rising up inside of me. I try to fight it back, but it claws its way out of my throat.

'I don't know if I can do it,' I say, each word forced through gritted teeth.

Jed stops walking. I continue for a few paces, but he grabs my arm. I turn to him, raising my eyes to his face.

'What do you mean?' he asks, frowning. 'Of course you can handle a few townies.'

'I don't mean it like that,' I say. 'I guess I mean ... I

don't know if I *should* do it.' He tilts his head questioningly. I let out a long breath. 'I don't know if I can live with myself after doing it.'

'Live with . . . ?' Jed repeats, not getting it. 'Clementine, you kill people all the time.'

I take a deep breath and push a strand of hair behind my ear, trying to form coherent thoughts and words.

'But it's different,' I say. 'I have these . . . rules. I only kill for profit, or out of necessity. That's it.' I guess a raid is for profit, but that's just a technicality and I know it. And of course, I can't bring myself to add that 'protecting Jed' seems to fall in the 'necessity' category now, as proven by Fort Cain.

'Or else what?' Jed asks, and I shake my head, unable to find the words. 'I feel like there's something you're not telling me. There's a story there, yeah?'

My stomach twists and turns.

'I killed for the first time when I was eight years old. A raider.' His eyebrows rise slightly. 'And I kept killing them, whenever they came to town. I was good at it. *Really* good at it.'

'Okay,' he says, when I pause. 'So you were defending yourself and your people. Nothing wrong with that.'

'Sure,' I say, thinking of beating that half-dead man's head in with a metal pot. 'The town loved me for it. They used to call me a hero. But it got out of hand.' Jed is quiet, waiting for me to continue. 'One day a man came to stay for a night. I was in town, freshly back from the latest hunt.' I take a deep breath. 'He was an older guy. Pretty charming, actually. Polite. Funny. Everyone liked him, except for me.'

'He was a raider,' Jed says. There's an odd look on his face, some emotion I can't discern, even though I haven't finished the story yet.

'Yeah. He had these tattoos, and this look about him, and he carried a huge gun with him even though he never threatened to use it. I knew what he was, and I hated that the townsfolk seemed to accept him despite it. This was in the early days of J—' I pause, remembering who I'm speaking to. 'Of your father's rule, I mean, so things were tense and confusing and everyone was still figuring out what it all meant. But I was angry. I wanted to fight. I wanted to protect my people. I thought I understood things, and that it was worth breaking the rules.'

'How did you kill him?' Jedediah asks. He stares down at the ground, not looking at me, and the emotion is gone from his face.

'I slit his throat in his sleep,' I say, remembering it as I say the words. He woke up halfway through, and fought me, but it was too late and he was losing too much blood already. I can still picture the light dying from his eyes. 'I burned the body, but I was an idiot. I kept the gun. So when Jedediah Johnson's crew came looking for the man they lost, they found it stashed under my pillow, and they knew.

'They didn't think it was me. I was just an eighteen-year-old townie girl to them – I had already been hunting bounties for two years, but they didn't know that. They thought it was my father, and while they questioned him, I ran. I thought they would figure it out, that they would come for me and leave the town alone, but ... they were dumber than I expected, I guess.' That was one time of many that I found myself wrong in my assessment of people. But that time, it was brutally punished. 'Later that night I saw the smoke. I went back, and tried to get in to save my family, but ... ' I trail off, absently raising a hand to touch the burns on my face. The blaze at Fort Cain has the memory vivid in my mind: the intense heat, the hungry flames, the screams. I take a deep breath. 'That's why I need to follow the rules. I need to ... make sure I stay aimed in the right direction. Make sure I stay on the right side. Like my people would've wanted me to.'

Several long seconds pass, and Jed says nothing. I glance at his face, uncertain. Maybe sharing this much was a mistake. But he's not even looking at me, still staring at the ground with his eyes distant, like he's lost in thought.

'Jed?' I ask. His head jerks up. He blinks at me, like he'd forgotten I was there, and his face stays guarded.

'Let's get some sleep,' he says. That's it. I take a deep breath, and hope the hurt doesn't show on my face.

'Okay,' I say, my voice coming out flat. I set up my blankets, and he sets up his a few feet away. I fight the cold, and my thoughts, for hours before I finally fall asleep.

XXI
The Raid

I wake early. The sun isn't up yet, the wastes still dark and blessedly quiet. I stand and stretch, shrugging off the sluggishness of sleep. It's quickly replaced by nerves, my entire body buzzing with a static energy that hisses up my spine and down each of my limbs.

Today's the day.

There's too much to think about right now – the raid, my rules, my conversation with Jed and its uncomfortable ending. I can't let myself worry about any of it right now. If I'm distracted today, I'll get myself killed. For now, I just need to push it all to the back of my mind.

I mechanically sort through my weapons, mostly as an excuse not to think. Pistol at my hip, knife strapped to my leg, one spare revolver with a few bullets left. Not much ammo left for my pistol either. When I came here,

I had so many beautiful weapons, and no end of ammo in sight. But the last several days have had a hell of a lot of shooting in them, more than I'm used to – and that's saying a lot, since I make my living shooting. But back in the east, it's all about the careful balance of power, and purposeful killings, and goods changing hands. Here, it's just charging into the fray, guns blazing, and hoping for the best. For someone like me, the chaos has proved to be livable – but not so much for all the dead townies in our wake.

By the time I've finished my routine, I'm not the only one awake. Dolly is up and watching me, carefully handling her own weapons, going through a process similar to my own. She and I exchange a nod across the open space between us. Near her, Kid and Wolf are starting to stir as well, and Tank is soon woken by a kick from the latter. Jed is still snoring. I let him; I want to enjoy the silence while I can.

Only when the sun is rising and the crew is packing up do I finally wake Jed, prodding him in the side with my boot until he opens one eye. I grab his hand and pull him to his feet, and together we fold up the blankets and stuff them into my bag alongside my paltry supply of remaining ammo. He says nothing about last night – nothing at all, actually, which is odd for him. I mirror his silence. When we're done packing, we set off.

I expected a serious atmosphere on the dawn of a

raid, or a ferociously excited one, but instead the crew meanders along and chats among themselves as if this is any other day. I guess it might be, for them. While this is huge for me – my first raid, the day I could easily lose my life or a far more integral part of myself – it's not the same for them. This is what they do, how they make their living. And even though that 'living' revolves around killing and stealing from helpless townies, I guess it's just another job to them. Maybe it's as easy for them as bounty hunting is for me.

But the atmosphere changes once the town looms on the horizon. First a hush falls over the raiders – not just Wolf's crew but all of them, chatter and complaints alike dying down to a complete silence. Then someone shouts, and the horde roars back in response. The mob draws together, individual crews dissolving into the singular, terrifying mass that I've seen before.

It feels unnatural looking at a raid from the other side. The mob swells around me, psyching themselves up for the attack. The typical shouts and war cries of raiders, usually a herald of danger, come from all around me now. My whole body is so tightly coiled that it feels like part of me will snap off. I try to keep my face cold and hard, like I'm used to doing this, but my heart is pounding. I can't stop thinking about the concerns I voiced to Jed, and how he hasn't spoken to me since I spilled them.

This thing inside me, gnawing and tearing, it's always hungry for more. If I feed it, it will only grow stronger. Already I can feel it clamoring inside me, making me feel equal parts excited and afraid. Soon the two become indistinguishable, one dizzying rush of adrenaline so intense that my hands shake. Bloodlust is thick and infectious in the air around me.

When a raider from another crew bumps into me, I snap at him, my gun instantly in my hand. It's a decision that could mean disaster, but luckily, he just slinks back with his head down. Jed glances sideways at me, but I refuse to look at him. I'm having a hard enough time keeping myself in check right now without thinking about him. I force myself to place my gun back in its holster, restless hands clenching and unclenching.

As we draw closer, I imagine watching the horde appear from the town. I know from experience what it feels like to see the raider mob for the first time – the awe, the fear, the helplessness. I feel none of that, staring down the town. Instead, I feel predatory. The closer we get, the more my nervousness dissipates, replaced by steely resolve.

This place is no Fort Cain. There's no metal gate, no huge wall, just a cluster of barely stable buildings patched together with scraps, a true western-wastes town. And the townies are nowhere to be seen. Unlike Cain, and the Nameless Town before it, there's no front line of armed townies waiting to meet us, no attempt at defense. The place just looks empty. The raider mob slows as it approaches. I slow with everyone else, frowning, my eyes scanning the town and finding no signs of life.

'Fuckers ran with their tails between their legs,' Wolf complains from ahead.

'Probably took all the supplies first too,' Tank says glumly.

The other raiders walk right in, eager to scour the buildings for anything left behind. I pause on the edge of town. Wolf's assessment does seem like the most likely case. It's not farfetched that this town, hearing how the others before it fell, would flee instead of standing their ground. And yet something gives me pause. I've learned to trust my instincts, and right now they're telling me that something isn't right.

But the crew is moving forward without me, Jed included. So I grit my teeth, try to subdue the rising urge to run, and advance into the town.

It's eerily quiet, made more so by the fact my senses are all on high alert, straining to find signs of danger in the seemingly dead town. My eyes dart around and my gun is ready. I'm careful to search every dark corner, not put my back to open space. After a few minutes, the effort starts to feel ridiculous. There's no one here. Every noise and movement I jump at turns out to be one of the raiders. They've diffused throughout the town, spreading out to cover as much ground as possible. And yet, my uneasiness only grows. These buildings aren't just empty of people, they're *completely* empty. I would have expected the townies to take all the food, and water, and weapons ... but the furniture? The silverware? Every blanket, every article of clothing? It's all gone. I guess it could be some kind of overzealous, burn-it-all method to ensure there was absolutely nothing the raiders could use to their advantage, but still. It's odd. I don't like odd, and I don't trust it.

After scanning a building to find it just as cleaned out as all the rest, I hurry forward to catch up to Jed. He turns and looks over his shoulder at me.

'What do you think?' he calls out to me. It's alarmingly loud in the quiet town, echoing off the buildings around us. I crouch down automatically, expecting some kind of response, but nothing happens. I slowly straighten up.

'Something's—'

Not right would be the next words out of my mouth, but I cut off at the sound of an explosion nearby. Jed and I both turn toward the sound. There's nothing to see other than a plume of smoke rising above the buildings. Shouts echo around the empty streets, the words unintelligible. I hesitate, torn; do we run toward the chaos, or away from it?

Before I can decide, there's another explosion, this time from the opposite direction. I turn that way instead, but once again, I can't see what happened. The shouts come from all around us now – and then, gunfire. Not a steady unloading of ammo, but short bursts, and no returning fire. I frown at Jed, who's staring in the direction of the latest explosion. He takes off in that direction. Cursing under my breath but with nothing better to do, I follow.

I turn the corner and slam into him. He staggers forward a few steps before coming to a stop again, and continues staring.

Ahead is the aftermath of the blast. From the looks of it, it must've been a grenade, and one that landed right in the midst of a raider crew. Not the one we were traveling with, which gives me a surprising sense of relief.

A few of the unfortunate raiders are splattered across the dusty ground, a couple have been flung away and lie unconscious, and one is holding the bloody stub of a leg and groaning. While Jed seems entranced by the gory sight, I tear my eyes away and scan the town around us. Was it another raider crew that did this? Or was it townies after all? There are plenty of windows in the surrounding buildings, good vantage points to throw an explosive from, but they're empty now.

On the other side of the carnage, a second raider crew turns the corner. They scrutinize the bloody remains and mutter among themselves, before their gazes find Jed and me. We stare at one another across the mess of dead and dying.

'You do this?' one of the men shouts at us, his words echoing up and down the street.

'Of course not,' I snap. 'We're with you.'

'Well, someone took 'em out,' the man growls. 'And ain't no townies to be found.'

We glare at each other. None of us move, but I size up his crew. There are only four of them, a mangy group aside from the bulky, red-faced man who's been shouting at us. Jed and I could probably take them, especially if we shot first, but I'm not eager to start a raider civil war right now. I know what these people are like. If they see a fight erupting, they'll join in, even if they don't know why it's happening. One little misunderstanding like this could rip the entire raider army apart.

Just when I'm starting to wonder if that's such a bad idea, Jed decides to open his mouth.

'Well, let's not get too hasty here,' he says, raising his hands in a 'stop' motion.

Out of all of the things that have come out of Jed's mouth, that's possibly the most reasonable sentence yet. But somehow, it incites a murderous rage in the other raiders. The leader lets out a shout as if Jed personally insulted him, and comes flying in our direction. The rest of them follow, their feet skidding and sliding across the bloody mess they have to cross to reach us, one of them stepping right on the stomach of the man who lost his leg.

I hesitate – unsure if I want to run or shoot – but Jed grabs my arm and yanks me back, making the decision for me. We tear down the street, the shouts of the raiders echoing after us.

'What did I say wrong?' Jed asks between pants for breath, casting a look over his shoulder at our pursuers. They're still coming, still yelling, and the situation still doesn't make much sense. Other raider crews are emerging from side streets and poking their heads out of buildings to see what the hell is going on. They all stare as we pass.

I don't answer him – partially because I have no fucking idea, and partially because I'm trying to figure out what the hell to do about the situation. Secretly, part of me is pleased at the turn of events; the immediate danger leaves no room for moral concerns, and the weirdness between Jed and me is gone, replaced by the camaraderie that comes with fighting for our lives together.

I'm guessing our best bet is to find the others. We may not really be part of the crew, but Wolf seems like the type who's always looking for an excuse to fight, and I'm sure he'd gladly jump in. Problem is, I'm not sure where he went. This town seems much bigger now that we're inside of it, a confusing maze of streets and broken buildings. I have no idea where to find them, though every other goddamn raider crew seems intent on gaping at us.

As I'm searching for the crew, I make a critical mistake, a wrong turn. Jed and I skid to a stop at a dead end. A brick wall looms up ahead, cutting off our escape. I scan the area, but there's no other exit, and the crew in pursuit of us has already reached the mouth of the alleyway. They stop there, completely severing our only escape route, while we stand with the wall at our backs. The red-faced leader's face splits into a grin.

'Got ya,' he says. 'Fuckin' cowards.'

The plus side to fighting in an alleyway is that they can't all come at us at once. The downside is that if any of them get a good hold on us, there's no way to escape. My pulse rises to a steady hammer as I raise my gun, Jed doing the same at my side. He opens his mouth, and shuts it again; maybe he's too afraid to talk, now that his previous harmless phrase sent these men into a mad frenzy.

'Calm the fuck down,' I say, hoping that speaking 'raider' might get the message through their thick skulls. 'We don't have time for this shit right now.'

Once again, that somehow seems to be the exact wrong thing to say. The man lets out a howl like an incensed animal – but before he can run at us, something falls from the sky and lands right in front of him. His howl cuts off abruptly as he looks down at it.

A grenade.

I yank Jed backward, sending both of us crashing to the end of the alleyway in a heap, just half a moment before the explosion. I press myself against the ground so hard I choke on dust. I wait a couple moments, and cautiously raise my head. Jed is coughing, his eyes watering, but he looks unharmed.

The raiders at the mouth of the alleyway didn't fare as well as us. The scene is almost hilariously reminiscent of the one we found earlier. With all of them packed so tightly around the entrance to the alleyway, not one of them managed to escape unscathed, all four raiders downed and bloody. I climb to my feet, helping Jed up, and we make our way out of the alleyway. Only once we're out do I realize how many eyes have watched this go down – at least a half dozen raider crews are all staring at us from different directions.

'It wasn't us!' Jed shouts immediately. He throws up his hands in surrender, looking from one group of raiders to another. 'I don't know what happened, but it was *not* us!'

I can tell from the muttering that not a single one of them believes that. And why should they? There's been no sign of anyone but raiders here, and they've thoroughly combed the town by now.

And yet ... someone did throw a grenade. Someone who definitely wasn't us.

Remembering the image of the grenade falling from above, I raise my eyes to the open sky. I sweep them left, and sweep them right, and catch just the slightest hint of movement . . . something that could be a pale face disappearing over the edge of a rooftop. My head snaps in that direction, and I stare hard at the building. Nothing now, and I can't be certain what I saw.

But somehow I am certain, and I think I'm finally catching on to what my instincts have been trying to tell me this whole time.

'Townies,' I say, my voice coming out quiet and dry, choked with dust. I cough to clear my throat, and raise my voice. 'Townies! On the rooftops!'

The eyes of all the raiders, formerly on us, rise upward. There's a moment of silence – a moment when I'm sure all of them are trying to decide whether I'm telling the truth, or just trying to shake off suspicion.

Then dozens of faces appear at the edges of the rooftops. A moment later, they begin to pelt us. A fork *dings* off a building to my left, a pot crashes into a raider in front of me, and an empty tin can smacks into the side of my head. I jerk back, my head ringing, and raise my arms to cover myself. The rain of various everyday objects continues, and I retreat back into the alleyway and press against the wall. Jed, caught out in the open, staggers left and right in an effort to avoid falling objects, and finally stumbles after me, yelping as a broken chair leg catches him on his way over.

Most of the other raiders are still caught out in the open streets. They seem baffled about how to handle this situation, some stumbling around in an attempt to dodge, others ducking into buildings, still more holding their ground and trying to shoot at the townies up above. None of it seems very effective. With the raiders too confused to fight back, the steady fall of objects only grows heavier. When one group of raiders clusters together back-to-back, trying to cover one another, one of the townies hurls another grenade.

Boom. Another bloody mess on the dusty streets.

'Spread out!' Jed yells, struggling to be heard above the constant clatters and thuds and dings of various things hitting the ground, and townies shouting in triumph, and raiders screaming in frustration and pain. With chaos all around us, Jed is staring out at the mess of a fight like it's a puzzle he's trying to solve. 'Spread out and find shelter!'

Clearly at a loss for what else to do, the raiders listen to him. The streets empty as raiders hide in buildings and other shelters, leaving only the dead and dying out in the open streets. The rain of objects from above gradually dies down, and the streets become silent and dead once again. I, along with the others, wait to see what will come next – and what Jed will tell us to do.

My head is still spinning from that blow from the can.

So what else do the townies have up their sleeves? If we're lucky, maybe it's nothing. Townies are simple things, after all. Maybe they didn't think any further than this clever little ploy. Maybe they thought they'd be able to pick off more of us before we realized what was happening. Though, judging from an explosion on the other side of town, some of the other crews haven't caught on yet. If we're lucky, maybe the townies will just focus their attentions elsewhere.

But luck is rarely on my side lately.

Before I can even catch my breath, the door to a nearby building bursts open, and townies pour out. There are more than I would've expected. Few of them are armed properly, but those that aren't still carry things like wooden boards and broken chair legs and metal pots. There's no fear, no hesitation – they flood out and run, yelling, at the closest raiders. A pack of them swarms Jed and me.

I thought it would be hard to kill townies. I thought – perhaps *hoped* – that some shred of my conscience would awaken and make me hesitate about pulling the trigger on people who are just trying to defend their homes. But, as it turns out, there isn't much time for conscience when the townies are running at me with weapons in hand. It's not even a matter of right or wrong. It's a matter of staying alive. A choice between them and me. A matter of necessity.

Without conscience hindering me, the raid becomes nothing more than a very easy fight. See target, pull trigger, body hits ground. Most of the townies don't have guns, and those who do hardly know how to use them. To a professional like me, they might as well not have any weapons at all. I shoot them down, one by one, before they're even close enough to endanger me. Quick and easy. Almost too easy, actually, and I start to get bored after a while. I put my gun away and grab my knife from its sheath on my leg, using that to take care of the next man who comes at me.

I laugh – and immediately sober as I catch myself doing it. I'm *enjoying* this, I realize; I'm enjoying slaughtering these mostly defenseless townies in their own home. I look around me, at the town swiftly being overrun by raiders. I see raiders killing people, torturing people, looting bodies and buildings, lighting fires and destroying things for the fun of it. Some of them are laughing, just like I was a moment ago. I lower my knife to my side, guilt creeping up on me as I look around at the chaos being wrought.

I search for Jed in the fight, and find him gleefully wrapped up in it, wielding two pistols he must have looted from someone. I try to catch his eye, but the sight of him taking out two townies at once and whooping excitedly stops me in my tracks. For him, this is just the same as killing raiders in the Nameless Town. I can't let that be the case for me; I have to keep myself under control. I turn away from Jed and head deeper into town, away from the worst of the fighting.

I can't handle being deep in the fray anymore, but I know that the raiders will be suspicious if I'm not doing something helpful. So I decide to search for loot, heading up to the rooftops where I suspect the townies have hidden their goods.

There isn't much to find; most of it was thrown down at the raiders, and what's left isn't useful. I pick my way among smashed furniture and tattered blankets. Some children hide among the wreckage, staying out of the fight below, but I ignore them and keep looking. Even though I've escaped the fight, the sound of gunfire and shouting is constantly on the edge of my consciousness, and it's almost physically painful to keep myself away. The outcome is obvious; these townies took out an impressive number of raiders, maybe enough to save the next town the army hits, but they're severely outmatched.

I walk to the edge of the building and look down on the town below. The ground is strewn with the remains of the townies' hail of junk, along with bodies from both sides. The fight rages on atop the wreckage. I search for Jed, but I can't find him in the midst of everything, not from this distance.

Instead, I see something else – and my body goes rigid, a sharp breath hissing through my teeth.

Vehicles are approaching. Five of them altogether, and they're not the shoddy, pieced-together scrap metal that people call cars out here in the west. They're big, intimidating trucks, all shiny and painted black. My heart sinks down into my stomach as I get a better look at them. I've seen these kinds of cars before. Everyone in the east has, and everyone knows that they can only mean one thing.

And evidently, people here are learning it too. Before long, people notice them coming, and a whisper starts up. It ripples through the town, even through the chaos, and the fighting comes to a pause. It stops townies and raiders alike, the eyes of both turning toward the east. The vehicles pull up to the front of town and stop there, engines growling loudly, the town quiet in their presence. One by one, the engines shut off, and silence falls. The whole town is hushed.

Then someone shouts it.

'Jedediah Johnson is here!'

XXII
The Raid Gone Wrong

Some of the raiders turn tail and run, while others rush toward the vehicles, shouting and brandishing their weapons. Townies flee, or fight with renewed vigor. Just moments ago there were two sides to this fight, but it soon dissolves into one very confused mess.

On the rooftop, I stand completely still. My hand is on my gun, my face turned toward the black vehicles that I've always known as a portent of death and loss. These are the cars that come when things are about to go terribly wrong. They show up to steal your supplies, to punish your resistance. They show up to drag people away kicking and screaming, people who will never be seen again. Now they've come so far from home, and they've come all this way for me, and for Jed.

Jed. I need to find him. We need to run. Not only is

this town about to turn into a massacre of townies and western raiders alike, but if they see Jed, it's all over. Our only hope is that with everything happening around us, we can escape without his father's crew noticing us. They can't know for sure that we're here, so if we manage to disappear quickly enough, maybe we'll have a shot.

I force away the childish fear that the sight of those vehicles ignited in me, and finally break my paralysis. I run for the rusty staircase I climbed to reach the rooftop, clamber down to the street, and keep running. I'm not even sure where I'm running, other than *away*, desperately hoping that Jed will have the same idea and head in the same direction . . . and desperately hoping that he was telling the truth when he said he didn't want to go back to his father.

But I don't see him anywhere as I run through town, searching every corner and hiding place. I find an elderly couple hidden away in a building on the edge of town, an injured raider dragging himself into an alleyway, a dying townie holding her hands to the sky and begging for Jedediah Johnson to save her. Jed isn't with them, or the mob of raiders racing to meet the eastern crew, or the stragglers fleeing town.

Among those stragglers I find Wolf's crew. The leader seems seriously displeased about leaving the fight, with Tank at one elbow prodding him forward and Dolly at the other, keeping an eye out for trouble. Kid, lagging behind the others, is the one who spots me. She slows down, raising a hand.

'We're getting out of here. You coming?' she asks. I hesitate, and shake my head. She looks over my shoulder at the town. 'He was right in the thick of the fight when they got here,' she says. 'Didn't see where he went afterward.' I nod again, a silent thanks. She bites her lip, hesitating for a moment before blurting out, 'I don't trust the guy. Talks too pretty.'

I'm not surprised. I remember the way Kid distrusted him from the beginning. And maybe she's right; Jed has lied before, after all, and he's pretty damn good at it. But still . . .

'I know,' I say. 'But I can't leave him.'

She sighs to herself, but doesn't argue.

'Good luck,' she says.

'You too.'

I stay on the edge of town, watching the crew disappearing into the vast expanse of the wastes before turning back to the town consumed by chaos. This could be my only chance to run. I glance at the wastes again, imagining myself shouting for Wolf and his crew to wait, imagining myself fleeing with them and leaving Jed behind. I imagine a life for myself with them as my family, my home. Then I curse and run back into the heart of town.

Jed could have turned against me the moment his

father showed up ... or he could be injured, or trapped, or captured. He could need me. And if there's a chance of that, I can't leave him behind. So I ignore my pounding heart and all my instincts screaming at me to run, and head right toward Jedediah Johnson's crew.

The infamous raiders are cutting their way through town, mowing down townies and western raiders alike. Some try to fight, but they don't stand a chance. Jedediah's crew is no unruly band of outlaws; they're professionals, better fed and better trained and much better armed than anyone around here. These western wastelands must be a joke to them. Even for me, a bounty hunter used to dealing with them, Jedediah's crew is a challenge. I might be able to take down a few of them, but I don't like my chances against the whole lot, especially when I'm alone.

Though I know that logically I don't stand a chance, hatred bubbles through my veins at the mere thought of Jedediah's crew, and having them so close at hand nearly makes me forget my goal. I know almost every one of them, by name and by face – and every crime they've committed, every town they've wronged. Some of them are faces that have haunted my nightmares for years; others are newer, but no less awful. I'd gladly kill each and every one of them, and do it slowly and with relish, without a shred of moral uncertainty to weigh on my conscience.

I try to push aside anger and fear alike, to not think, to let my body move mechanically. All that matters right now is finding Jed. But he's nowhere to be found. It's like he vanished as soon as his father's crew appeared. But did he go toward them, or away? Impossible to tell.

I scour streets and buildings. I find raiders, and townies, and plenty of bodies belonging to both sides, but not Jed. I carry on, my search growing more frantic. Then I round the corner and run into a familiar face.

Not a face I know personally, but one I've seen on wanted posters all over the eastern wastes. One of Jedediah Johnson's crew members – Maria Heartless, they call her. A revolver is in her hand and pointed at me; I can tell she knows my face as well. We end up at a standstill, each staring down the barrel of the other's gun.

'Well, well, what a surprise,' she says. Then, she raises her voice to a shout, turning her head so the sound carries behind her. 'I found the bounty hunter! He's here somewhere!'

The moment her attention shifts, I slam into her. She fires her gun, but the shot goes wild. I slam her back against the closest building. She grunts as she hits crumbling brick, but it doesn't faze her. She slams the butt of her pistol up against my chin, and then into my face as I jerk back. I gasp, blood gushing from my likely broken nose, and keep grappling with her. A close-quarters fight is my best bet, but she's not easy prey. She's lean with muscle and full of fire, matching me blow for blow.

We fight hard and dirty. She yanks my hair, and I spit blood in her face; I knee her in the stomach, and she hits me in my broken nose again, sending a jolt of agony all the way down my spine. I pull a brick free from the wall behind her, and send it crashing toward her face – but she's quick, too quick, and ducks her head to the side just in time to avoid the blow. The contact with the wall sends pain up my arm, my knuckles scraping excruciatingly against the brick and my own momentum throwing me off balance. She slips from my grasp, and I whirl around to find her with her gun aimed at my head.

She laughs, clucking her tongue at me like I'm a disobedient child. Fury threatens to make me do something stupid, but I force it down. My body is already shaking from the brief struggle. The days with scarce food and water have not been kind to me, and I'm at a disadvantage with that gun in her hands. I know when I've lost.

I lower my hands to my sides, ready to admit defeat and let her drag me off to who-knows-where. At least this way, I can buy Jed some time to escape.

She laughs and smashes the butt of the gun right into my nose once more. I stumble back, and before I can recover she hits me again in the forehead, this time causing my head to smack back against the bricks. I drop to my knees, my head spinning, the taste of blood in my mouth.

The woman grabs a fistful of my hair and drags me down the street. I struggle and fight and claw at her hand, but I'm weak and hazy minded, my vision obscured by blood running down my face, my feet scrabbling against the ground. I find myself helpless as she drags me, past fleeing raiders and townies and straight into the arms of her crew.

She throws me on the ground, and I land heavily on my hands and knees. I turn my face upwards to see a huge man towering above me. He's broad shouldered, arms knotted with muscle, with a shaggy beard and hard eyes.

I realize, with a jolt, that I recognize him. He was one of the tax collectors I saw in Sunrise, the giant one who hardly spoke. I wouldn't have guessed that Jedediah Johnson would have the guts to go collect taxes himself, but I suppose it makes sense. And he's exactly what I expected Jedediah Johnson to be: tough, intimidating, emotionless. This is the face of my real enemy, and now I'm at his mercy.

He raises a gun to my forehead, cold steel pressing against my skin. I swallow my fear and meet his eyes.

'Where is he?' he asks. His voice is gravelly and quiet, barely audible above the sounds of the fight.

'He's dead,' I say calmly. 'Died in the fire at Fort Cain.'

His face betrays nothing, but one booted foot shoves me so I land on my back in the dirt. He places the boot on my chest, squeezing the breath out of me, gun still aimed at my head.

'Last chance,' he says, his voice as soft and stoic as before. 'Where is he?'

'Like I said.' I turn my head to the side, spit blood, and turn back to him. 'Jed's dead.'

His finger tightens on the trigger.

'Stop.'

Both of our heads whip toward the familiar voice. I'm not sure which of us is more surprised to see Jed standing there, pointing a gun at the man above me. My heart sinks. The rest of the crew – those who aren't immersed in the fighting, at least – all turn to Jed as well, gasps and murmurs running through their ranks.

'You idiot,' I say, struggling for breath with a boot crushing my chest. I try to shove it off, but the huge man doesn't budge. 'You're supposed to run!'

Jed doesn't even look at me. His eyes stay locked on the man above me – on his father. Jedediah Johnson.

'Back up,' Jed says, his gun hand steady.

You idiot, I think again, though I don't have the breath to speak anymore. This will only get both of us killed. Does he really think he can help me? That his word will sway his father not to kill the bounty hunter who kidnapped his son?

And yet, Jedediah Johnson steps away from me and lowers his gun to his side without a hint of hesitation. I scramble away in the dust, panting for breath and trying to process what's happening. Did he just take an order from Jed? I stare at the man, trying to understand. After a moment, he smiles, an expression that looks strange and foreign on his formerly serious face.

'Hey, boss,' he says.

XXIII
A Snake by Any Other Name

At first, I don't understand. The word 'boss,' the way the raiders snap to attention, the utter adoration in their expressions. To say the crew is happy to see Jed would be a massive understatement. They look at him like a god descended from heaven in front of them. They seem to have forgotten about me entirely. I slowly get to my knees, but my legs give out when I try to rise any farther than that. So I stay down, my eyes locked on the man I thought I knew. The blow to my head is still making things murky for me, and this feels surreal, dreamlike.

'Ah, hello, boys,' Jed says, in a voice that's unfamiliar – odd and lilting, smooth on the surface with something dangerous lurking just beneath. He walks into the midst of the crew. The raiders eagerly gather around, but keep a respectful distance. He smiles at them, making eye contact with each and every one of them – and completely ignoring me. My whole body is numb, my brain full of static.

'It's so good to be back together,' Jed says. More of the crew members are breaking off from the fight in the town, drawn to him like a magnet. They form a loose circle, all eyes on him. He pauses briefly, stepping up to the big man who nearly shot me. He bumps knuckles with him amiably before continuing. 'And wow, jeez guys, I am *so* touched that you all followed me across the wastes to this hellhole.'

'As if we had a choice, Jedediah,' a woman says with a half smile.

Jedediah. And there it is, finally, making its way into my shell-shocked brain. Not Jed, but Jedediah. Not the son of a ruthless dictator, but ...

'No,' I breathe. It isn't possible. There's no way it was really him the whole time, no way I fell for a stupid trick and became *friendly* with the man who burned down my home. No way I saved the life of the man who murdered my family.

But the evidence is right in front of me. 'Jed' was a lie. He never existed. All along, there's only ever been Jedediah Johnson.

The one and only, as he said himself not too long ago. All of his long-winded stories, stories I thought he was telling about his father ... He's been rubbing the truth in my face this whole time.

He drops his old identity like a snake shedding its skin. His posture straightens, his eyes sharpen, his smile becomes unfamiliar. He rolls his shoulders back and cracks his neck and, in the time it takes me to blink twice, he has become a stranger. I saw glimpses of this man at times. I saw him when I first put a gun in his hands, and when he looked at the fire at Fort Cain – a fire, I finally realize with a growing horror, he must have started himself. He orchestrated the fall of Fort Cain, leading us to the raiders, and eventually ... right here.

And I helped him. How many times did I save his life? Risk *my* life for his? How many times did I propel him toward this very moment?

Jedediah frowns at the woman who interrupted him.

'Sh, I'm talking right now,' he says in a hushed whisper, waving his hand to silence her, and then grins again. 'Anyway, welcome to the western wastes, I guess. What a shitfest, right?' He spreads his hands wide, inviting commentary now, and earns a few chuckles from his crew.

It's ridiculous, how they pander to him. I don't understand. What power does this small, ridiculous man have over a crew of the best raiders in the wastes? I'm barely aware of the next couple minutes of Jedediah's speech; I spend it watching him, studying his face and the faces of his crew. By the time he finishes, and his crew cheers for him, I feel like I'm even further from understanding him than when I started out.

'So,' Jedediah says in a conversational tone, turning in a circle and looking at his crew. 'We're all reunited, then. Good. I think there's just one more thing to address before we all have a well-earned rest.' He un-holsters his gun and spins it around his hand. 'Which one of you had the bright idea of pretending to be me?'

Silence falls. Jedediah looks from one face to another, and everyone avoids his gaze. He frowns at the lack of an answer, and raises his hands wide open, gun dangling haphazardly from his fingers like he's forgotten he's still holding it. Everyone's eyes are trained on that weapon, my own included.

'C'mon guys, it's a simple question,' he says. 'All the towns said Jedediah Johnson was coming through with his crew. Clearly, one of you was claiming to be me.' No one responds. Jedediah sighs, lowering his hands to his sides. He twirls his gun around one finger, looking down at his shoes. He stays like that for a long few moments, his expression pensive, and then his head jerks up. '*Oh*, I see. You guys think I'm going to be mad, is that it?' He laughs, a little too loudly, and shrugs his shoulders. 'I'm not mad, guys. I mean, I get it. You couldn't exactly admit that I was missing, right? Would really fuck up our reputation. So instead someone had to step up, make it look like we had everything under control, right? And it worked! It totally worked.'

I stay quiet as I watch the scene unfold, moving only my eyes to take in the lowered heads and overly stiff statures of Jedediah's crew, so at odds with their leader's smooth and casual movements. I have the distinct impression that everyone knows something I don't.

Finally, someone steps forward, separating himself from the rest of the crew. He's a thick-necked man with his face almost entirely concealed by his hair. I've seen him before, I realize. He's the other tax collector I saw, way back in Sunrise.

'Er, boss,' he says, brushing hair out of his eyes, only to have it fall back into place the moment he lowers his hand.

'Yes, Mop?'

The man cocks his head to one side.

'Boss?' he says uncertainly. 'My name is—'

'I know, I know,' Jedediah says, waving his words aside. 'We're doing nicknames now. That's what they do out here in the west. Isn't it cool?'

'Oh,' the newly deemed Mop says, brushing hair out of his eyes and frowning. 'Do I have to be Mop?'

'What's wrong with Mop?'

'Well, it's just—' he starts, and then halts abruptly as Jedediah stops spinning his gun. The weapon falls perfectly into place in his palm, and he taps it against the side of his leg. Mop swallows. 'Never mind,' he says.

'Anyway, what were you saying?' Jedediah asks, smiling.

'It was Frank that did it.' He pauses and licks his lip. 'We thought no one would take us seriously if they knew our leader got 'imself kidnapped an' such. So, uh, Frank decided to say he was you.'

'Oh? Frank?' Jedediah turns, scans his gathered crew, and points with his gun. A few people step aside to avoid the end of the barrel, but one steps forward. It's the huge, quiet-voiced man from before, the one who I initially mistook for Jedediah. He's as stoic as before, his shoulders braced and his face stone-like. 'Is this true?' Jedediah asks, leaning his head back and squinting up at the big man. Frank lets out a long sigh, and slowly nods. Jedediah scratches his head, frowns, and glances at Mop.

'But Frank hardly talks.'

'Yeah, well, he only really said "I'm Jedediah Johnson" a couple times, and that seemed to convince people.'

Jedediah looks at Frank.

Frank clears his throat. 'I'm Jedediah Johnson,' he says in his quiet, gravelly voice, staring straight ahead.

'That *is* pretty convincing,' Jedediah says, nodding to himself. He puts his hands on his hips and chews his bottom lip thoughtfully. 'Well, if anyone was gonna step up and pretend to be me, I'm glad it was a big, handsome guy like you.' He reaches up to clap Frank on the shoulder, and then gasps with sudden excitement. 'Oh, I've got it! Tiny! I'll call you Tiny. It's ironic, see? What do you think?'

Frank grunts and shrugs, which Jedediah apparently takes as a sign of agreement, because he gives the man another excited fist-bump, his hand tiny next to the raider's giant fist. Mop, meanwhile, seems progressively more bewildered.

'You're really not mad? 'Cause usually, when you say "I'm not mad, guys"' – he does a rather poor and high-pitched imitation of Jedediah's voice – 'it actually means you're *really* mad . . .'

'Oh? So you thought I was going to punish Tiny?' Jedediah asks, raising an eyebrow.

'Well,' Mop says, trying again in vain to push hair out of his face. 'I thought for sure you would punish *somebody* . . .'

'Quite right,' Jedediah says, and shoots Mop in the head.

His body teeters for a moment, topples backward, and lands in the dust with a heavy thud.

The rest of the crew step aside to avoid the fallen body, but otherwise show no reaction – no anger, no horror, not even the barest hint of surprise. Aside from my sharp intake of breath, there's total silence. Jedediah sweeps his eyes over his crew, nods to himself, and resumes twirling his gun.

'Sorry about that,' he says, 'but, well, you know how it is. Gotta punish somebody, y'know, and it can't be Tiny. He's my biggest and most favorite crew member. Everyone on board with this?' When Jedediah looks around, his crew mumbles quiet assent. Apparently deciding that's not good enough, he whirls abruptly and points his gun at one particular man. 'Yes, Eyepatch?'

At the end of his gun is a scrawny man donning – surprise, surprise – an eyepatch over his left eye. The man gulps and stands up straighter, his visible eye bulging.

'Right, boss!' he shouts in Jedediah's face. Jedediah blinks rapidly.

'Woah, 'Patch,' he says. 'Relax, buddy.' He chuckles, and then turns back around. When his back turns, Eyepatch lets his shoulders slump, releasing a gust of breath like a balloon deflating.

'Well, I'm glad we're all on the same page,' Jedediah says. 'And now ... ' He splits into a broad grin, putting his gun away and holding his hands up. 'Let's celebrate!'

While the raiders celebrate, I sit locked in a basement.

The room is dark and musty, with no windows and a single door, at the top of a set of stairs in the corner. There's no furniture, nothing at all except dust and cobwebs. I already spent a solid thirty minutes shouting and hammering at the door with my fists. Now I sit winded and defeated in the corner, listening to the sounds of revelry above. Despite the bumpy initial reunion, the crew does seem genuinely happy to have their leader back – or else they've grown exceptionally good at faking it for him. And Jed seems happy to be back with them as well. I hear his voice occasionally, cheering and celebrating, cutting through the other noise to reach my ears.

But 'Jed' is wrong, I remind myself. It's Jedediah. Jedediah Johnson. The infamous shark, the ruthless dictator. The stranger.

The deception sits heavily in the pit of my stomach. I can't believe I was stupid enough to believe everything he told me, to grow to trust him, maybe even like him. I traveled with him. I put a gun in his hand and expected him to watch my back. I spent a cold night pressed against him. I imagined a future with us together; I let myself believe that he could be the home I was looking for.

The all-encompassing shock has finally left my body, and in its wake, my emotions roil and churn every time I think about it. Anger. Disgust. Disappointment.

Hurt.

It's been a long time since I felt that one. A long time since I let anyone get close enough to hurt me.

I curl my hands into fists and dig my nails into my palms. I force myself to take long, slow breaths, and focus on the rise and fall of my chest until I have myself under control again.

I can't believe I was this fucking stupid. I thought my situation was bad before, stranded out in these hellish western lands, surrounded by raiders. Now I've ended up in an even worse one: held hostage by a crazy dictator who I had almost started to believe was my friend.

I know I should be spending my time productively, trying to think of a plan, a way to escape, but it's too hard. I'm too exhausted, body and mind. It's hard enough to keep my thoughts from spiraling into despair. I don't even raise my head as I hear the door open. Only when footsteps reach the bottom of the stairs do I look up and see Jedediah.

He drops to a crouch a few feet in front of me, and places a folded blanket and a metal canteen on the floor.

'Got you some water,' he says, pushing it toward me.

I kick the canteen, sending it skidding back across the floor to hit his foot. He slowly slides it back toward me.

'I know you're upset, but you do need to drink,' he says. When I still don't move to touch it, he shrugs. 'Well. I'll leave it here. And the blanket, in case it gets cold down here.' He scrutinizes me, and when he speaks again, his voice is soft. 'I thought about keeping you in a car, but I know places like this make you feel safe.'

The memory of that conversation, of the personal things I shared with him, sends a fresh burst of humiliation and hatred through me. I kick the canteen again, this time sending it flying across the room with a clang of metal. Jedediah rocks back on his heels, looking at the fallen canteen for a long few moments before turning back to me.

'I'm sorry,' he says. 'I really do mean it. Things got out of hand.'

'Out of hand,' I repeat.

'Well, yeah,' he says, gesturing vaguely. 'I mean, coming out here was part of the plan, but I didn't expect things with Saint to happen quite like they did, and Tiny pretending to be me required some serious improvising, and . . . well. You know how these things are. Or maybe you don't. I suppose you'll have to take my word for it.'

I stay quiet for a few moments, my anger stewing, until what he said hits me.

'What do you mean, part of the plan?'

'Surely you didn't think I'd end up all the way out here by accident,' he says, half-smiling. 'Give me some credit, Clem. Haven't you heard I'm a genius?'

I say nothing, too busy fighting back an urge to punch him. I may have hit him several times, but that was before; before I was at his mercy, before I saw him murder one of his own men for no good reason. Now I really have no clue who the man is front of me is, or what he's capable of doing. Jedediah glances at my clenched fists, one eyebrow rising as if he's curious to see whether I'll do it. After a few moments pass, he stands up, brushing himself off.

'Well,' he says. 'We'll have plenty of time to talk about it later. I have to get back to my party.' He walks backward toward the stairs, still keeping his eyes on me. 'I would invite you, but I'm afraid that might be a little awkward for everyone involved. I'm sure you understand. Don't worry. They'll come around eventually.' Before I can even begin to decipher what that means, he waves at me, turns, and climbs the stairs. Without looking back again, he's gone, leaving me even more confused than before.

XXIV
The Grand Plan

I wake to the sound of the door slamming. I scramble up, pressing my back against the wall and facing the stairs. I was on the verge of giving up yesterday, but now, after a night's rest – albeit a shitty one spent on a cold floor – I'm feeling a little differently about the situation. I'm more than ready to launch myself at Jedediah the moment he reaches the bottom of the stairs.

But the man coming toward me isn't Jedediah. It's Frank – or Tiny, or whatever his name is now. He pauses as he reaches the bottom of the stairs, regarding me warily. I stare back at him. After a moment, he swings his gaze to the blanket Jedediah gave me, sitting folded and unused in the middle of the floor. His eyebrows rise slightly, though his face remains otherwise expression-less. He walks over to the canteen, lifts it up, and shakes it to judge the amount of water inside. Finding it full, he shakes his head and mutters under his breath.

He gives me another long, searching look, picks up both the blanket and canteen, and walks over to me. I stay perfectly still as he draws near, my fists clenched. Unlike Jedediah, this man would have no problem beating me down in a fight. But he makes no aggressive moves toward me. Instead, he sets down both blanket and canteen in a slow and almost gentle way, then turns and leaves.

When the door shuts again, I grab the canteen and pull it toward me. I open it, take a good sniff, swirl it around and sniff it again. It smells like water, and a quick taste reveals nothing out of the ordinary. It tastes like nice, clean, bottled water.

As much as I want to reject Jedediah's hospitality, I can't take revenge if I end up dead of dehydration. I swallow my pride along with the water.

As I rest and drink over the day, life gradually returns to my body – and with life, the will to fight.

Later in the day, Jedediah comes for another visit, this time bringing a can of beans. I can smell meat cooking outside, but he didn't bring any. A gesture intended to show that he knows me, I assume, just like the bomb shelter thing. But if he thinks he's going to trick me into trusting him again, he's dead wrong.

I stay in the corner and bristle silently as he sets the

opened can in front of me and sits, cross-legged, a few feet away. After a few minutes of silent standoff, the smell of food becomes too tempting. I reach out and grab the can, dragging it over to me. It's warm, and I eat it quickly, while still keeping one eye on Jedediah. He watches me, one hand propping his chin up.

When I'm done eating, I slam the emptied can down on the floor and stare at him. He maintains eye contact, and the corner of his mouth curls up, like he thinks we're playing some sort of game. And maybe we are, from his perspective. Either way, I'm tired of the silence and the waiting.

'You planned all of this?' I ask in disbelief. My voice comes out rusty from disuse, and I clear my throat. 'Me taking you, ending up all the way out here.' He says nothing, just waits, and I grind my teeth. 'How the fuck did you—' I start, and then stop. Everyone has always said that Jedediah Johnson is a genius ... and there's a question much more important than *how* he did it. *'Why?'*

'Ooh, man, I've been so excited to explain this,' he says, his eyes lighting up. He leans forward, clasping his hands together. 'Well, as you know, I had a pretty sweet setup back in Wormwood. Nice mansion, lots of towns to give me whatever I needed, plenty of guards, etcetera, etcetera. But, after a while of that, it actually got rather boring. Who would've thought?'

I study his face, sure that he must be joking, but he looks earnest.

'You got bored,' I say flatly. 'Bored with … what? Having enough food and water and men to not have to worry about anything? Most people would kill for that.'

'Well, yeah,' he says, shrugging. 'It was nice for a while, but I wanted more.'

And there's the truth of it. He can claim boredom all he wants, but in that *more*, and in his eyes, is the real reason: hunger. Hunger on a scale more grand than I could even imagine.

'When I heard what things were like out in the west,' he continues, 'I thought it sounded perfect. Total lawlessness, and so many little towns in need of my guidance … But my crew disagreed. They liked things the way they were, didn't want to risk it all. So I thought to myself: "Hmm, how can I get them to follow me across the wastes?"'

'You can't be serious,' I say.

'Yes,' he says, looking immensely satisfied with himself. 'That's where you came into play.'

I stare at him. I knew Jedediah Johnson was evil, I knew he was some kind of mad genius, but I never would have expected him to be completely batshit *insane*. And as he spews out this fucking ridiculous plan, he's smiling at me like we're two friends sharing an inside joke. He doesn't say anything else, clearly waiting for my reaction.

'You're out of your fucking mind,' I say.

His smile fades, and is replaced with an expression of puzzlement and hurt. His confusion baffles me. Did he really expect me to say something different? Apparently so, judging from the wounded-puppy look he's giving me. I guess he truly, honestly thought I would be ... what, pleased? Impressed?

'But we talked about this,' he says. 'When I said the eastern wastes are better than the west, you didn't argue.'

'I didn't argue that *maybe* life was better for the townies there,' I say, loath even to admit that. 'Doesn't mean I think you're anything less than a power-hungry, maniacal piece of shit.'

Jedediah sighs and sits back on his heels. He's quiet for a couple minutes.

'You know,' he says thoughtfully, 'you and I are really quite similar when you think about it.'

My eyebrows shoot up despite my determination not to show a reaction.

'In the end, we both want to make the world a better place,' he says. He's very serious now, all of the gleeful triumph from before leaving his voice. He speaks more slowly than usual, like he's puzzling the words out as he says them. 'And we both know violence is the way to do it.'

'You literally burn people inside their homes if they

disagree with you,' I say, my hands clenching into fists. 'We're nothing alike.'

'Okay, so, a minor disagreement about methods.'

'And you think *tyranny* is the way to make the world a better place.'

He frowns at that.

'I just don't get it,' he says. 'The towns under my care have rules. And protection. And of course I demand a little something in return, but I think that's really quite reasonable.'

'Reasonable,' I repeat flatly.

'I'm not a cruel man. I just do what I have to do. The same as you, Clementine.'

He says it so calmly, so casually, as if it's not even in question. As if the things he's done are truly reasonable – things like burning Old Creek to the ground. Rage rises inside me, and I barely keep myself from wrapping my hands around his throat. The only thing that stops me is the knowledge that he surely has someone outside, waiting to intervene if he's in trouble. When I decide to kill Jedediah, I want to make sure I succeed.

'You're fucking insane,' I tell him. 'And I'm going to kill you when I get a chance.'

Jedediah stares at me for a moment, and then throws back his head and laughs. He keeps laughing as he stands up and moves toward the door. When he's almost there, he finally stops and looks back at me, shaking his head.

'You're not going to kill me,' he says, still smiling. He says it with such confidence that I don't know how to react other than with an incredulous stare. 'Anyway, I suppose it doesn't really matter if you agree or not. I don't need your help. I've already won.'

I stay silent as he walks to the door, steps outside, and locks it.

'We'll see,' I whisper to myself in the darkness of my cell.

The next morning, Jedediah's crew stomps around and shouts to one another outside. The words are indecipherable, but they sound busy. I sit and listen carefully, even walk up to the door and press my ear against it in an attempt to hear better, but I gather nothing other than the fact that a lot of movement and noise is happening. After a few minutes, I retreat back to the basement floor to wait. There's nothing else I can do.

Soon the door opens, and Tiny walks down the stairs. A rope hangs from his hands. I stand and back against the wall, my hands curling into fists. I don't give a damn that Tiny is twice my size, and that he'll undoubtedly beat the shit out of me. Whatever he wants to do to me with that rope, there's no way I'm letting it happen without a fight.

The raider descends to the bottom of the stairs, where he stops, rope dangling from his hands. We stare each other down, and he wraps an end of the rope around one massive hand.

'Wrists,' he says, and demonstrates holding them out. I shake my head – that's better than a noose, but not *much* better. He steps forward, and I step to the side. He sighs, and raises his free hand to rub at his forehead.

'I'm guessing you have orders not to hurt me,' I say, and spit at his feet. 'Good luck with that.'

He looks down at his spittle-covered boot impassively, sighs again, and walks back up the stairs without further argument. I stay where I am, bracing myself for whatever comes next.

A few minutes later, Tiny returns with Jedediah behind him. The bastard's usual blasé demeanor is gone for once. He moves quickly down the stairs and stops there, staring at me and tapping one foot against the floor. I set my jaw and glare at him.

'Okay, what's the issue here?' he asks, running a hand through his hair. Tiny stands behind him with the rope in hand, waiting silently. Jedediah looks at him, and at me. When nobody says anything, he throws his hands up with a groan. 'Both of you seriously need to work on your verbal communication skills,' he mutters, and focuses on me. 'Okay, Clem, so here's the deal. I like you, I respect you, and all of that jazz, but I'm afraid I simply must insist on tying you up for the journey.'

A journey. So that's what this all the noise is about. I

want to ask where we're going, but I won't trust whatever answer he gives anyway.

'Not gonna happen,' I say.

'This is really unfair,' he says, in a voice like he's scolding me. 'You dragged me around in ropes for days, Clementine. *Days*. It's really uncomfortable, you know. And I'm just asking for a few hours in return.' I merely glare at him in response. After a moment, he turns and grabs the rope out of Tiny's hands. 'Would it make you feel better if I did it myself?' he asks, taking a step toward me. I don't move, which he seems to take as encouragement, moving forward and raising the ropes.

I stay completely still until he's just a step away. As soon as he's close enough, I smash my fist into his jaw. His head jolts to the side, and he swears, stumbling back. I lunge forward again – and a goddamn truck slams into me.

That's what it feels like, at least. I'm smashed face-down on the floor, breath forced out of my chest. I try to struggle, but my arms are pinned down by an ironlike grip. I can barely move, barely breathe with my face pressed against the concrete.

'Careful with her,' Jedediah says from somewhere above me. 'She barely got me. I'm fine.'

Barely got him, my ass. It may not have been my best punch – didn't knock him out this time, after all – but I'm sure he'll have a bruise to show for it. When Tiny loosens his hold on me just a bit, I take full advantage of it by resuming my struggles. He's no longer crushing me against the floor, but he keeps my arms tightly pinned. With all of my struggling, I barely manage to lift my face off the concrete, which just gives me a better view of Jedediah crouched in front of me. He holds one hand against his face, but he doesn't look angry, just vaguely frustrated. The rope dangles loosely from his grip.

'Oh, Clementine,' he says, rubbing his jaw. 'You really do like to make things difficult, huh?' When I say nothing, he raises his eyes to Tiny and nods. 'Okay, hold her.'

I struggle the entire time they spend tying me, though it does nothing, especially since I'm starting to lose the feeling in my hands due to Tiny's grip. When he finally releases me, I drop to the floor, breathing hard. I wriggle my hands, testing the binds, and can barely move my fingers.

'Good work,' Jedediah says, fist-bumping Tiny. He smiles at me. 'Hold tight, I'll be back soon.'

They leave me tied on the floor, simmering in my anger, for five minutes. Finally, Tiny returns to retrieve me. I guess I should consider it a compliment, that Jedediah would dedicate his biggest crew member to personally escort me. Despite my boiling frustration, I know better than to fuck with him, especially after that display of strength before. He's a bit rougher with me after witnessing me punch his boss in the face, dragging me along by one arm with a grip that will leave bruises, but I keep my mouth shut and my face blank.

Outside, I wince at the brightness of the sun. A couple days in a basement was almost enough to make me forget about the intense light and heat, already at a sweltering level at this point of the day. A bead of sweat trickles down my forehead. Never thought I would miss being cooped up in that basement, but this is a reminder that the wastes are just as shitty.

Tiny drags me through the eerily quiet town. The crew has cleaned out the bodies from the last fight, leaving behind nothing but dust and useless junk. While other raiders might leave a mess, Jedediah's crew is thorough and efficient, leaving an empty ghost town in its wake.

The crew waits on the edge of town, lounging around the vehicles. Some are seated on the hoods or leaning against the sides of their cars, others sitting on the ground or standing around in clumps, most of them talking among themselves and roughhousing. There's an atmosphere of thinly veiled energy and excitement – whatever Jedediah has planned, they seem pretty thrilled about it. I listen as we approach, straining for a hint about where we're headed. Are we going 'home,' to the eastern wastes? Or somewhere else entirely? I hear nothing that helps me guess.

As Jedediah approaches, the crew snaps to attention instantaneously. Their conversations die, their postures straighten, and anyone seated scrambles to their feet. The friendly banter and play fighting dies down, and their eyes all move to watch him. They stand, and listen, and wait for instruction. The immediate shift is almost absurd, and all at the approach of a single, rather scrawny man who is humming cheerfully to himself as he walks.

I have to marvel at the hold Jedediah has over his crew, the seemingly effortless authority he exudes. These men and women are all hardened raiders. Every one of them is bigger than him, older than him, or at the very least tougher than him. Most look like they could snap their leader in half with one arm tied behind their back. And yet, they all look at him with such deep respect – perhaps even awe. They look at him like he's more than a crew leader. I can see why they call him a king.

'All right, boys and girls, we all good here?' Jedediah asks, looking around. Despite my surprise about his crew's behavior, he acts completely casual. I suppose he's grown to expect it at this point. 'All buildings cleared out, all bodies searched, all crew members accounted for?' Several crew members mutter assent, some variations of 'yes boss' and 'all covered,' and Jedediah nods with a satisfied grin. 'Great. Let's move out.' He swirls a finger in the air, and they move to obey.

I still have no clue where we're going, but apparently everyone else does, because there are no questions asked as everyone piles into the vehicles. One by one, the roars of the engines start up. Tiny, Jedediah, and I are the last to pile in, squished up against one another in the back-seat of a car. I'm forced to sit in the middle.

Tiny sits on one side, stoic as usual and keeping his eyes fixed on me like he's expecting me to try something even with my wrists tied. He takes up so much space that he practically fills two seats, forcing me to squish up against Jedediah in the seat and a half left over. I try to wriggle away, but there's nowhere to go. At odds with Tiny's seriousness, Jedediah bounces in his seat, alternating between staring out the window and shooting me grins. He seems to expect me to share in whatever he's pleased about, though I'm far from happy and haven't a fucking clue what's going on.

The ride is completely silent, with the exception of Jedediah occasionally asking a question – usually some variation of 'How much longer?' or 'Are we almost there?' The two raiders sitting up front repeatedly remind him we'll be there tomorrow. Jedediah keeps looking at me, practically begging me to show some curiosity, but I don't give him the satisfaction. It's not like I can change where we're headed, or that the knowledge will do me any good. No matter where we go, my goal is the same: to kill this madman before his bullshit plan gets any further. Wherever we go, I'll find a way. So, I'm perfectly content to stay silent, especially if there's any chance that it will upset Jedediah.

We travel all day. I steal an occasional glance out the window, careful not to seem *too* interested, but never see anything other than empty wastes. It's impossible for me to tell where we're going, and nobody drops any hints. Even Jedediah quiets down after a while, and then dozes off. Tiny, as usual, remains silent.

When we stop for the night, they move me to the trunk. I fight and kick, scuffling with Tiny as he drags me out of my seat. But in the end, the fight drains out of me, and Tiny carries me and dumps me in the trunk without much effort. Jedediah stands beside him, looking down at me. I glare at him, trying to channel as much hate as I can into my gaze.

'Sorry about this,' Jedediah says. His expression makes a good show of genuine regret, though I know better than to believe anything he says or does at this point. 'But, well ... you know how it is.' He blows me a kiss, and Tiny slams the trunk shut.

In the darkness, I will myself not to break down. It's cramped in here, and uncomfortable, and the air tastes stale ... but the physical discomfort is nothing in comparison to the overwhelming sense of humiliation. It's been a long time since I've been made to feel like a helpless child, and the feeling claws and chews at my insides. My chest feels tight, and my eyes burn. I shut them, forcing back any hint of tears. Like hell am I going to give Jedediah the satisfaction of knowing he's gotten to me. I just need to be patient. Bide my time. And when the opportunity comes, I'll fucking kill him for doing this to me.

In the morning, I'm more sore than ever, my old lingering injuries added to the fresh bruising from my scuffle with Tiny. I inadvertently wince as the huge man drags me out of the trunk, but cover it with a scowl. I put up a struggle, though it's an admittedly pathetic one. Once I'm planted back in my seat, though, exhaustion takes hold. Despite my intentions of being difficult, I soon doze off.

'We're here!'

Jed's cheerful announcement jolts me awake. I raise my head and look around, trying to gather my wits in preparation for whatever is in store. But nothing could prepare me for what I see when I'm half-dragged out of the vehicle. I stand there, blinking in the sunlight and staring up at what is apparently our destination.

'What the fuck is this?' I ask. The building is a fucking mansion, huge and imposing and absurdly luxurious for the wastes ... *especially* the western wastes. I didn't know a place like this could survive in this violent cluster-fuck of a region. I've never seen anything like it before. The only thing that comes close is Jedediah's home in

Wormwood, but even that pales in comparison to whatever the hell this place is. At least Jedediah's place is functional, practical, more of a fortress than anything. This place is a goddamn palace. There's nothing functional about it – no fence, no guard towers, no gates. It's like whoever set this place up was so cocky they thought they'd never have to worry about defending it.

'This,' Jedediah says, grinning up at the building and radiating pride, 'is the former dwelling of the former Queen of the Wastes, or so they say. Supposedly, she was the big boss in the west before Saint came along and shook things up.' He looks over his shoulder at me and his crew, who are exiting their vehicles and joining me in staring. They may have known where they were headed, but judging by the looks and whispers, they weren't prepared for this either. Jedediah is nothing but pleased, throwing his arms wide as if to embrace the sprawling palace. 'And now, it's mine.'

A rather unimpressed silence follows the announcement.

'Never heard of this so-called queen,' I say. Jedediah turns to frown at me, and then at his men who seem similarly lost. He lowers his arms and sighs.

'Seriously?' he asks. 'The fucking Queen, guys! She was a huge deal! People said all roads lead to her palace, she was stunningly beautiful and widely beloved, etcetera? She disappeared a short while ago and nobody knows why? None of this ringing any bells?'

He looks around at his men, who shrug and shift uncomfortably. Finally, though, Eyepatch brightens up.

'Oh, *oh*, is she the one who bathed in blood to stay beautiful forever?' he asks.

'Y'know, I *have* heard that,' Jedediah says, nodding. 'And that she had some way of purifying water, but that one's gotta be bullshit. You know how these things get twisted up.' He shrugs, and turns back to the huge palace. 'Anyway,' he says, 'the point is, this place is fucking awesome. It's the perfect home for the new ruler of the western wastes.'

XXV
The New King

This place may be impressive on the outside, but the inside is like something out of a horrifying fever dream. The Queen's former abode was clearly once luxurious, but apparently the Queen losing her throne was not a peaceful matter. Now the place reeks of death and fear. The front doors are ripped off their hinges. The entrance room is coated in blood, the paintings on the wall splattered with it, the tile's color indistinguishable between the bloodstains and the dust blown through the open doors. A toppled statue rests in the middle of the room, riddled with bullet holes. And of course, there are the bodies, decomposing in the heat. The place reeks of rotting flesh, so thick that I choke on it.

Jedediah's crew is quiet and grim as they enter the building, guns at the ready, expecting trouble. But

Jedediah strolls ahead, humming loudly as he walks through the carnage. Tiny drags me along just behind his leader, following as Jedediah walks right over the grisly scene at the entrance and through a set of ripped-apart double doors on the other side.

Through those doors is the throne room. I recognize it only by the huge painting on the wall, depicting a gorgeous woman seated on a dignified chair. The Queen and her throne, I presume. Now, though, the room is less defined by the throne than by the piles of bodies.

Whatever happened in here, it must've been huge and wild and vicious, and of course there was no one left to clean any of it up afterward. There are bodies everywhere, some evidently raiders and others wearing a crown emblem, along with other unidentifiable wastelanders. Jedediah picks his way among the half-decomposed bodies, making his way to the center of the room, where he stops abruptly. He turns in a circle, surveying the room, and stops facing us. He spreads his hands wide once more.

'Ta-da!' he says. 'Our new headquarters.'

His words echo around the room, emphasizing just how silent and dead this place is. His crew shifts uneasily, much more disturbed by the carnage than their leader is. Jedediah's smile fades, and he lowers his hands.

'Don't you love it?' he asks, puzzled.

'Er, yeah, it's great, boss,' Eyepatch says. He clears his throat. 'It's just . . . a bit messy.'

'We're going to clean it up, of course. The place stinks,' Jedediah says with a roll of his eyes. 'Well, rather, you guys are going to clean it up. I have other important things to do. Plan-making for conquering and such.' He turns his back to us and finishes his stroll across the room, where he plops down onto a dilapidated wooden chair. After a moment, I realize that must be the throne, though it looks absolutely nothing like the portrait on the wall behind it. It's just a shoddy wooden thing, one leg half-broken so the whole thing slants forward, and clearly has never been as grand as the throne in the picture. Jedediah leans back in the chair, placing his hands on the armrests and crossing his legs at the ankle. He looks very, very pleased with himself. 'See? It's perfect.'

There, sitting in his 'throne,' Jedediah Johnson finally looks like the man I always thought he was. I may have been surprised when I first saw him, and surprised by him many times since then, but now it finally fits. A man sitting on a throne in a room full of bodies, and smiling about it. *That's* the real Jedediah Johnson. That's who he is. Not the man the legends say he is, and not the Jed I traveled across the wastes with, but this man.

I stare at him as his crew spreads out, grabbing bodies and wreckage to drag out of the room. They're quiet as they work – not happy about moving into a new place occupied by half-rotted bodies, I guess. Or maybe they're finally realizing that their leader is a complete lunatic who has gotten them in way over their heads. Either way, they still do as he says.

'Maybe I'll drop the name and just start calling myself "the King,"' Jedediah muses, tapping his fingers on the armrests. He catches me looking, and grins at me across the room. 'Westerners are all about their nicknames. What do you think?'

'I think it suits you,' I say.

While Jedediah's crew busies themselves cleaning up the carnage, I'm dragged along by Tiny, joining Jedediah on a tour of the place once he's done lounging on his throne. Jedediah insists on checking out each and every room. Most of them are filled with the same gruesome scenes we witnessed in the throne room, but Jedediah grows progressively more excited by each one. In one he finds a small handheld radio, which he insists on carrying with him, clicking it on and off as we walk, though there's nothing but static on any of the stations. Remembering Saint's broadcast, I wonder if the Queen ever listened in when she was still around. I wonder how many people are still out there, with no idea what's happened, waiting to hear his broadcasts again.

Aside from the gore, the place *is* impressive. There are guest rooms with real beds, bathing rooms with huge tubs, a dining hall with actual silverware. The latter seems to have had real plates at some point too, though now the room is covered with shattered ceramic and glass, spoons and forks scattered across the floor.

But all of it pales in comparison to the master bedroom. It must be where the Queen slept, and it's even more luxurious than the room Jedediah left behind in Wormwood. Thankfully there are no bodies in it, though someone has done some impressive finger-painting with blood on the walls, and the pictures have all been torn down and ripped apart. The dresser is tipped over, the floor covered with feathers from some thoroughly murdered pillows, and the mattress on the bed is riddled with stab wounds, but even so, the room is incredible.

Jedediah, oblivious to the mess, stares at the room in awe. He drops the radio he was playing with on top of the fallen dresser, crosses the room, and flops down on the middle of the huge bed.

'Yeah, this will do,' he says, half-smiling at the ceiling. After a moment, his head lolls to one side, and he looks over at me and Tiny. 'You can go now, Tiny,' he says, flapping a hand. The huge man hesitates, looking down at me. After a moment, Jedediah's eyebrows draw together. 'I said you can go,' he repeats, his voice growing hard. Tiny releases his grip on my shoulder. He sighs once, loudly, before leaving us.

'What do you think?' Jedediah asks once the two of us are left alone, and after I spend several quiet seconds contemplating how hard it would be to kill him with my hands still tied. I raise my eyebrows at the question.

'Does it matter?'

'Of course,' he says, as if the question surprises him. He gestures impatiently. 'Come, sit.'

I stay where I am. He lets his hand drop and sits up, stretching his arms above his head and scrutinizing me.

'Are you still angry?' he asks.

'What?'

'I asked,' he says, raising his voice, 'are you—'

'Am I "angry"?' I repeat, cutting him off. 'That I fell for your stupid act? That I started to believe you might not be a total monster?' I grind my teeth, humiliation burning deep in the pit of my stomach. 'What the fuck do you think?'

'Well, "monster" is a little strong. Lying and tricks aside, I thought we kind of bonded,' he says with a shrug. My blood boils. I take a deep breath, trying to force my temper back before I do something stupid.

'You're the man who burned down my home. Killed my family. Did this to my face,' I spit at him. 'If I had known that, we would never have "bonded."'

'And I'm the man who traveled with you across the wastes,' he says. 'The man who saved your life, whose life you saved. You asked me about my life and told me—'

'Because you lied,' I snap, before he can continue. The reminder of those conversations churns my stomach. 'If I had known who you were, those things would never have happened.'

Jedediah sighs again, rubbing at his temples as if to ward off a headache.

'Well, you kidnapped me from my home with the intention of exchanging my life for money,' he says. 'And I forgave you.'

'You literally fucking planned that yourself!'

'Well ... you got me there,' he says. 'But still. You didn't know that at the time.'

I let out a wordless sound of frustration, unable to put into words how aggravating he is. He looks almost amused.

'I'm still the same person I was, Clem,' he says. 'You're just mad because you started to like me.'

'You are *not* the man I thought I knew,' I say.

'How so?'

'I ... ' I begin, and pause, fumbling for an example. 'For starters, the man I knew wouldn't have shot one of his own crewmates for no goddamn reason,' I say, thinking of Mop.

'Just because you don't understand doesn't mean there was no reason,' he says, and for once he actually sounds annoyed. He sighs and lowers his voice, jabbing a finger at the door. 'You don't know what it's like to be in charge of these kinds of people, okay?'

'These kinds of people are *your people*.'

'And sometimes I have to make hard decisions to keep them that way.'

'Hard decisions,' I repeat. 'Like burning down Old Creek. Is that what you're trying to convince me?'

'Clementine—'

'Like locking my family in their home and burning—'

'You killed my father.'

That shuts me up. I stare at him, words dying in my throat.

'What?' I ask. He says nothing. 'What the fuck are you talking about?'

'That raider you killed,' he says softly, once it's clear I'm ready to listen, 'in Old Creek. He was my father.' I open my mouth, shut it again, and he continues. 'And I was upset. I was angry. I had just started taking control of the eastern wastes, and my hold was still fragile, and I was . . . I was young, you know, and I was scared, and I couldn't . . . ' He pauses. 'So I burned Old Creek to the ground.' He leans back, resting his hands against the mattress. He half-shrugs, like he's trying to act nonchalant and not quite pulling it off. 'I'm not proud of it.'

I search for words and can't find them. All I know is that my anger is dying down, suddenly and swiftly, to a small shriveled ball of confusion and shame. I killed his father. I killed his father just like he killed my parents, and he forgave me for it. He could've killed me a hundred times now, a thousand times, and he didn't. Even with that knowledge, he was kind to me. He wanted me to stay with him.

I take a deep breath.

'I didn't know,' I say finally, not sure what else to say.

'Well, obviously. I didn't tell you until now.'

'Smartass.' The comment comes out automatically, as if my brain forgot for a moment that things have changed, that we have all the reasons in the world to hate each other. Jed and I pause for a moment. Very slowly, the corner of his lips curls upward.

He stands up and crosses the room to me. Without hesitation, he takes out a knife and cuts through the ropes binding my wrists. I rub at the chafed skin as blood flows back into my hands.

'Well,' he says. 'I'm going to go celebrate my conquest of the western wastes.' Seeing my questioning look, he shrugs. 'So easy I might as well have done it already.' He pauses for a moment, looking up at me. I stare down at him. He's probably right; there's no way these western townies or raiders will stand a chance against him. He'll conquer them as certainly as he conquered the east.

I could stop it now, before it happens. I could wrap my hands around his throat and squeeze the life out of him. He'd be dead before Tiny or any of his other goons knew what was happening. For a moment I start to raise my hands, but I force myself to stop. Killing him would mean ... what? I once thought it would save the wastes, that people would love me for it, call me a hero. I thought it would lead me to a home. Now, I'm not so sure that's true. Without him, the western wastes will remain in shambles, and perhaps the east will become the same. There will be no home for me there.

Is it possible there could be one for me here, with Jedediah? With *raiders*? Is a home worth betraying my past and everything I thought I knew?

I don't know what's right. Not for me, and certainly not for the wastes. I don't know what the right direction to aim is, not anymore.

'You know, I really did think about leaving this all behind,' Jedediah says, pulling me from my thoughts. 'When I told you that I wanted to stay with you, that I didn't want to go back, it wasn't a lie. But ... ' He shrugs. 'People need me,' he says, his voice very quiet and somber. 'Really. Even if they don't know it.'

He steps past me without waiting for me to respond.

'You can do whatever you like,' he says over his shoulder, and leaves me there.

The Queen's palace is full of shitty whiskey and fist-fights. Eastern or western, it seems, all raiders celebrate much the same. Most of the revelry takes place in the throne room, which has been successfully cleansed of bodies and the most obvious of the bloodstains, though the scent of death still lingers. Jedediah left up all of the paintings and sculptures and other decorations depicting the former Queen, in various states of destruction.

I lurk in the back of the room. Jedediah's crew cast me suspicious looks, and suspicious double-takes upon seeing that I'm not restrained, but they leave me alone. Maybe they think I've joined their side, or maybe they think I can't possibly be a threat, or maybe they think nothing and just follow Jedediah's lead.

The raider king watches the party unfold from his throne, body sprawled out across it in a very unking-like way. Every so often he raises a half-empty bottle of whiskey to his mouth and takes a long swig – or pretends to, rather. I watch carefully, and note that he doesn't actually swallow afterward, just wipes his mouth with the back of his hand. Every so often, he 'accidentally' spills some, so the level gradually lowers.

Part of me is tempted to go talk to him . . . or shout at him, or throttle him, or *something*, but most of me is still too busy processing everything. Our last conversation explained a lot, and also raised so many questions. I've held a grudge against him for what he did to my family for years . . . and he seemingly forgave me in a matter of days for doing the same to him.

What the hell am I supposed to do with any of this? I don't need this kind of emotional complexity on top of all the shit I'm already dealing with. I don't even know why I'm still here. I should leave this all behind, forget about the infuriating enigma that is Jedediah Johnson. I should go . . . where? To the eastern wastes? So I can go back to barely surviving off bounties, and always feeling like an outsider?

Maybe I shouldn't leave. Maybe I should stay, and support Jedediah. Maybe he's been right the whole time, that having him in charge is better than lawlessness. Maybe that's what this place needs right now: a ruler with an iron fist, a ruler not afraid to embrace the violence of the wastes.

Maybe I should stay. Maybe I should kill Jedediah in his sleep, just like I killed his father.

When someone taps me on the shoulder, I nearly punch them in the face out of sheer instinct. Thankfully I restrain the impulse, because I have a feeling Tiny would hit back a lot harder. As I stare at him, he wordlessly holds up a pack of cards.

'What?' I say. 'Seriously?' He says nothing, just continues holding the cards up. 'Did Jedediah send you?' I ask. He shakes his head.

For some reason, I'm inclined to believe the quiet giant, and playing cards with him sounds a lot better than drowning in my thoughts.

Tiny carries a table and two chairs to a corner of the room, and scatters the raiders already hanging out there with a look. Within moments, we have a corner to ourselves. I sit while Tiny deals out cards. No words are exchanged, but I pick up on it quick enough; we're playing War.

It's a mindless, easy game, and I spend most of my time watching Tiny. His huge hands handle the cards with a surprising gentleness – though he's clumsy, frequently dropping cards and struggling to shuffle them. Despite the rough way he handled me as a prisoner, there's no hint of anger or aggression toward me now. I'm still suspicious that he's doing this just to keep an eye on me, but most of the time, he's watching his leader instead.

'So,' I say, and Tiny turns to look at me. 'How long have you worked for Jedediah?' He shrugs, his eyes going back to the cards. 'A long time?' He nods. I pause for a few moments, running my thumb over a card, which has a bloodstain in one corner. 'You knew his father,' I guess, and after a moment, he nods again. 'You worked for his father, and now for him.'

'Hmm,' Tiny agrees. I eye him, wondering if he knows what Jedediah knows. I could ask him, but instead another question jumps out of my mouth.

'Is it true that Jedediah's father killed his mother?'

Ever since I found out who he really is, that question has been lurking in the back of my mind. How much of what he told me on our journey was true? How much of that persona was really him?

Tiny pauses. His eyes flick behind me, toward where I know Jedediah is sitting. For a moment I think he's going to ignore the question, but just when I'm about to give up and continue playing he gives a small bob of his head.

So it's true, then. I almost wish it weren't. This would be so much easier if Jedediah had lied about everything.

I flip over another card over and collect his when I win.

'Can I ask you something else?' He continues shuffling his cards without looking at me. 'Do you think Jedediah is a good man?'

He pauses, his hand resting on a card. He taps one finger against it, considers for several long seconds.

'Doesn't matter,' he says, finally.

'Hmm,' I say.

'Hmm,' Tiny agrees, and we continue our game.

At the end of the night, I find myself back in Jedediah's room. I expected him to be at his party until dawn, but instead he slips in a few minutes after me, and flops facedown on the bed.

'You're not going to convince me you're drunk,' I say. He laughs, the sound muffled by the bedding, and turns his head to face me.

'So, you're still here,' he says.

'Yeah.'

'For how long?'

I shrug. He rolls over onto his side, propping his chin up with one hand.

'Does this mean you're back on my side?'

'Was I ever on your side?' I ask, raising my eyebrows.

'Sure you were. You saved my life more than a couple of times, I seem to remember.'

I want to say *That was different*, but really, is it? If someone walked in right now and came at Jedediah with a knife, I have the feeling I'd still leap to defend him, even if I willed myself not to.

I lean back against the headboard, sighing, well aware that I still haven't answered his question.

'You honestly believe that you're going to make this place better,' I say.

'I wouldn't be doing this otherwise.'

'And you honestly think you can pull it off.'

He shrugs.

'Nobody here can stand up to my crew,' he says. 'They're the best.' As usual, his confidence is at an absolutely ludicrous level. But this time, I believe he may be right. Jedediah has only a few dozen men and women at his disposal, but they're the best of the best. Even if that raider army held together as a unified group – which they didn't, in the end – I don't think even *they* could have fought Jedediah's crew. And who else could possibly stand up to him? 'You still think I'm wrong,' he says, watching me think.

'No,' I say, and am surprised at how confidently my answer comes out. 'I think ... I think you're right. I think this place needs guidance. I think it needs a ruler.'

His eyebrows rise in clear disbelief.

'Well, this is an awfully convenient time for you to change your mind,' he says.

'I've been thinking about it a lot,' I say. 'About how you were with all the townies, and with the raiders, and with me ... ' I trail off, not sure how to put it into words. 'You're the kind of man that people can believe in.'

As he searches my face, his eyebrows gradually lower.

'Huh,' he says. 'You really mean it.'

In response, I reach over and squeeze his arm. The touch feels strange, almost taboo, after the events of the last few days, but I let it linger for several seconds before pulling back. Jed smiles at me, and contentedly curls up in bed, making no move to get closer to me.

As he starts to snore, I grab the radio and slip out of the room.

I stop in the hallway with it clutched tightly in my hands, listening for any approaching footsteps, but none come. It's just me, and this radio. An awful lot of people listened to Saint's broadcast not too long ago. I wonder how many wastelanders are still tuning in, waiting for news about him ... or someone else like him.

Me, a radio, and a decision I have to make.

Jedediah Johnson is a liar, a shark, a tyrant, and certainly out of his damn mind. Yet still, people love him. Follow him. Trust him. Does he deserve that trust? Does he deserve the loyalty of men like Tiny, or women like me? I think it's time to find out.

I click the radio on and raise it to my mouth.

XXVI
It All Comes Tumbling Down

The morning begins with a bang.

Several bangs, actually, along with a very loud thud. My eyes fly open at the noise, but I remain still, staring at the ceiling. An explosion shakes the building, and some dust and bits of plaster rain down from the ceiling and onto the bed. Beside me, Jedediah finally sits up, clutching the blanket to his chest.

'What?' he asks the air, not awake enough to form a complete sentence. When the air doesn't answer, he scrambles out of bed. Feet still bare, hair sticking up in tufts, he crosses to the door and yanks it open, looking up and down the hallway outside. 'Tiny?' he calls out.

I sit up, but stay where I am. A burst of gunfire comes from outside, followed by a yelp from Jedediah, and another burst of gunfire. I scramble to my feet, rushing for the door – but a moment later, Tiny bursts inside and slams it closed behind him. Jedediah is clutched in his arms like a child's toy, looking rattled but unharmed. Tiny sets him down, and he sways on his feet. He gathers himself after a moment, gives Tiny a cursory fist-bump, and turns to me.

'People are here,' he says, rubbing at one of his eyes. 'Angry people. Lots of angry people. Raiders, and townies, and … fuck. Everyone. All these westerners.' He crosses the room to the window, looks outside. When he turns back, his face is very pale and confused. 'Why are so many angry people here?'

'Broadcast,' Tiny says.

'A broadcast?' Jedediah says, and seems to finally realize. 'They heard I'm here, and taking over. They … shit. *Shit.* This isn't how we do things. We're supposed to take it slow. Divide and conquer. How did this happen?'

Tiny says nothing, but his eyes quickly find the radio sitting on the dresser. Jedediah's gaze follows, and pauses there. He opens his mouth, hesitates, and whirls to Tiny again. 'Frank,' he says, his voice very serious. 'Go make sure everyone is together. It's gonna be a fight.'

Without a word, Tiny is out the door, slamming it shut behind him and leaving us alone. Jedediah, meanwhile, rushes over to the bed and rummages under it. He grabs a bag I never saw him stash, and his shoes. I turn away from him and walk to the window. I can't see anything from here, but I can hear the noise – a lot of gunshots, and a lot of yelling. I don't need to see it to guess what's happening. That broadcast I sent out last night must have reached a lot of people and pissed them all off, raiders and townies alike.

'You called them here,' Jedediah says from behind me. I turn to find him staring at me with naked confusion and hurt on his face. 'After everything you said yesterday?' He pauses, searching my face. 'I didn't think you were that good of a liar,' he says, sounding almost impressed. 'Damn.'

'It wasn't a lie,' I say. I take a deep breath. Words aren't my strong point, but I want to say this right. 'I think the wastes need a leader. Whether you're the right man or not, I'm not too sure, and I don't think I'm the right person to choose anyway. So, I'm going to leave it up to you.' Jedediah stares at me wordlessly, and I continue after a brief pause. 'If you deserve to rule the wastes, then prove it. No crew to do your dirty work, just you and your damn words. Start from scratch and make your way to the top again, if you can.'

'How exactly am I supposed to do that with no crew?' he asks, searching my face.

'Do what you've been doing,' I say. 'Make people love you.' I grit my teeth, wrestling with the next words, but they tumble out of my mouth anyway. 'You're way too damn good at it. Don't force your way in with a crew. You have to do this on your own. If you let the people choose for themselves, they might just choose you.'

He scrutinizes my face. Whatever he finds there makes his expression soften. He opens his mouth, shuts it, opens it again – as if, for once, he's the one struggling to find the right words to express himself. He takes a step toward me.

'Clementine,' he says. 'You should probably know—'

At that moment, something huge slams into the door – once, and then again. We both turn toward it, and Jed steps in front of me. A moment later, a man bursts through the door, ripping it off its hinges. He's big, dark-skinned, scarred, and ... familiar. He pauses, looking at us.

'Oh,' Tank says. 'It's you two.'

'Hi there,' Jedediah says, sounding as casual as ever, though I can see the tension in his body. I'm tense myself. Nobody was supposed to make it to this room so quickly. Now we're trapped, and I'm unarmed and unprepared.

But here's Tank, and standing in the doorway is Kid and the rest of the crew.

'Well, well,' Wolf says behind her, 'if it isn't our old friends.' He steps into the room, an assault rifle aimed at me – clearly prioritizing me as the threat. 'You fucking piece-of-shit liars.'

'Seriously? This is the guy?' Kid asks, jerking the barrel of her shotgun in Jed's direction. She eyes him up and down, looking thoroughly unimpressed. 'A lot smaller than Saint.'

'And *this* scrawny fucker thinks he can come along and attempt the same damn thing right after we kill Saint,' Wolf says, shaking his head. 'But you know what really pisses me off? This fucker had the gall to talk himself up in the *third person* while he was with us. What kind of crazy asshole—'

'Yeah, he's a crazy bastard,' I say, cutting him off. They all look at me, and I take a deep breath. I'd much rather fight my way out of this situation, but right now talking is my only option. 'But maybe that's exactly the kind of leader the wastelands need.'

Wolf turns to me, surprised.

'Wait,' he says. 'Aren't you the one who sent out that broadcast in the first place? Bringing everyone here to take this guy down?'

'Yeah . . . well . . . it's a complicated situation.'

'Listen,' Jedediah says, and I relax. He'll take charge now; he'll convince them, like he convinced me. 'I'm going to do things differently around here. I'm *not* going to be a second Saint—'

Bang.

I don't even have time to react. My eyes stay on the raiders in the doorway, who mostly look as surprised as

I am – aside from Kid, who has stumbled back a few steps from the recoil on her shotgun. Slowly, very slowly, I turn my eyes to Jed.

I missed him stumbling back. I missed him hitting the floor. He's sprawled there now, facedown, surrounded by a metric fuck-ton of blood. It's pooled around him, splattered on the walls, on the bed. On me too, I realize, looking down at myself in stupefaction.

'*Kid*,' Wolf is yelling, though it sounds very distant to my ears, 'are you fucking serious? I told you we were gonna do it *right* this time. I had this whole fucking speech planned out—'

I feel numb. Distant, like I'm watching this scene unfold in a dream, like I'm not really here. This can't possibly be happening. This isn't how things were supposed to be. Jed wasn't supposed to die. I wish that I had a gun, that I could mow down each and every one of these raiders. I can vividly imagine it: slicing Tank's throat, planting a bullet in Wolf's forehead, ripping Kid limb from limb. If I only had a weapon – but I don't. I can't. And what would be the point?

I guess I should've expected this. I'm the one who brought them here.

I thought it was the right decision – to give Jed a chance to prove himself. I was so sure he could do it too. I thought I was giving a choice to myself, to him, to the people. Now, that choice has been snuffed out.

Was it the right thing to do? Was it best for the wastes, or will people be better off with him in the ground? Jed could've almost certainly led the wastes to a new age … but would it have been an improvement? I'm not sure. We all know he was a good leader, but whether he was a good man, and whether that matters, is something I don't think I'll ever be sure of.

Dolly watches me from across the room as the rest of her crew bickers. I meet her eyes for a moment. I picture myself walking over and knocking her out, taking her gun, killing each and every member of her crew while she watches. I could make her feel the way I feel – like some vital part of her was just ripped out of her and thrown away forever.

I savor the mental image for a moment, and then walk past Dolly and into the hallway outside. Nobody stops me.

XXVII
Afterward

A fight rages in the rest of the Queen's mansion, westerners embroiled in a bloody tussle with Jedediah's men.
There are western raiders with their brutal weapons,
townies with their makeshift tools, some who are difficult to tell apart but working together – mostly. I see five
of them surrounding Eyepatch, who still manages to kill
two men before finally going limp.

I walk past the scene in a half daze, ignored by all. My
mind keeps flashing back to that gunshot, to the sight of
Jed's body surrounded by blood. Somewhere inside of
me is a violent rage, and a sickening sadness, but both
are smothered by numbness. I walk, barely aware of the
danger around me until a knife flies right past my face,
hits the wall, and clatters to the floor.

I stop, and my wits finally return, the sound of the

fight wiping away my haze. I grab the knife and gut the man nearest me before he knows what hit him. It feels good, doing what I'm best at, and so I keep doing it, hacking and slashing my way through the fight, cutting down townies and western raiders and Jedediah's crew members alike. For a while, it's enough to keep me numb. I embrace the violence, lose myself in it.

No rules, not anymore. They've gotten me nowhere.

But gradually, the rush of it fades away and leaves behind ... nothing. I pause over the body of my latest victim, breathing hard as I watch the life bleed out of the man. He was one of Jedediah's men – I'm sure I'd know his name if I committed enough thought to it, but right now looking at his face just sickens me. I wipe my knife on my pants and step back. So now I do ... what?

I don't know. I feel like all desire and purpose have drained out of me, so I turn to the next possible thing: logic. I can't stay here. Step one is to get out of this bloodbath. And then ... And then figure out what's next, I guess.

Of course, there are a few people who try to stop me on my way, mostly western raiders who are eager to fight regardless of the reason why. I take them out easily. Fighting feels mechanical, instinctual, mindless. As my body goes through the motions, my mind is still back in that room, staring at Jed's body facedown on the floor.

More than angry or sad, I am tired, and lost, and afraid to find out what comes next.

It takes a familiar face to jolt me out of my haze again. An unexpected face, waiting around a corner: Cat, the poacher. The bounty hunter freezes, but I waste no time in holding my knife to her throat.

'Wait,' she yells, before I can cut her open.

Surprising both of us, I do. I'm not sure what initially gives me pause, but upon getting a better look at her, that pause stretches out further. She's in bad shape – out of breath and covered in blood, and the wound on her leg seems to have reopened. Her face is ashen, and she sways on her feet.

'What the fuck are you doing here?' I ask, still itching to slice her throat, but holding myself back.

'Looking for you,' she says. 'And Jedediah.' I stare at her. 'I know you're with him now, and listen, I've seen the goddamn light or whatever too. I'm sick of these crazy-ass western wastes. I want Jedediah's ass back on that throne, and my ass back in the east. That work for you?'

'Jed is … Jedediah's dead,' I say, my voice deadly calm. Letting any hint of emotion out could start a flood of it, and I can't afford that right now.

'Well, shit,' Cat says. 'Fuck it all then. I just wanna get the fuck out of here.'

I lower my knife.

'Yeah,' I say. 'Me too.'

Regardless of everything that's happened between us, I'm not eager to go back to being alone – especially not now, when I'm stranded in the middle of the torn-apart western wastes and surrounded by warring raiders. And as far as allies go, Cat seems like my best bet. At least she's not a raider.

'Thank fucking Jesus,' she says.

'The closest exit is—'

'Well, hold up, first we need to find Bird.'

Of course, it has to be complicated. I sigh, already regretting my decision to be civil.

'I didn't realize I was signing up for a rescue mission,' I say.

'Well, I'm not leaving her behind,' Cat snaps. I open my mouth, about to argue, ready to explain to her how impossible it will be for us to get out of here alive without the side mission to rescue her insane companion, but I stop myself. I would have done it for Jed, I realize.

'Fine,' I say, mentally cursing at myself even as I agree. 'I'll find her. You wait outside.'

'It'll be faster if we both look.'

'It'll be slower if I have to rescue you too.'

I can see that her pride wants her to argue, but she glances down at her injured leg and shuts her mouth. She nods curtly.

'We have a spot where we were supposed to meet,' she says. 'I'll be waiting there.'

I nod at her, and she leaves. More than anything, I want to follow her out, get myself free of this situation. But instead, I plunge back into the fray.

I go to the place where I'd go in Bird's position: the worst of the battle, the spots where the fighting is thickest. Filled with a renewed vigor, I punch and slash and shoot my way through the fight, picking up weapons when I can find them, using my fists when I can't. It would be easy to let myself go here, to give myself over to violence, but purpose keeps me going. It helps me stay aware. Maybe that's what I've been lacking, all this time.

But my purpose proves a lot more difficult than I initially thought it would be. Bird isn't anywhere to be found. I consider the problem in between taking out raiders and townies. Bird is tough, and dedicated to her partner. She would find her way to Cat if she could. And she should be able to. She may not be as good as me, but she's still pretty damn good, and these westerners should be easy enough to take out. So if she can't, that means she's hurt. Or dead.

For now, I have to ignore that second possibility. Instead I focus on the former idea. So maybe she's hurt. If she's hurt ... then I'm looking in exactly the wrong kinds of places.

I disentangle myself from the fighting, pausing to kill an idiot townie who decides to pursue me, and instead start to check the places I haven't been looking. The quiet places; abandoned rooms, hallways occupied only by corpses, cramped closets, places where an injured woman with some serious issues might drag herself if she was in trouble.

And finally, in the dining room, I find her.

She's curled up under the table, rocking and shivering, cradling an arm against her chest. Sitting on the floor near her is a bloodied knife. My heart sinks. If she's hurt badly, getting her out of here will be the least of my concerns. There's no way we'll make it across the wastes with both her and Cat useless. But getting a closer look, I realize there's no blood on her, no sign of actual injury.

'Come on, we need to go,' I say. She doesn't even look at me. 'Cat's waiting.' She pauses at that – only to resume rocking, ducking her head lower.

My first instinct is to leave her behind. I'll tell Cat I couldn't find her, or that I found the body. Hell, I should probably kill her myself just to make sure the lie doesn't come back to bite me. I tighten my grip on my knife, but then pause.

I'm not leaving her behind.

'Fuck,' I say, shoving the knife into my leg holster. Who knew a journey to the west would turn me into a goddamn bleeding heart?

Sighing at myself, I lower to a crouch beside Bird.

'Let me see it,' I say. When she doesn't respond, I grab the arm and yank it toward me – maybe a little more roughly than necessary. She smacks my face with her free hand, making high-pitched sounds of protest. I release her after I see the problem: a rip in her sleeve.

'Ugh,' I say. 'Can't you subdue the crazy long enough for us to get out of here?' Of course, she doesn't respond to that, just resumes rocking and whimpering to herself. Grumbling, I reach down and rip off a piece of my shirt. I fight with her for the arm again, and wrap the piece of fabric across her revealed skin, circling it twice and then tying it off tightly while she smacks me in the face. Once it's done, I shove her back, struggling with the urge to bash her head in. 'See? I'm trying to fucking help,' I say, pulling back.

She pauses, looking at the arm and seeming to finally realize what I was doing. She flexes her arm, scrutinizing the knot, and then looking at my dirty, bloodstained shirt.

'Unsanitary,' she proclaims quietly.

'Oh come on,' I say. 'It's good enough for now, right? Considering the imminent danger?'

She grabs the bloodied knife off the floor, scrambles to her feet, and races for the door. Cursing under my breath, I follow.

Bird weaves an unpredictable path through the

building with occasional pauses to stab someone. She's so fast that I can do little but struggle to keep up, and take out anyone who gets in my way. I want to ask if she has any idea where she's going, but I can't spare the breath.

Her path seems random, but after several minutes of winding her way through rooms and halls and stabbing her way through raiders, she bursts through a door into open air. I follow her outside and skid to a stop, blinking in the sunlight. I take a moment to catch my breath – and it then hitches as I realize we're not alone. Cat is standing nearby, waiting as she promised, but she's not the only one. Beside her stands Tiny, huge and silent, his eyes locked on me.

'Bird!' Seemingly oblivious to the hulking man standing nearby, Cat grabs her partner by the shoulder, yanks her close, and plants a noisy kiss on her mask. 'You asshole!' Bird ducks her head and rubs bashfully at the spot on her mask.

Tiny stares at me over the tops of their heads, waiting for the sickeningly affectionate reunion to finish before he steps forward. I keep an eye on his gun, but he doesn't reach for it.

Instead, he juts out a fist and lets it hang in the air. After a moment, I bump my own knuckles against it, and we both let our hands fall.

'I'm sorry things turned out this way,' I say. I'm

confused about a lot of things right now, but I do mean that.

'Hmm,' he says, and then stares out at the wastelands ahead. He doesn't look as torn up as I'd expect, just vaguely troubled. I wonder if he feels as uncertain as I do about Jedediah's death, and whether it's for the best. There are still a million questions churning through my head, but right now, there's only one that's important.

'So what do we do now?' Cat asks. Silence hangs in the air for a few moments before I realize all three of them are looking at me, waiting for an answer. I blink at them, startled. Gradually, the initial shock fades and a strange calm settles over me. They're looking to me to lead them. This feels . . . right, somehow.

'I think we start in the east,' I say.

'Start?' Bird asks.

'The east is gonna be a fucking mess,' Cat says, almost simultaneously.

'So we put it back together,' I say.

'How are we gonna do that?'

'One piece at a time.' I glance around at them. Cat and Bird shrug at each other, and Tiny just watches, silently waiting.

'Gonna be hard,' Cat says. 'Been a long time since they've been without a leader.'

'Oh, they're gonna have one,' I say.

Behind us, I distantly hear the fight continuing

inside the former Queen's palace; the sound of the raider army and Jedediah's men tearing one another apart. Jedediah's crew will be done for, especially with their leader gone. The raider army will be left limping, and likely dissolve into individual crews again. Everything restored to its natural balance – but in the wastes, balance never lasts for long. It's too ripe with opportunity.

I smile out at the expanse of wastelands in front of me, vast and empty and waiting. So many little towns out there, left alone and uncertain about what comes next. Both the east and the west will be left bleeding from all of this. Someone has to rise to the challenge of handling the aftermath.

People need me. Even if they don't know it.

Like with most things, I think Jed had the right idea about that. Time and time again, I've found myself wrong about people. I overestimate them, and end up disappointed – like the townies we've encountered who fell apart at the first sign of trouble, like those raiders who killed Jed before he had a chance to speak, and like Jed himself in the end. He got greedy, he got cocky, and he paid for it.

I won't make the same mistake.

I've always placed so much value on freedom. But what does that really give people? The right to die free, and little else. Townies know nothing about the world beyond their own walls. How did I ever think they were capable of making their own decisions? All the towns that turned me away when I would've helped them … All the people who saw me as a monster when I was just trying to protect them. Clearly, they have no idea what's good for them. But I do.

So, I think it's time to do what's best for them – even if they hate me for it. I'll save them, even if they don't deserve it. I can't help but care, but I'm tired of chasing love. All I need is a few people to support me … a few whom I'm already starting to gather. The rest will fall in line. They'll respect me, at least, and that will be good enough.

All this time I've spent searching for a new home, without realizing I could *make* one. By force, if I have to.

'The King is dead, long live the Queen?' Cat mutters, looking at Bird. Overhearing it, I grin.

And we set off to make our new world.

Acknowledgments

First of all, thank you to my critique partner Leigh Mar, who was the first person to read the first draft of *Raid*, and who gave invaluable feedback and encouragement that helped shape it into an actual story.

Thank you to my amazing agent, Emmanuelle Morgen, for always believing in my writing and for preventing me from panicking when deadlines loom a little too close for comfort.

Thanks to Lindsey Hall, whose insightful editing made this book bolder and immeasurably better. Thank you to Lisa Marie Pompilio for designing the badass cover, as well as to Ellen Wright, Nazia Khatun, Sarah Guan, Gleni Bartels, and the rest of the team at Orbit, who have been amazing during the publication process for both *Bite* and *Raid*.

As always, thank you to my family for encouraging me to chase my dreams, and for not judging me when those dreams included writing violent books about cannibals. A special thanks to my mom and gramma for all the support, and to my dad, who checked Barnes & Noble every day for a week to see if my book was back in stock yet.

And lastly, thank you to everyone who read and enjoyed *Bite* and/or *Raid*. Hearing from you always makes my day!

extras

www.orbitbooks.net

about the author

K. S. Merbeth is obsessed with SFF, food, video games, and her cat. She resides in Tucson, Arizona. You can find her on Twitter @ksmerbeth.

Find out more about K. S. Merbeth and other Orbit authors by registering for the free monthly newsletter at www.orbitbooks.net.

if you enjoyed
RAID

look out for

WAKE OF VULTURES

by

Lila Bowen

Nettie Lonesome lives in a land of hard people and hard ground dusted with sand. She's a half-breed who dresses like a boy, raised by folks who don't call her a slave but use her like one. She knows of nothing else. That is, until the day a stranger attacks her. When nothing, not even a sickle to the eye can stop him, Nettie stabs him through the heart with a chunk of wood and he turns to black sand.

And just like that, Nettie can see.

But her newfound sight is a blessing and a curse. Even if she doesn't understand what's under her own skin, she can sense what everyone else is hiding — at least physically. The world is full of evil, and now she knows the source of all the sand in the desert. Haunted by the spirits, Nettie has no choice but to set out on a quest that might lead her to find her true kin ... if the monsters along the way don't kill her first.

CHAPTER

1

Nettie Lonesome had two things in the world that were worth a sweet goddamn: her old boots and her one-eyed mule, Blue. Neither item actually belonged to her. But then again, nothing did. Not even the whisper-thin blanket she lay under, pretending to be asleep and wishing the black mare would get out of the water trough before things went south.

The last fourteen years of Nettie's life had passed in a shriveled corner of Durango territory under the leaking roof of this wind-chapped lean-to with Pap and Mam, not quite a slave and nowhere close to something like a daughter. Their faces, white and wobbling as new butter under a smear of prairie dirt, held no kindness. The boots and the mule had belonged to Pap, right up until the day he'd exhausted their use, a sentiment he threatened to apply to her every time she was just a little too slow with the porridge.

'Nettie! Girl, you take care of that wild filly, or I'll put one in her goddamn skull!'

Pap got in a lather when he'd been drinking, which was pretty much always. At least this time his anger was aimed at a critter instead of Nettie. When the witch-hearted black filly had first shown up on the farm, Pap had laid claim and pronounced her a fine chunk of flesh and a sign of the Creator's good graces. If Nettie broke her and sold her for a decent price, she'd be closer to paying back Pap for taking her in as a baby when nobody else had wanted her but the hungry, circling vultures. The value Pap placed on feeding and housing a half-Injun, half-black orphan girl always seemed to go up instead of down, no matter that Nettie did most of the work around the homestead these days. Maybe that was why she'd not been taught her sums: Then she'd know her own damn worth, to the penny.

But the dainty black mare outside wouldn't be roped, much less saddled and gentled, and Nettie had failed to sell her to the cowpokes at the Double TK Ranch next door. Her idol, Monty, was a top hand and always had a kind word. But even he had put a boot on Pap's poorly kept fence, laughed through his mustache, and hollered that a horse that couldn't be caught couldn't be sold. No matter how many times Pap drove the filly away with poorly thrown bottles, stones, and bullets, the critter crept back under cover of night to ruin the water by dancing a jig in the trough, which meant another blistering trip to the creek with a leaky bucket for Nettie.

Splash, splash. Whinny.

Could a horse laugh? Nettie figured this one could.

Pap, however, was a humorless bastard who didn't get a joke that didn't involve bruises.

'Unless you wanna go live in the flats, eatin' bugs, you'd best get on, girl.'

Nettie rolled off her worn-out straw tick, hoping there weren't any scorpions or centipedes on the dusty dirt floor. By the moon's scant light she shook out Pap's old boots and shoved her bare feet into the cracked leather.

Splash, splash.

The shotgun cocked loud enough to be heard across the border, and Nettie dove into Mam's old wool cloak and ran toward the stockyard with her long, thick braids slapping against her back. Mam said nothing, just rocked in her chair by the window, a bottle cradled in her arm like a baby's corpse. Grabbing the rawhide whip from its nail by the warped door, Nettie hurried past Pap on the porch and stumbled across the yard, around two mostly roofless barns, and toward the wet black shape taunting her in the moonlight against a backdrop of stars.

'Get on, mare. Go!'

A monster in a flapping jacket with a waving whip would send any horse with sense wheeling in the opposite direction, but this horse had apparently been dancing in the creek on the day sense was handed out. The mare stood in the water trough and stared at Nettie like she was a damn strange bird, her dark eyes blinking with moonlight and her lips pulled back over long, white teeth.

Nettie slowed. She wasn't one to quirt a horse, but if the mare kept causing a ruckus, Pap would shoot her without a second or even a first thought – and he wasn't so deep in his bottle that he was sure to miss. Getting smacked with rawhide had to be better than getting shot in the head, so Nettie doubled up her shouting and prepared herself for the heartache that would accompany the smack of a whip on unmarred hide. She didn't even own the horse, much less the right to beat it. Nettie had grown up trying to be the opposite of Pap, and hurting something that didn't come with claws and a stinger went against her grain.

'Shoo, fool, or I'll have to whip you,' she said, creeping closer. The horse didn't budge, and for the millionth time, Nettie swung the whip around the horse's neck like a rope, all gentle-like. But, as ever, the mare tossed her head at exactly the right moment, and the braided leather snickered against the wooden water trough instead.

'Godamighty, why won't you move on? Ain't nobody wants you, if you won't be rode or bred. Dumb mare.'

At that, the horse reared up with a wild scream, spraying water as she pawed the air. Before Nettie could leap back to avoid the splatter, the mare had wheeled and galloped into the night. The starlight showed her streaking across the prairie with a speed Nettie herself would've enjoyed, especially if it meant she could turn her back on Pap's dirt-poor farm and no-good cattle company forever. Doubling over to stare at her scuffed boots while she caught her breath, Nettie felt her hope disappear with hoofbeats in the night.

A low and painfully unfamiliar laugh trembled out of the barn's shadow, and Nettie cocked the whip back so that it was ready to strike.

'Who's that? Jed?'

But it wasn't Jed, the mule-kicked, sometimes stable boy, and she already knew it.

'Looks like that black mare's giving you a spot of trouble, darlin'. If you were smart, you'd set fire to her tail.'

A figure peeled away from the barn, jerky-thin and slithery in a too-short coat with buttons that glinted like extra stars. The man's hat was pulled low, his brown hair overshaggy and his lily-white hand on his gun in a manner both unfriendly and relaxed that Nettie found insulting.

'You best run off, mister. Pap don't like strangers on his land, especially when he's only a bottle in. If it's horses you want, we ain't got none worth selling. If you want work and you're dumb and blind, best come back in the morning when he's slept off the mezcal.'

'I wouldn't work for that good-for-nothing piss-pot even if I needed work.'

The stranger switched sides with his toothpick and looked Nettie up and down like a horse he was thinking about stealing. Her fist tightened on the whip handle, her fingers going cold. She wouldn't defend Pap or his land or his sorry excuses for cattle, but she'd defend the only thing other than Blue that mostly belonged to her. Men had been pawing at her for two years now, and nobody'd yet come close to reaching her soft parts, not even Pap.

'Then you'd best move on, mister.'

The feller spit his toothpick out on the ground and took a step forward, all quiet-like because he wore no spurs. And that was Nettie's first clue that he wasn't what he seemed.

'Naw, I'll stay. Pretty little thing like you to keep me company.'

That was Nettie's second clue. Nobody called her pretty unless they wanted something. She looked around the yard, but all she saw were sand, chaparral, bone-dry cow patties, and the remains of a fence that Pap hadn't seen fit to fix. Mam was surely asleep, and Pap had gone inside, or maybe around back to piss. It was just the stranger and her. And the whip.

'Bullshit,' she spit.

'Put down that whip before you hurt yourself, girl.'

'Don't reckon I will.'

The stranger stroked his pistol and started to circle her. Nettie shook the whip out behind her as she spun in place to face him and hunched over in a crouch. He stopped circling when the barn yawned behind her, barely a shell of a thing but darker than sin in the corners. And then he took a step forward, his silver pistol out and flashing starlight. Against her will, she took a step back. Inch by inch he drove her into the barn with slow, easy steps. Her feet rattled in the big boots, her fingers numb around the whip she had forgotten how to use.

'What is it you think you're gonna do to me, mister?'

It came out breathless, god damn her tongue.

His mouth turned up like a cat in the sun. 'Something nice. Something somebody probably done to you already. Your master or pappy, maybe.'

She pushed air out through her nose like a bull. 'Ain't got a pappy. Or a master.'

'Then I guess nobody'll mind, will they?'

That was pretty much it for Nettie Lonesome. She spun on her heel and ran into the barn, right where he'd been pushing her to go. But she didn't flop down on the hay or toss down the mangy blanket that had dried into folds in the broke-down, three-wheeled rig. No, she snatched the sickle from the wall and spun to face him under the hole in the roof. Starlight fell down on her ink-black braids and glinted off the parts of the curved blade that weren't rusted up.

'I reckon I'd mind,' she said.

Nettie wasn't a little thing, at least not height-wise, and she'd figured that seeing a pissed-off woman with a weapon in each hand would be enough to drive off the curious feller and send him back to the whores at the Leaping Lizard, where he apparently belonged. But the stranger just laughed and cracked his knuckles like he was glad for a fight and would take his pleasure with his fists instead of his twig.

'You wanna play first? Go on, girl. Have your fun. You think you're facin' down a coydog, but you found a timber wolf.'

As he stepped into the barn, the stranger went into shadow for just a second, and that was when Nettie struck. Her whip whistled for his feet and managed to catch one ankle, yanking hard enough to pluck him off his feet and onto the back of his fancy jacket. A puff of dust went up as he thumped on the ground, but he just crossed his ankles and stared at her and laughed. Which pissed her off more. Dropping the whip handle, Nettie took the sickle in both hands and went for the stranger's legs, hoping that a good slash would keep him from chasing her but not get her sent to the hangman's noose. But her blade whistled over a patch of nothing. The man was gone, her whip with him.

Nettie stepped into the doorway to watch him run away, her heart thumping underneath the tight muslin binding she always wore over her chest. She squinted into the long, flat night, one hand on the hinge of what used to be a barn door, back before the church was willing to pay cash money for Pap's old lumber. But the stranger wasn't hightailing it across the prairie. Which meant . . .

'Looking for someone, darlin'?'

She spun, sickle in hand, and sliced into something that

felt like a ham with the round part of the blade. Hot blood spattered over her, burning like lye.

'Goddammit, girl! What'd you do that for?'

She ripped the sickle out with a sick splash, but the man wasn't standing in the barn, much less falling to the floor. He was hanging upside-down from a cross-beam, cradling his arm. It made no goddamn sense, and Nettie couldn't stand a thing that made no sense, so she struck again while he was poking around his wound.

This time, she caught him in the neck. This time, he fell.

The stranger landed in the dirt and popped right back up into a crouch. The slice in his neck looked like the first carving in an undercooked roast, but the blood was slurry and smelled like rotten meat. And the stranger was sneering at her.

'Girl, you just made the biggest mistake of your short, useless life.'

Then he sprang at her.

There was no way he should've been able to jump at her like that with those wounds, and she brought her hands straight up without thinking. Luckily, her fist still held the sickle, and the stranger took it right in the face, the point of the blade jerking into his eyeball with a moist squish. Nettie turned away and lost most of last night's meager dinner in a noisy splatter against the wall of the barn. When she spun back around, she was surprised to find that the fool hadn't fallen or died or done anything helpful to her cause. Without a word, he calmly pulled the blade out of his eye and wiped a dribble of black glop off his cheek.

His smile was a cold, dark thing that sent Nettie's feet toward Pap and the crooked house and anything but the stranger who wouldn't die, wouldn't scream, and wouldn't leave her alone. She'd never felt safe a day in her life, but now she recognized the chill hand of death, reaching for her. Her feet trembled in the too-big boots as she stumbled backward across the bumpy yard, tripping on stones and bits of trash. Turning her back on the demon man seemed intolerably stupid. She just had to get past the round pen, and then she'd be halfway to the house. Pap wouldn't be worth much by now, but he had a gun by his side. Maybe the stranger would give up if he saw a man instead of just a half-breed girl nobody cared about.

Nettie turned to run and tripped on a fallen chunk of fence, going down hard on hands and skinned knees. When she looked up, she saw butternut-brown pants stippled with blood and no-spur boots tapping.

'Pap!' she shouted. 'Pap, help!'

She was gulping in a big breath to holler again when the stranger's boot caught her right under the ribs and knocked it all back out. The force of the kick flipped her over onto her back, and she scrabbled away from the stranger and toward the ramshackle round pen of old, gray branches and junk roped together, just barely enough fence to trick a colt into staying put. They'd slaughtered a pig in here, once, and now Nettie knew how he felt.

As soon as her back fetched up against the pen, the stranger crouched in front of her, one eye closed and weeping black and the other brim-full with evil over the bloody slice in his neck. He looked like a dead man, a corpse groom, and Nettie was pretty sure she was in the hell Mam kept threatening her with.

'Ain't nobody coming. Ain't nobody cares about a girl like you. Ain't nobody gonna need to, not after what you done to me.'

The stranger leaned down and made like he was going to kiss her with his mouth wide open, and Nettie did the only thing that came to mind. She grabbed up a stout twig from the wall of the pen and stabbed him in the chest as hard as she damn could.

She expected the stick to break against his shirt like the time she'd seen a buggy bash apart against the general store during a twister. But the twig sunk right in like a hot knife in butter. The stranger shuddered and fell on her, his mouth working as gloppy red-black liquid bubbled out. She didn't trust blood anymore, not after the first splat had burned her, and she wasn't much for being found under a corpse, so Nettie shoved him off hard and shot to her feet, blowing air as hard as a galloping horse.

The stranger was rolling around on the ground, plucking at his chest. Thick clouds blotted out the meager starlight, and she had nothing like the view she'd have tomorrow under the white-hot, unrelenting sun. But even a girl who'd never killed a man before knew when something was wrong. She kicked him over with the toe of her boot, tit for tat, and he was light as a tumbleweed when he landed on his back.

The twig jutted up out of a black splotch in his shirt, and the slice in his neck had curled over like gone meat. His bad eye was a swamp of black, but then, everything was black at midnight. His mouth was open, the lips drawing back over too-white teeth, several of which looked like they'd come out of a panther. He wasn't breathing, and Pap wasn't coming, and Nettie's finger reached out as if it had a mind of its own and flicked one big, shiny, curved tooth.

The goddamn thing fell back into the dead man's gaping throat. Nettie jumped away, skitty as the black filly, and her boot toe brushed the dead man's shoulder, and his entire body collapsed in on itself like a puffball, thousands of sparkly motes piling up in the place he'd occupied and spilling out through his empty clothes. Utterly bewildered, she knelt and brushed the pile with trembling fingers. It was sand. Nothing but sand. A soft wind came up just then and blew some of the stranger away, revealing one of those big, curved teeth where his head had been. It didn't make a goddamn lick of sense, but it could've gone far worse.

Still wary, she stood and shook out his clothes, noting that everything was in better than fine condition, except for his white shirt, which had a twig-sized hole in the breast, surrounded by a smear of black. She knew enough of laundering and sewing to make it nice enough, and the black blood on his pants looked, to her eye, manly and tough. Even the stranger's boots were of better quality than any that had ever set foot on Pap's land, snakeskin with fancy chasing. With her own, too-big boots, she smeared the sand back into the hard, dry ground as if the stranger had never existed. All that was left was the four big panther teeth, and she put those in her pocket and tried to forget about them.

After checking the yard for anything livelier than a scorpion, she rolled up the clothes around the boots and hid them in the old rig in the barn. Knowing Pap would pester her if she left signs of a scuffle, she wiped the black glop off the sickle and hung it up, along with the whip, out of Pap's drunken reach. She didn't need any more whip scars on her back than she already had.

Out by the round pen, the sand that had once been a devil of a stranger had all blown away. There was no sign of what had almost happened, just a few more deadwood twigs pulled from the lopsided fence. On good days, Nettie spent a fair bit of time doing the dangerous work of breaking colts or doctoring cattle in here for Pap, then picking up the twigs that got knocked off and roping them back in with whatever twine she could scavenge from the town. Wood wasn't cheap, and there wasn't much of it. But Nettie's hands were twitchy still, and so she picked up the black-splattered stick and wove it back into the fence, wishing she lived in a world where her life was worth more than a mule, more than boots, more than a stranger's cold smile in the barn. She'd had her first victory, but no one would ever believe her, and if they did, she wouldn't be cheered. She'd be hanged.

That stranger – he had been all kinds of wrong. And the way that he'd wanted to touch her – that felt wrong, too. Nettie couldn't recall being touched in kindness, not in all her years with Pap and Mam. Maybe that was why she understood horses. Mustangs were wild things captured by thoughtless men, roped and branded and beaten until their heads hung low, until it took spurs and whips to move them in rage and fear. But Nettie could feel the wildness inside their hearts, beating under skin that quivered under the flat of her palm. She didn't break a horse, she gentled it. And until someone touched her with that same kindness, she would continue to shy away, to bare her teeth and lower her head.

Someone, surely, had been kind to her once, long ago. She could feel it in her bones. But Pap said she'd been tossed out like trash, left on the prairie to die. Which she almost had, tonight. Again.

Pap and Mam were asleep on the porch, snoring loud as thunder. When Nettie crept past them and into the house, she had four shiny teeth in one fist, a wad of cash from the stranger's pocket, and more questions than there were stars.